CLAIMING BAILEY

DISCOVER OTHER TITLES BY SUSAN STOKER

Ace Security Series

Claiming Grace

Claiming Alexis

Claiming Bailey

Claiming Felicity

Badge of Honor: Texas Heroes Series

Justice for Mackenzie

Justice for Mickie

Justice for Corrie

Justice for Laine (novella)

Shelter for Elizabeth

Justice for Boone

Shelter for Adeline

Justice for Sophie

Justice for Erin

Justice for Milena (March 2018)

Shelter for Blythe (July 2018)

Justice for Hope (TBA)

Shelter for Quinn (TBA)

Shelter for Koren (TBA)

Shelter for Penelope (TBA)

Delta Force Heroes Series

Rescuing Rayne

Assisting Aimee

Rescuing Emily

Rescuing Harley
Marrying Emily
Rescuing Kassie
Rescuing Bryn
Rescuing Casey (January 2018)
Rescuing Sadie (April 2018)
Rescuing Wendy (May 2018)
Rescuing Mary (November 2018)

SEAL of Protection: Legacy Series

Defending Caite (September 2018)

SEAL of Protection Series

Protecting Caroline
Protecting Alabama
Protecting Fiona
Marrying Caroline (novella)
Protecting Summer
Protecting Cheyenne
Protecting Jessyka
Protecting Julie (novella)
Protecting Melody
Protecting the Future
Protecting Alabama's Kids (novella)
Protecting Kiera (novella)
Protecting Dakota

Beyond Reality Series

Outback Hearts
Flaming Hearts
Frozen Hearts

CLAIMING BAILEY

ACE SECURITY

BOOK 3

Susan Stoker

Published by Montlake Romance, Seattle

www.apub.com

ISBN-13: 9781542049023
ISBN-10: 1542049024

Cover design by Eileen Carey

Printed in the United States of America

CLAIMING BAILEY

Chapter One

Nathan Anderson shook his head in disgust and glared at the steering wheel of his Ford Focus. His brothers, Logan and Blake, told him over and over that one day the car was going to give up the ghost, but he'd ignored them. Marilyn, named after the iconic movie star, was old, but she was the first thing he'd purchased when he'd left home after graduating high school, and he just couldn't bear to part with her. The black paint had long ago begun to peel off, she was rusting in places, and the trunk only stayed shut because of the rope used to tie it down.

After several mornings of Marilyn barely turning over when Nathan tried to start her, it looked like she'd finally had enough. Figured she'd do it when he was sitting with a trunk full of groceries in a supermarket parking lot.

Nathan took out his phone and tapped on Logan's number. It went to voice mail. Not bothering to leave a message, Nathan tried Blake and turned the phone off in frustration when it too went to his brother's voice mail. He considered trying to get ahold of either Grace or Alexis but figured they were probably with his brothers since they were rarely away from each other.

His friends Felicity and Cole weren't around either. Felicity wasn't due back until later tonight from some sort of mysterious trip to Chicago that she refused to talk about, and Cole was up in Denver getting marketing ideas for the gym he and Felicity co-owned.

Nathan sighed and drummed the steering wheel with his index finger, trying to figure out who else he could call.

He wasn't a man who made friends easily, more comfortable with his computer and numbers than with people. Over the years he'd found that he pretty much didn't like most people. They lied, were rude, and didn't give a crap about anyone but themselves. And that went for almost every situation . . . in line at the store, on the road, and in business. They almost always put their own wants and needs first. Alexis tried to tell him that he just hadn't hung around the right people, and he supposed that was true, but it didn't make his feelings any less accurate.

Alexis and Grace were exceptions. Nathan vaguely remembered Grace from growing up. While they went to the same high school, it wasn't until he and his brothers had come home to Castle Rock to start their security business that he'd gotten to know her better. They saved her from her horrible parents who emotionally abused her for years, and she and Logan were now married and expecting twin boys, literally any day now.

Alexis's family had also been victimized by Grace's parents, and at first Nathan had been annoyed that Blake had invited Alexis to work with them at Ace Security. But over time, he'd found out that she wasn't like most women he'd known. She was quiet and easygoing, and not afraid to say what she was thinking. They could sit together for hours in the office, and she wouldn't say a word. He liked that about her.

Where his brothers were didn't really matter at the moment. What mattered was getting Marilyn started and getting his groceries put away.

Nathan pulled his lanky six-foot-two frame out of his small car after popping the hood. He propped it up, then leaned over the engine. He stared down at the hunk of metal as if he knew what he was doing, hoping he'd somehow magically see what was wrong. He knew nothing about cars, only that when he turned the key, the engine started . . . usually.

He was staring down into the hunk of steel that was Marilyn's engine when a slight cough sounded behind him, causing him to whirl around and curse himself for being caught unawares. He knew better than to leave himself vulnerable, especially since the Inca Boyz had tried to kill Alexis and vowed vengeance against her and his family.

The Inca Boyz were a gang from Denver who had gotten into the business of hiring themselves out as thugs online. The Anderson brothers had nearly put them out of business after working with the police to take them down. The leader of the gang, Donovan, had recently gotten out of jail, and all three of the brothers were on high alert, not knowing what the man would do, or if he'd try to get revenge on them for taking down his gang.

Nathan looked in shock at the woman standing in front of him. The first thing he noticed was her height. She had to be almost a foot shorter than he was, and the top of her head came to his shoulder. She had colorful sleeves of tattoos on both arms, her lips were pulled up into a smirk, and her eyes danced with humor. Her black hair blew around her in the evening breeze, the strands looking alive as they swirled around her head. She had high cheekbones, a small nose, and full lips that Nathan suddenly wanted to see wrapped around his dick.

He was shocked at the image that burst into his brain as if it were a memory instead of a fantasy. This woman on her knees in front of him, her tattoos bright against her pale skin, her lips wrapped around him as she took him deep into her mouth, her nipples peeking out between the curls of her black hair as she leaned into him.

The vision was surprising. He'd lost his virginity in high school at prom, and the experience hadn't been great. His date had obviously faked her orgasm and looked unimpressed as he'd tried to make it good for her.

He'd slept with a grand total of two more women in the last ten years. He'd learned a bit about what women liked and how to please them from those experiences, but he'd found that it was easier to jack off than to try to woo and date women simply to get his rocks off. Nathan's three sexual encounters had left him feeling as if he were missing something.

And now he finally knew what that something was. Passion.

He felt it simply by looking at the petite woman in front of him.

Her arms were crossed now, and her eyes had narrowed in irritation as she waited for him to say something.

"My car won't start." As far as enticing opening lines, it sucked, but Nathan had never been good at flirting.

"What did it sound like when you turned the key?"

Her voice was husky, and Nathan imagined it would only get huskier after she'd had an orgasm . . . or two.

He cleared his throat and tried to think about things like fixed and current assets and the profit-and-loss statement for Ace Security he was working on for the current quarter. But it was no use; his dick had gotten hard at the sound of her voice, and it didn't want to be denied. Nathan turned so he was facing the engine again, trying to spare the woman his inappropriate hard-on.

"Not it. She. Marilyn's her name. She didn't do anything."

"Men and their cars," the woman joked.

Nathan turned his head to see her join him at the front of his car. She braced her hands on the edge of the hood and leaned over, the muscles in her upper arms flexing as she moved, making her tattoos jump enticingly. He wanted to spend hours examining them. Piecing together what each one meant to her and why she'd wanted to get them inked on her body for all eternity.

"I don't know why men think cars are female," she continued, thankfully oblivious to his thoughts. "Seems to me that they act much more like men. They do what they want no matter how well someone takes care of them, and in the end will always let you down when you need them the most."

She didn't look at him as she spoke, but continued to stare down into the wires and steel that was Marilyn's engine. Her words saddened him and made him want to hunt down every man who'd ever let her down.

"I disagree," Nathan said softly, his eyes trained on the woman's face. He ran his hand over the side of the car and said, "Marilyn might look rough on the outside, but when treated right, she purrs. Not only that, but she's mine to take care of and protect. In return for making sure she's got what she needs to stay healthy and happy, she stands by me, supports me, and helps me get where I want to go. It's a give-and-take relationship."

The woman turned her head. "Are we still talking about cars?"

Nathan shrugged, keeping eye contact while memorizing everything he could about her. She was wearing a lot of makeup. Her eyes were dark chocolate brown and smoky, and met his without hesitation. Her lips were covered with dark lipstick, and long chain earrings brushed her shoulders with every movement.

"I'm just telling you why I see my car as female."

She rolled her eyes and looked back down at the engine, her earrings swinging with her movements. Reaching forward, she bent over the edge of the hood and stood on her tiptoes to reach a wire. Her arms were stretched out, and once again Nathan's mind sank into the gutter. His fingers clenched around the metal of the hood, and he locked himself in place so he didn't move.

He'd only had sex in the missionary position. Of course he knew other positions existed, but he hadn't been with any woman long enough to experiment. But in his mind he could clearly picture himself standing behind this woman as she leaned over his car, holding on to her hips as he took her from behind. His thoughts astonished him, as he'd believed himself to be immune to the lusty thoughts most men had. He'd honestly thought something was wrong with him, but this slight woman was proving that everything he'd thought about himself, and sex, was wrong.

"There."

The word was short and to the point. She stood upright next to him and wiped her hands on her jeans.

"What?"

"That should solve your problem for now."

"You fixed her?"

"For now, yeah," she semirepeated.

"Damn," Nathan breathed, impressed.

"What? You didn't think a woman who looked like me would know anything about cars, did you?"

"Honestly? No."

"You think I was gonna mug you?" She folded her arms across her chest now, her eyes shooting daggers at him.

Nathan held up his hands in capitulation. "The thought never crossed my mind. And there's nothing wrong with the way you look. I don't know what you *think* you look like, but trust me, you're the most feminine woman I've seen in a long time."

Her lip curled up in derision. "You don't have to lie. I already fixed your car. You're honestly gonna stand there and tell me my tattoos didn't make you nervous?"

Nathan's brows drew together in confusion. "Why would your tattoos make me nervous?"

She waved a hand in the air. "Just forget it. The wires to your battery are completely corroded. The connection is shot. It'll hold long enough for you to get where you're going, but I highly suggest you get this hunk of junk into the shop. Remember, if you take care of her, she'll take care of you . . . right?"

Nathan nodded absently, still stuck on her tattoo comment. "You wanna know what I thought when I first saw you?" he asked.

She looked surprised at his question but merely shrugged, as if she didn't care one way or another.

"I thought you were the sexiest woman I've ever seen in my life. And that you were so out of my league, there's no way you'd ever give a man like me a chance."

She stared up at him with her mouth slightly agape, as if he'd suddenly sprouted wings and was about to rise up into the sky.

He didn't give her a chance to respond. "Your tattoos are gorgeous. They fit you perfectly. I don't know you, but they seem to match what I imagine your personality to be. Slightly impulsive, passionate, with a no-holds-barred attitude, and when you find something you want, you go after it with determination and don't let anyone stand in your way."

"Oh," she murmured, looking away from him for the first time.

"Me? I'm a nerd. I'm more comfortable with my spreadsheets. Sexy women never seem to take a second glance at me, and I'm not fishing for compliments, just being factual. So, no, I wasn't thinking that you'd know anything about cars when I turned around and saw you. I've got two gallons of ice cream in a cooler in my trunk that I need to take into the office, and my nine-months-pregnant sister-in-law would kill me if it melted. So, yeah, I'm thrilled you know something about cars because the only thing I know is how to turn Marilyn on and that I need to fill her up every two hundred miles, or she'll let me know I'm neglecting her."

Nathan knew his words were full of innuendo, but he couldn't stop himself.

The fascinating woman in front of him licked her lips, but he didn't think she was purposely trying to be sexual. Which, of course, made it all that much more sexy.

"Yo! Sis! We going or what?"

Nathan turned his head to see a boy with black hair hanging out the window of a classic car. He had no idea what make it was—he really didn't know cars—but it looked sleek, shiny, and well cared for. The kid's upper body was hanging out of the front seat, his hands braced on the window frame.

The woman in front of him didn't respond, but reached around and pulled a card out of her back pocket. "Your car really does need some work. I'm happy to help. I work at Clayson's Auto Body off Wolfensberger Road. It's a bit out of the city, but if you're interested . . ."

Nathan immediately held out his hand and took the business card. "I'm interested. I'll call for an appointment tomorrow."

She nodded and gave him a small smile. It wasn't the smirk that had been on her face earlier. The one meant to keep people away. This was genuine and open.

"I'll make sure to tell my boss you'll be calling . . ." Her voice trailed off once more, this time in an obvious attempt at getting his name.

"Nathan. Nathan Anderson," he readily supplied, expecting her to reciprocate.

"Later, Nathan." She nodded at him and backed away toward her car.

Nathan opened his mouth to say something else, anything to prolong their chat, but she'd turned away and was striding confidently toward her car. He took a moment to admire her ass in the tight jeans as she walked, but didn't say another word as she climbed into the driver's side and drove out of the parking lot without another look back.

Reluctantly, and rather bemusedly, Nathan closed the hood of his car and got back inside. This time Marilyn started up without any issues, just as the woman said she would.

Looking down at the business card in his hand, Nathan swore he could still feel the heat of her body in the paper. Clayson's Auto Body. There was a picture of a car with its hood up on the front along with the address, phone number, and e-mail of the business. He turned it over absently and froze.

Written on the back was a hastily scrawled note that simply said, *Tell 'em Bailey sent you.*

It was obviously something she'd written ahead of time on all the cards she carried, but that wasn't what stopped Nathan in his tracks.

Bailey.

Was it a coincidence that the woman he'd been searching for over the last few months was also named Bailey? He and Alexis hadn't found hide nor hair of Donovan's ex-girlfriend. And they'd looked.

Was it possible that the petite dynamo who had knocked him off-kilter and made him feel lust for the first time in his life was *the* Bailey they'd been searching for? And what about the little boy? He knew his brothers thought it was possible the kid was Donovan's, but he hadn't been convinced then, and after seeing the boy, wasn't convinced now.

Nathan had more questions than answers as he pulled out of the supermarket parking lot. The second she'd handed him the card, he knew he'd be calling the shop as soon as they opened simply to give him an excuse to see her again. But he'd also been obsessed with finding the elusive Bailey for a long time, and he had a feeling she'd just miraculously fallen in his lap.

Chapter Two

Bailey Hampton absently nodded and responded to her brother Joel as they drove home from the supermarket. She'd seen the man staring down into his engine as if it held the answers to the meaning of life and simply couldn't walk away.

She tried to tell herself it was because it was an opportunity to bring business to the shop, but there was more to it than that, and she knew it.

There was just something about the man that did it for her. Even though he so wasn't the kind of guy she'd ever been attracted to. He'd been honest in his evaluation of himself. He did kinda look like a nerd, but there was something else she saw lurking behind his eyes. Passion. And not just for sex. Somehow Bailey knew that when he found something he liked—be it math, food, friends, family, or a woman—he put one hundred percent of himself into it. And that intrigued her.

Her choice in men had sucked, like really, *really* sucked, so she supposed it was probably a good thing that Nathan was as different as night and day from the men she'd been with in the past.

Bailey wasn't a saint. She'd slept with way too many men to count, including her English teacher her senior year—it had been the only way she'd passed his class.

She'd grown up in the poorest part of Denver and had barely graduated from high school. She'd become involved with the Inca Boyz at fourteen and had slept with most of the guys in the gang over the years. At first being around the gang members had been exciting, the danger and drugs was exhilarating. But as she'd gotten older, day after day of life around the gang was the same. Drinking, doing drugs, breaking into people's houses, having sex with anyone who wanted it when *they* wanted it, and she'd become more and more dissatisfied.

She sometimes wondered if the loss of her mother when she was little had somehow contributed to her needing attention and affection from men. But at some point the feelings of excitement and belonging she got from being around the dangerous men in the gang had morphed into powerlessness and degradation.

She was more than a sex toy. More than just someone to hang on the arm of the president and look pretty. She wanted more, and she was slowly coming to the realization that she deserved it.

She'd started tinkering with cars in middle school. Bailey used to hang out at the auto body shop her pa worked at after school, and had slowly picked it up. Her pa used to say she could take any car from the junkyard to the highway. And he'd been right. He'd died when she was twenty, and she'd suddenly found herself in charge of her little brother. At first she was pissed. She was the girlfriend of the president of the Inca Boyz gang—she didn't need a kid to worry about.

But as time went by, she'd learned to appreciate Joel's easygoing nature and personality. He was open and loved everyone he met. It had been tough to find and afford childcare, so she'd starting bringing her brother along when she hung out with Donovan and his Inca Boyz crew. It had been the worst mistake she'd ever made . . . and she'd made some big ones in her life.

Within two years, Joel's sunny disposition had changed to closed off and angry. Bailey hadn't understood why until the day she'd walked in on Donovan and Joel sitting on the couch watching hard-core porn on Donovan's laptop while Joel puffed on a joint.

She'd never brought her brother around the gang again and had started making plans to get away from Donovan and the gang life once and for all. She might be white trash and have done lots of things she now regretted with the men in the Inca Boyz gang, but there was no way she was going to let Donovan turn her sweet brother into a junkie, asshole killer like him.

So while Donovan and his two brothers were away doing something that was probably illegal, Bailey fled. She'd packed up everything she could fit into her restored 1969 Chevy Chevelle and headed south.

She'd gotten hired on by a man named Clayson Davis in a small auto body shop outside of Castle Rock. It wasn't far enough from Denver for her comfort, but it would have to do until she could save up enough money to get farther away. Bailey's ultimate goal was to open her own shop, but for now she was content to be left alone, to do an honest day's work, and to raise her brother the way Pa would've wanted.

". . . don't ya think?" Joel asked, bringing Bailey back into the conversation with a jolt.

"Sorry, I was thinking. What was that?"

"For my birthday party . . . it would be cool to have it at Chuck E. Cheese's," Joel repeated.

Bailey mentally cringed. There was no way she could afford it. The plan was to have Joel's tenth-birthday party at Philip S. Miller Park. It was near their house, had great trails, and there was a lot of free stuff Joel and his friends could do. She would have snacks, and they would invite everyone to bring their bikes.

"Maybe next year, bro," Bailey said. "You were all excited about the park. What happened?"

Joel looked away from her and out the side window and shrugged.

Bailey sighed in frustration. She knew Joel was having a hard time acclimating to the new school. He was the new kid, and as much as she hated to admit it, Donovan's actions had damaged her brother. Joel was confused and didn't understand why they'd moved. It broke her heart, but she just had to give him time, and love, and hopefully he'd get back to the person he'd been before Donovan had tried to turn him into an Inca Boy.

"Did you give out the invitations to the kids in your class?"

Joel didn't turn his head and merely shrugged again.

Bailey tried again. She reached out and put her hand on his shoulder. "What's wrong, bro?"

"Rob's birthday party is next week, and he's having it at Chuck E. Cheese's."

Bailey felt herself tense. The feelings of inadequacy and failing her brother crept up her throat. She forced them down and, in a voice that was huskier than normal, said, "Just because *he* is doesn't mean that *you* have to. It'll be a nice change to have yours somewhere different."

"He laughed when he saw my invitation. His were from the store and were cool," Joel mumbled.

Shit. Bailey put her hand back on the steering wheel and tried not to let the tears that had welled up in her eyes spill over. She and Joel had spent one evening making his invitations. She wasn't much of an artist, but she'd managed to draw pretty good bikes on the front of each of the twenty-two invitations. They'd laughed and joked with each other as they'd created them, and it was a memory she'd hold in her heart forever.

But now that memory was tarnished. Joel was embarrassed by his invitations. She knew money mattered, but back when she was growing up, it hadn't become an issue until middle school. Apparently in today's society, it mattered much earlier than when she was a kid.

Bailey frantically thought about what she could say that would make Joel feel better. "I'm sure all the parties are held at that pizza place. Yours will be unique. It'll be fun, you'll see."

Joel merely shrugged and kept his eyes on the passing scenery.

Her attempt at cheering him up was lame at best, and Bailey knew it. Kids were cruel. It was part of the reason she'd begun hanging out with older boys, and why she'd been sucked into the gang life. She'd been made to feel welcome, despite the fact that her pa was a mechanic and they didn't have much money. Despite the fact that she didn't have the most expensive clothes. Despite the fact that she hadn't lost her baby fat until she was a junior.

Bailey pulled into the driveway of their rental house, which was conveniently located near the auto body shop. The house was small and had two bedrooms and a main living area. The kitchen was tiny, but since Bailey didn't cook, it worked for her. She was making enough to keep Joel and her fed as well as clothed . . . if buying clothes from Walmart counted as clothed, but compared to where she'd been a few short months ago, it was perfect.

Bailey cut the engine, and Joel immediately climbed out of the car. He began to walk up to the door but stopped short when Bailey called, "Please help me with the groceries, bro."

He turned and faced her, and Bailey almost took a step back at the look of hate in his eyes. She'd seen that look before, right when they'd moved to Castle Rock, but she'd hoped that time would erase it.

"Carrying shit is woman's work."

She tried not to flinch or lash out at Joel. He was only repeating what he'd heard from the Inca Boyz. He was frustrated and upset about the invitations to his birthday and didn't know how to properly express his feelings. Bailey kept her voice even. "You know that's not true, Joel. You eat the food as much as I do. The polite thing to do is to help me."

She held her breath waiting for his response.

After a tense few moments, Joel finally shrugged and reluctantly walked back toward the car.

Her breath came out in an inaudible whoosh. Thank God he hadn't pushed. It was getting harder and harder to know what the right response was to his moods. She'd backed down with Donovan all the time, even though she knew she shouldn't have. She should've been stronger with him. Stood up to him. But she hadn't. Especially right before she'd left. When she first met Donovan, he was nice. Gentle with her, had even wooed her—well, as much as a gang member could—before he'd taken her to bed. But in the months before she'd left, Bailey hadn't seen any gentleness in him. When she disagreed or contradicted him, he'd hit her, or make her have sex with one of his brothers . . . even though he knew she didn't like either of them. Remembering how cruel Donovan had been at the end made her shudder. She took a deep breath, forcing the memories away. Her ex wasn't here now. She was safe.

She and Joel loaded up their arms with the grocery bags, and Bailey unlocked the front door. "Wait here," she commanded as she did every time they came home.

She always checked out the house before Joel was allowed to enter. The last thing she wanted was to come home and find Donovan or one of the Inca Boyz lying in wait. Joel knew if she screamed, he was to run. He was supposed to go into the woods and make his way to the auto body shop. If it was after closing time, he knew where the spare key was hidden and that he was to go inside and immediately call 911.

The little house looked like it had that morning when they'd left for school and work. The crappy brown couch against the wall, the TV with the antenna covered in tinfoil, the surprisingly comfortable recliner Clayson had given her not long after they'd moved in. Turning her head to the small kitchen, Bailey saw the dishes they'd used that morning still sitting in the sink waiting to be washed.

She stepped past the small end table next to the couch and quickly entered the short hallway that led to the bedrooms. She pushed open Joel's door, and her eyes swept the room, finding nothing amiss. It was a mess, with the few toys he'd brought with him from Denver and clothes strewn all over the place. She could almost not even see the navy-blue thrift-shop comforter because of clothes—both dirty and clean, she assumed—thrown over it. The stained carpet peeked out from under toys, more clothes, and shoes.

An old television sat on a broken table with a game system sitting next to it. She hadn't wanted to bring it with them, as Donovan had given it to Joel, but Bailey knew her brother loved playing the few video games he had, and she didn't have the heart to leave it behind. Not to mention she knew he'd never forgive her if she denied him the ability to play his precious *This Is War* game. It was way too advanced for a fourth grader, but Donovan hadn't cared when he'd bought it for her brother. Hell, he'd probably been happy it was so violent. It was just one more way to mold Joel into the proper Inca Boy.

Bailey quickly backed out of the room, took the few steps to her own bedroom, and opened the door. It was just as she'd left it. Nothing out of place and almost nothing personal to see. Nothing except for the picture of her, Joel, and Pa on the decrepit dresser against the wall.

Her eyes flicked to the duffel bag sitting by the window. Her go-bag. It had a change of clothes for both Joel and her, five hundred dollars sewed into the lining, a knife, and the gun she'd stolen from Donovan before she'd run. It wasn't much, but if she had to get out fast, she wanted money to start over someplace new and a way to protect Joel. He was all that mattered.

Bailey sighed and thought about her brother as she quickly checked the only bathroom in the house. Her only goal in life was to try to raise Joel to be a good man. So far she was failing, though.

She glanced down at her arm. Bailey hadn't thought twice about getting herself inked. All the Inca Boyz had tattoos, and she wanted to be just like them. To fit in. So she'd let the guys in the gang talk her into ink after ink. Guns, roses, barbed wire, skulls, knives, even the stupid cartoonlike logo they'd adopted as their signature. Now both arms were covered from wrist to shoulder with the ink. It represented a time in her life she wasn't proud of, and would rather forget altogether.

But her arms weren't what she regretted the most. It was the tattoo on her lower back that made her skin crawl. She hadn't wanted it, but Donovan had insisted. Actually, he'd forced her to get trashed; then he had his brothers hold her down while his friend inked her. She'd pleaded with them to let her up, told him that she loved him but didn't want to be branded with the ink. The men had ignored her and talked above her as if she wasn't even there.

"Everyone will know who she belongs to."

"Every time you fuck her, you'll see it."

"Make it bigger than usual." That had been Donovan. *"I want a good target when we gangbang 'er."*

Bailey had passed out before the tattoo had been completed. She hadn't felt truly contaminated and ashamed of who she was until she'd been allowed to look in a mirror. The writing was fancy and would've been beautiful if it wasn't for the words.

PROPERTY OF INCA BOYZ
D'S WHORE

And the tattoo was huge. The first phrase went from one side of her waist to the other, and she could easily see the *P* and the *Z* from the front. The other two words were smaller, but the two arrows pointing down to her ass made it all the more humiliating.

Not a second went by that Bailey didn't feel dirty because of the words inked on her body. She'd been a whore. And she knew that while she might've left Denver, she *was* still Inca Boyz property. And they didn't like losing what was theirs.

The way Bailey figured it, if she could outrun and hide from them until Joel was at least sixteen, he'd be okay. He was a smart kid, even though he was almost ten. Six years felt like an eternity, but if she was careful, she could last that long.

The tattoo on her lower back itched, and it felt like bugs were crawling on her skin, but that was nothing new. She always felt like that and had learned to ignore it, mostly.

She quickly headed back to the front door and smiled at Joel. Even though he was upset with her about his party, he still looked nervous and scared.

"All's good, bro. Let's get this stuff into the fridge before it goes bad. Yeah?"

He didn't say anything, but brushed past her and the bags she'd put on the floor to head into the kitchen. Bailey heard him put the bags down before heading for his room as she came into the living area.

Deciding to give him some time, she didn't make him come back and help her put away the groceries. She'd learned that when his brain was on overload, it was a better idea to give him the time and space to work through whatever was bothering him.

As Bailey put away the groceries, she thought about the man in the parking lot. She usually didn't stop and help people—men, especially—when they had car trouble. But something about the tall, slender man had made it almost impossible to walk away.

He'd been staring down into his engine as though if he looked at it long enough, it would magically fix itself. He was nothing like the gangbangers she'd hung out with. At first he seemed almost shy and not sure of himself at all. But the more they'd talked, he'd seemed to gain confidence. He'd called himself a nerd, and she supposed he probably was at that. But with every word out of his mouth, she got more of a read on his personality and who he was as a person.

She's mine to take care of and protect. In return for making sure she's got what she needs to stay healthy and happy, she stands by me, supports me, and helps me get where I want to go. It's a give-and-take relationship.

He'd been talking about his car, but she could easily see him treating a woman he was with in the same way. She'd never been in a give-and-take relationship; it had always been her giving and an Inca Boy taking.

I'm more comfortable with my numbers.

Bailey had no idea what kind of women he'd been hanging around with, but they were obviously all idiots. Nathan was attractive, no doubt. But she had a feeling he didn't think so. Bailey had been with men more handsome than Nathan. Men who women literally drooled over as they walked down the street. But they'd been so into what they looked like and what they were feeling that they didn't have the slightest idea how to make their partner feel good.

But the fact that Nathan was buying ice cream for his sister-in-law cemented the fact that he liked to take care of women. No man had ever taken what *she* liked into consideration.

Not in the bedroom.

Not when they went out to eat.

Not in any way.

I thought you were so out of my league, there's no way you'd ever give a man like me a chance.

She was out of *his* league? Not hardly. He might've been driving a piece-of-crap car, but it was obvious he wasn't hurting for money. His clothes weren't from Walmart, and the watch on his wrist was worth several thousand dollars. She'd been trained by the gang to recognize quality when she saw it, and Nathan Anderson might've thought she was out of his league, but she wasn't even worth the gum on the bottom of his shoe. If he knew what she'd done and where she was from, he wouldn't even have let her look at his engine.

Sexy women never seem to take a second glance at me.

You're passionate, with a no-holds-barred attitude, and when you find something you want, you go after it with determination and don't let anyone stand in your way.

God. Every word out of his mouth had made her yearn for the thousandth time that she was a different person. That she was the person Nathan saw. But she wasn't. She was filth. A whore who'd slept with more men than she could count. She certainly didn't feel as though she was standing up for herself, especially when it came to the Inca Boyz.

Bailey heard Joel stomping around in his room, and it was enough to cause the tears she'd been holding back to break through.

Sliding down the wall in the kitchen, ignoring the way the cabinet handle dug into her back as she moved, Bailey hugged her knees and buried her head between them . . . and cried. She had no idea what she was doing with Joel. She was probably screwing him up worse than Donovan ever could. She didn't have the money to get him the things he wanted and needed—she was barely scraping by with her salary from the auto body store. She'd never earn enough to start her own business. She'd never get out of Colorado, and it was only a matter of time before the Inca Boyz found her and retrieved their property.

Ironic that she had more self-esteem when she was hanging out with the gang and being treated like shit than when she'd escaped that life. She might be only twenty-four, but she felt like she was eighty-four. Crushed by the weight of her life and the responsibility to raise her brother to be a good man.

Joel didn't come out of his room for the rest of the night.

Bailey fell asleep on the crappy couch, as usual, a knife hidden under the cushion, ready and willing to die for her brother, even if he couldn't stand her.

Chapter Three

"Bailey! Phone!"

Clayson's voice rang out through the garage, and Bailey's heart started to thud in panic. No one ever called for her . . . except Joel's school.

She grabbed for a rag to wipe her hands and hopped off the small stepladder in front of the SUV. Unlike most of the other mechanics, she needed the extra inches to reach the innards of the engine. She'd been teased, but didn't care. Her height was what it was. She quickly strode into the small office off the bays of the garage.

Clayson was sitting at his desk holding the ancient phone receiver out to her.

The owner of the body shop met her eyes straight on, but Bailey couldn't read anything in them. She gave him a small half smile and nervously took hold of the phone.

"Hello?"

"Hi. Is this Bailey?"

"Yes. Who is this?" But she knew. From four words, she knew exactly who was on the other end of the line.

"Nathan Anderson. We met last night and you gave me your card."

"Right." Bailey wasn't trying to be gruff or coy, but she'd had a hard night, her self-esteem was as low as it'd been in a long time, Joel was still giving her the silent treatment, and now the first man she'd been remotely interested in for way too many years was speaking in her ear, and it made goose bumps travel down both arms as if he was right there beside her, nibbling on said ear.

"I'd like to make an appointment to bring Marilyn in."

At the reminder of the silly name he'd given his car, Bailey couldn't stop the twitch of her lips. "You could've done that with Clayson. You didn't have to talk to me personally."

"But I wanted to."

His voice had dropped, and Bailey shivered. As if Clayson knew exactly what was being said, he pushed the appointment book over in front of her. The older man didn't use a computer; he still used the archaic schedule-book-and-pencil method for scheduling appointments. She swallowed hard and forced herself to sound as businesslike as possible.

"When is good for you?"

"When is your schedule open?"

"What do you mean?" Bailey asked, her brows furrowing in confusion at the question.

"I want *you* to work on Marilyn. Not someone else. So when do you have time in your schedule to take a look at her?"

"Oh, um, Clayson's isn't that kind of garage. We don't schedule specific mechanics for specific vehicles. We can all work on all the cars that come in. It just depends on who is doing what at the time."

"I trust *you*. Not anyone else."

She spun so her back was to Clayson. She liked him, but she really wasn't comfortable having this conversation in front of him. "Everyone here at Clayson's is more than qualified to look at your car, Nathan. Besides, I already told you, it's not a big deal. I'm pretty sure all you need, for now, is a new battery."

"Great. So when can you look at her and let me know for sure?"

Sighing, Bailey knew he wasn't going to drop it. He wanted her to look at his car, and no one else would do. Fine. She'd just tell him a time, and he'd never know whom it was who serviced it.

"How about Friday at four. Will that work?"

"And you'll look at her?" Nathan insisted.

Bailey looked up at the ceiling. God, he was persistent. "Yeah. I'll be here." She usually picked Joel up at school around three, and Clayson allowed him to hang out at the garage from three thirty until she was off at five. It wasn't ideal, but she wasn't about to leave him home by himself. Not with the Inca Boyz breathing down her neck.

"Great. I'll see you Friday. Take care of yourself until then," was Nathan's unusual response.

"I always do," was her retort.

If possible, Nathan's voice dropped even more as he said, "I know you do, pixie, but soon you'll have help."

Bailey's mouth opened to ask what the hell he meant when the dial tone sounded in her ear. She pulled the handset away from her ear and stared at it in disbelief. She'd have help? Pixie? *What the fuck?*

"Friday at four. Got it," Clayson told her as he scribbled in the appointment book. "Name? Car? Problem?"

Placing the handset back in the cradle, Bailey shook her head in exasperation. God, Nathan might say he was a nerd, and he might say that he didn't like people that much, but he sure was bossy and good at getting people to do what he wanted. Most nerds she'd known growing up were soft-spoken and reluctant to push their will on anyone. Nathan sure as heck wasn't like any of the boys she'd known in the past, that was for sure.

She took a deep breath to get her emotions under control. She wasn't pissed—Nathan hadn't really done anything to be mad at—but she was confused, her blood seemed like it was flowing faster through her veins, and she could feel her heart beating fast. It was bewildering, and she didn't like it. At all.

"Nathan Anderson. He has a Ford Focus. Probably around a mid-two-thousand model. I helped him in a parking lot in town yesterday.

His car wouldn't start, and it looks like it's a simple matter of replacing either the battery or the connections, which were extremely corroded."

Clayson nodded and leaned back in his chair, his hands clasped behind his head as he eyed Bailey closely. "He bothering you?"

Surprised, she blurted, "No!"

"Good. Because if anyone thinks he can put his hands on you without your say-so, he's got another thing coming. Me an' the boys'll take care of 'em. Just let us know. Okay, sweetheart?"

Bailey swallowed hard against the lump that rose in her throat at his words. Clayson reminded her a lot of her pa. Her dad had never liked Donovan or any of the boys in the gang. Bailey didn't know if her pa knew exactly what she did outside his house, but she had a feeling he did. He'd died while helping a friend work on his car when the lift the car had been on collapsed, pinning her dad underneath. The day before he'd been killed, he'd taken her head in his hands and told her that he worried about her. That he loved her more than anything, and he'd kill any man who hurt her.

At the time Bailey hadn't thought much about her dad's words, but now she knew without a doubt that he would've put a bullet in Donovan's head if he knew what the gang member had turned her into.

She probably should've been worried about the threat she heard in Clayson's voice, but she wasn't. It wasn't like the four other mechanics were gang members. They were rednecks and a little rough around the edges, but she honestly liked them. Duke, the youngest, was around her age and was brash and bold, as only a man who had the entire world in front of him could be. He was typically the one to volunteer to come in and work on Saturdays when they had enough business to do so.

Henry was in his late twenties and newly married. He'd only known his new wife for six months, and she was already pregnant. He'd told them all that when you met the person you were meant to spend the rest of your life with, you better get started on that. Bailey hoped like hell the couple made it. She knew firsthand how well relationships could start, and how fast they could turn bad.

Ozzie was probably about ten years older than she was, and she'd been scared of him at first. He had a beard down to his midchest, and not a pretty, groomed beard either. It was shaggy and rough, which made him look at least ten years older. He also had a patch over his right eye. She hadn't heard the story of how he'd lost his eye, but she'd gotten the impression it had something to do with a chick.

Bert was the oldest mechanic and had started the shop with Clayson. They'd worked together for twenty years, and Bailey had caught him studying her on more than one occasion. He always wore jean overalls, and his beer belly stuck out from his middle. It was a good thing the man had long arms; otherwise he'd need a stepladder to reach engines just like she did, except in his case it would be because the bulk of his stomach wouldn't let him lean over properly.

All in all, she liked the men she worked with. They respected her as a mechanic, which meant the world to her.

She hadn't been sure she'd even be able to find a job at an auto body shop because of her gender and the way she looked. But Clayson had been desperate. The day she'd walked in inquiring about the **Now Hiring** sign in the window, he'd pointed to a car in one of the bays and told her that for her job interview, she had to tell him what was wrong with the vehicle. After a thorough examination of the car, and feeling horribly out of place with not only Clayson watching her work, but the other four mechanics as well, she told the owner that not only were the brake pads worn, but there was brake dust inside the drum. She'd gone on to report that the radiator fan was shot, and there was a leak in the coolant hose. Clayson had immediately offered her the job.

The guys treated her like a little sister, which was fine with her. The last thing she wanted was to have to fend off unwanted romantic attention from a coworker. She'd written off men for good, knowing no one would want to date a former whore.

"It's fine, Clayson. I appreciate the concern, but I'm good."

"Mmm," the owner of the shop murmured noncommittedly. "I've got lots of paperwork to get done this week. I'm sure I'll be around on Friday afternoon."

Bailey barely resisted the urge to roll her eyes at the protective older man. She'd never admit it, as it would embarrass both Clayson and her, but it felt good to be worried about. "I'm sure you will," she told him. "Gotta get back to work." She gave her boss a half wave and headed back out into the garage bays.

She wasn't really worried about Nathan Anderson. He'd bring his car in on Friday, she'd be cold and professional with him, and he'd get the hint that she wanted nothing to do with him.

As Bailey stepped back up on the stool and got to work putting the guts of the vehicle she'd been working on back together before Clayson had called her into the office, she ignored the little voice inside her head that called her a liar.

Chapter Four

"Something wrong with your car?" Blake asked Nathan after he'd hung up the phone. He and Logan had walked into the office in the middle of his short conversation.

"Yeah. Don't think it's anything major, though."

"That's good. I'm surprised that heap is still running," Logan observed from the other side of his desk, not able to keep the smirk off his face.

"I take good care of Marilyn," Nathan protested. "She might look rough on the outside, but on the inside she purrs like a cat."

Blake's grin took over his face as he said dryly, "Are we still talking about your car?"

Nathan was taken aback, as that was almost exactly what Bailey had asked him the night before. And speaking of his favorite mechanic . . .

"I'm pretty sure I found Bailey."

His words had the effect of a grenade lobbed into the office. Both Logan and Blake's heads whipped around and they stared at Nathan.

The questions came at the same time.

"What?"

"Where?"

"She's here in Castle Rock," Nathan told his brothers calmly.

"No shit?" Logan asked. "So all that detective work you and Alexis did finally panned out."

Nathan shook his head. "Nope. We had no leads to where she was. All we had was what the women in the gang said about her."

For some reason Nathan had been obsessed with finding Bailey from the get-go. He didn't know what she looked like, didn't know much about her at all. But he did know how the people she hung out with described her.

Even though she was the prez's woman, she still talked to us.

She had the greatest laugh.

The bitch sure did love that kid.

She was almost like a sister to me.

I don't blame her for bolting.

The women in the gang hadn't had many good things to say about each other, but not one had really bad-mouthed the mysterious Bailey. They weren't exactly nominating her for sainthood, but they weren't purposely throwing her under the proverbial bus. But knowing there was a child involved had really touched Nathan's heart.

His own mother hadn't given one little shit about his brothers or him. He didn't know if the child was somehow related to her—maybe her own kid—or if it was a street kid she'd taken responsibility for, but it had made Nathan all that more determined to find her.

Anyone who would risk her life to get away from the Inca Boyz—and take a defenseless kid with her—was someone he wanted to know. Needed to know.

"Then how'd you find her?" Blake asked, leaning against his desk and crossing his arms.

"She found me, actually." At the looks of exasperation and impatience on his brothers' faces, he elaborated. "Marilyn wouldn't start last night. I couldn't get ahold of either of you and was trying to figure out how to solve whatever problem she had by myself, when a woman came up to me and offered to help."

"Damn," Blake breathed. "Bailey?"

"Yup. Although I didn't know it was her at the time," Nathan told him. "We shot the shit for a bit, she gave me a card to the auto body shop she works at, and left."

"You let her leave?" Logan asked, his eyebrows raised in bewilderment.

"She didn't introduce herself right off the bat, so I didn't know it was her."

Blake said, "How do you know her name is even Bailey?"

"She wrote her name on the back of the card."

"That doesn't mean she's Donovan's Bailey," Logan argued reasonably.

Nathan's hands clenched into fists. "She's not Donovan's," he gritted out between his teeth.

Blake and Logan looked taken aback at the fierceness of their brother's words. Nathan was the easygoing one. The man who let things roll off his back. Yes, he'd been intense in his search for the mysterious Bailey, but he hadn't ever gotten defensive about anything they'd said before. Not like this.

Blake held his hands up in capitulation, and Logan merely nodded his acquiescence as he clarified, "Just because her name is Bailey doesn't mean she's the ex-girlfriend of the leader of the Inca Boyz, Nathan."

"True. But I have a feeling that she is. Not only was she skittish as could be, but both of her arms are covered in tattoos." Nathan held up a hand to forestall the protests he knew were coming and continued. "I didn't get a good look at them, but one was that stupid-ass white cartoon logo they've adopted as their symbol."

"Damn," Blake breathed. "She's pushing her luck living so close to Denver."

"There's more," Nathan said.

"More? Damn." Blake pushed off his desk, walked around it to pull out his chair, and settled into it. "Let's hear it."

"She's got the kid the gang women mentioned with her."

"Donovan's kid?" Logan asked.

Nathan felt his fingernails cutting into his palm as he clenched his fists again. "No," he bit out, agitated again. "Kid called her sis, and she said he was her brother. I believe her. They look similar. I don't know exactly how old either of them is, but if he was hers, she would've had to have had him when she was around twelve."

"Not unheard of in the gang lifestyle," Logan observed dryly.

"Look. If she had Donovan's child, we would've known about it. Someone would've said something by now. Hell, Alexis would've gotten an earful when she was undercover. You think that bitch Kelly who was jealous as shit of Bailey would've stayed quiet about it?"

His brothers were silent. They both knew Nathan was right.

"I just have a hunch, this is her," Nathan insisted.

"What's the plan?" Logan asked.

"I'm bringing my car to her shop on Friday, and I'll go from there."

The three brothers eyed each other for a long moment before Logan stated, "You like her."

Nathan didn't quibble. "I like her. Not only that, but she intrigues me. At first I thought she was probably a hard-ass gang bitch, but if she was, why leave without a trace? Why did Kelly hate her so much? When I couldn't find any trace of her, she impressed me with how well she covered her tracks. She had to be clever to do that. She was a puzzle I needed to solve."

"Then you met her," Blake said.

Nathan nodded. "She's nothing like what I imagined. Oh, she's got her shields up pretty high to protect herself, which doesn't surprise me. But for someone who lived the gang life for as long as she did, if you take away the tattoos, she could be the girl next door. She's scared to death and doing a piss-poor job of hiding it. Not to mention she loves her brother. The look in her eyes when she looked over at him reminded me of the loyalty we share."

"She might have run because of him," Logan stated flatly.

Nathan simply nodded.

"If Donovan or any of the others threatened him, she could have left to protect him," Blake agreed. "If that's the case, I don't even need to meet her to know I like the woman."

Nathan looked at his two brothers. The three of them understood sibling loyalty. They'd been through hell in their childhood, dodging their mother's fists, and doing their best to protect each other. Logan had been thc onc who took most of her rage, and he did it willingly, knowing it meant his brothers would be spared.

"For now, I'm going to bring my car to her shop and see if she'll open up to me. She's closed off and ultrawary, and I can't blame her. But if we're going to make sure Donovan and his crew leave her alone, I need to get her to trust me."

"You think she knows Donovan's out?" Logan asked, the anger simmering in his eyes.

Nathan knew the fact that the gangbanger was already out of jail stuck in both his brothers' craws. Donovan had been released early for good behavior and because of jail overcrowding. The man had been responsible for taking lewd pictures of Logan's wife and Alexis's brother. Not to mention, Donovan's brothers had kidnapped and planned to kill Alexis. Thankfully they failed. No, the Inca Boyz gang wasn't on the top of the Anderson brothers' list of friends.

If Kelly's rants had been correct, Donovan, and what was left of the Inca Boyz, would probably be looking for Bailey right this second. Nathan's only consolation was that if he and Alexis hadn't been able to find her, most likely Donovan couldn't either.

"I doubt it," Nathan answered his brother. "I have a feeling if she knew Donovan was out of jail, she'd bolt."

"Sorry we weren't around yesterday to help you out," Blake said. "I took Alexis out to dinner, and afterward we went to Rock Park and hiked it."

"I thought it closed at sunset?" Nathan asked.

Blake shrugged. "It does. But when she starts to feel claustrophobic, she needs to hike, to feel more in charge of herself. I parked on Gilbert Street, and we hiked up to the trail on the back side."

"She still having nightmares?" Nathan asked. Alexis hadn't said anything to him, not that she would, but she was still having trouble dealing with what had happened to her after the Inca Boyz had kidnapped her and buried her up to her neck.

"Some," Blake confirmed. "But she's seeing someone, and we're working it out."

"I didn't see that you'd called until a few hours afterward," Logan told Nathan. "Grace is exhausted. I know she is more than ready to have our boys. She lay down for a nap and was so uncomfortable, I climbed in bed with her. It seems that she can only sleep if she's sitting up against me." He shrugged, a half smile on his face as he thought about his pregnant wife. "We both ended up falling asleep."

"It's fine," Nathan assured both his brothers. "Bailey got Marilyn started again, and all's well."

"I'll make sure I've got my phone from now on," Logan assured his brother.

"Me too," Blake agreed. "Although if we're in the mountains, I might not have reception, like last night."

"Seriously, it's good," Nathan said again. "You guys have your women to look after now. They should always come first."

"Maybe so," Logan said in a serious voice, leaning his elbows on his desk. "But that doesn't mean that you'll ever be less important in our lives. We might've been apart for ten years, but that doesn't mean that I didn't think about you both during that time. We're brothers. We're blood."

"Thanks," Nathan said immediately, feeling respect and love for his siblings well up in his chest. All three of them had left home right after graduating from high school, mostly to get away from their abusive mother. Letters were few and far between in the years between leaving and coming back home to Castle Rock after their father was murdered.

Nathan had missed his brothers more than he realized. Missed their support and simply having someone there who understood what he'd been through, because they'd been right there with him.

Nathan had always felt restless and unsettled after high school, and he knew now it was because he hadn't been with his brothers. They were fraternal triplets, they had the same blood in their veins.

"You'll let us know Saturday what happens with Bailey?" Blake asked.

Nathan nodded. "Of course."

Deciding it was time to change the subject, Nathan asked Logan, "You decide what you're naming those babies of yours?"

The other man shrugged, but the look of pride and anticipation was clear in his dark eyes. "We've got some names in mind, but nothing concrete. Grace says she wants to wait and see her sons before she decides. Something about knowing what name will be right for them after she meets them. I don't really care, as long as everyone is all right when it's all said and done."

"The doc have any idea when she'll have them?" Blake asked.

"Soon, is all he'll say. It could be today, or two weeks from now. It's up to those babies. And if they're as stubborn as their mama, I'm putting my money on two weeks from now," Logan said, his voice gruff as if he was trying to keep both the emotion from overtaking him and also keep from laughing.

Blake leaned over, took out his wallet, and put two twenties on the desk in front of him. "Forty bucks says it'll be this weekend."

Nathan smiled and reached for his own wallet, taking out a couple of bills and putting them on top of his own desk. "I'm in on this bet. I say it'll be another two weeks."

"What're we betting on?" Alexis chirped as she strode into the room.

Blake immediately pushed away from his desk and went to meet her. He put one hand behind her neck and the other around her waist and pulled her into him, kissing her as if he hadn't seen her for days instead of only hours.

He pulled back, but didn't release her. "You have a good morning?"

She smiled up at him and nodded, her hands resting on his biceps. "Yeah." Then she turned her head and looked over at Nathan. "So . . . what're we betting on?"

"When Grace is gonna have those babies she's been hauling around."

"I'm so in on that. What dates have been taken so far?" She jumped in immediately.

"Blake took this weekend, and I'm saying in two weeks," Nathan told her.

"Then I'll take next weekend. Honey, you'll spot me the ante, won't you?" she asked, smiling up at Blake and blinking innocently.

He rolled his eyes and grumbled good-naturedly, but walked her back over to her desk before adding two more bills to the pile.

"You know if Grace finds out we're betting on this, she's gonna lose her mind," Logan observed.

"Betting on what?" Grace asked as she waddled into the large office space.

Logan was out of his chair and by his wife's side before the last word had left her mouth.

"What are you doing here? How did you get here? You better not have driven," he barked, as he led Grace to the sofa they'd added to the office after Grace had gotten pregnant.

Grace put her hand on Logan's forearm, on top of the pink tattoo of two birds in flight, and stroked it gently as she said softly, "Felicity's back from Chicago and dropped me off. We both know I can't fit behind the wheel of our car anymore."

Logan kissed her temple after he got her settled onto the cushions, and sat next to her.

"Now . . . what are we betting on?" she asked stubbornly.

"When you'll give birth," Alexis told her with a smile. "Blake says this weekend, I say next weekend, and Nathan says in two weeks."

Grace turned to glare at her brother-in-law. "Two weeks? Lord have mercy. If I had my way, I'd have them today. I'm so done with being pregnant."

Everyone laughed, and Logan reassured his wife that she'd have their twins when they were good and ready to come out, and not a second before.

Nathan looked at his family as everyone got settled. Grace and Alexis were perfect for his brothers, and he genuinely liked them both. He hadn't ever been jealous of his siblings . . . until now. Somehow, meeting Bailey and seeing through his brothers' relationships what he was missing made his life seem empty. He had a small house, enjoyed living alone, but he realized suddenly that he was lonely.

He might not like people in general, but he liked Grace and Alexis. And he liked his brothers. He enjoyed spending time with them, but it wasn't the same as having a woman sleep next to him. Or the same as hearing her breathe as she slept. To wake up and know someone was by your side. To eat meals made by someone else. To say nothing, but watch television or a movie with someone.

And he wanted that.

Wanted it with Bailey.

Which was insane. He didn't know her, and she didn't know him.

But as surely as he knew he'd lay down his life for his brothers and their women, he knew Bailey was meant to be his.

There had to be a reason he'd been so determined to find her.

He wanted to claim Bailey as his own, and her brother too.

As the gentle banter continued around him, Nathan made a vow right then and there to do whatever he could to bring Bailey into the fold. He might not be suave, or the best conversationalist, or even the most interesting man, but Bailey needed family. Needed someone to have her back.

And that someone was going to be him.

Chapter Five

At ten till four, Nathan pulled Marilyn into an empty space in front of one of the garage bays at Clayson's Auto Body and climbed out. Seeing no one inside the bays, he pushed open the front door to the business and looked around.

Clayson's was a typical garage. The waiting room wasn't large, but it had a television, a small table with a few magazines on it, a counter with a cash register, and four hard plastic chairs. It was serviceable, if not that comfortable, but clean.

Nathan had just opened his mouth to call out to see if anyone was around, when an older man with black hair liberally streaked with gray came out of a door in the back of the room. He ambled up to the counter, leaned over it on both hands, and pierced Nathan with a stern look.

"Nathan Anderson. Good to see you."

Nathan didn't get upset at the protective vibes emanating from the man. If nothing else, he was glad about them. Happy that Bailey had someone looking out for her. He didn't recall meeting the man in front of him before, but it was obvious the older man knew who he was. "Yes," he answered with a nod of his head.

The men eyed each other for a moment before Clayson cut to the chase. "Don't fuck with Bailey."

"I won't," Nathan returned simply. He stood with his hands in his pockets and met the man's gaze head-on.

It took another few moments, but the man must've seen whatever he was looking for in Nathan's eyes as he nodded once, then turned back toward the door behind him. Right before he went through it, he looked back at Nathan and said, "Well? Come on."

Without hesitation, Nathan veered around the counter and followed the man into the back room of the garage.

He entered an office, which was much more comfortable-looking, and cluttered, than the sparse public waiting area. But instead of noticing the furniture, or caring about the piles of papers, Nathan's eyes immediately went to Bailey.

She was sitting on the couch next to her brother. They were hunched over a book on his lap, and she was pointing at something on the page. She wore a dark T-shirt under a pair of overalls that were smeared with grease. On her feet she had a pair of black steel-toed boots. Her hair was pulled back into a messy ponytail that she was twirling around one finger as she concentrated on what was in the book in front of her.

The boy had on a pair of jeans that looked too short for his lanky frame, and a T-shirt that had a picture of Batman on it. He looked frustrated about something, no doubt whatever it was in the textbook in his lap.

At his entrance, they both looked up, and Nathan knew without a doubt that they were indeed brother and sister. They both had the same black hair, but the boy was going to be big. Not fat, but tall. He was also built very differently than Bailey. He was stocky and well on his way to being a formidable figure of a man.

Nathan gave the couple on the couch a chin lift in greeting and said, "Hello."

"Oh crud, is it four already?" Bailey said, looking at her left wrist as if she was looking at a watch . . . except there was no watch there. She leaned over and kissed the top of the boy's head and stood up. "Joel, keep working on those math problems. When I'm done, I'll take another look at it. Don't worry, we'll figure it out." Then she looked up at Nathan.

"Hi, Nathan. You park outside the bay doors?"

He nodded, not particularly liking the businesslike tone of her voice, but he didn't get a chance to say anything else.

"Great." She held out her hand. "Give me your keys, and I'll get right to work. If it's only the battery, it shouldn't take longer than around half an hour, forty-five minutes tops, to get it switched out and those connections cleaned."

Nathan wanted to prolong his time with her, but couldn't figure out how without looking like he was *trying* to prolong his time with her. So he merely fished his key ring out of his pocket and dropped it into her hand, making sure to brush his fingertips against her palm as he did.

Her hand twitched under his, but she quickly closed her fingers around the keys and turned to the older man. "Clayson, if you'll take his info, I'll let you know when I'm done."

"Take your time, hon," the older man said without concern.

"Thanks." And with that, she was gone.

Nathan's eyes flicked to Joel, who hadn't moved from the couch, to Clayson.

The older man was looking at him with a smirk now, as if something about what had just happened amused him. But he merely held out a clipboard with a piece of paper on it. "If you can fill this out, we'll have all the info we need. Bailey'll come in and let you know what's wrong before she does any work, along with the estimate."

Nathan nodded and took the clipboard and pen from the man. He looked around at his seating options, and decided to take a chance and sit next to Joel.

He settled into the seat Bailey had occupied, feeling a thrill when the warmth from her body still lingering in the cushion soaked into his backside.

The form had basic information on it, and Nathan was done with it in only a few minutes. He glanced over at the math problems Joel was working on and blinked. His words came out without thought. "What the hell are you doing?" They weren't rough or mean, but completely baffled.

The boy looked up at him in surprise and said simply, "Math."

"That doesn't look like any kind of math I've seen," Nathan said, his eyes on the worksheet in front of the boy and his eyebrows drawn down in confusion.

"That's what Bailey says too," Joel responded.

Nathan looked up at him for the first time. "Your sister is right."

Joel didn't look confused or upset at his statement, and Nathan was pleased to know he was right about them being siblings.

"It's Common Core math."

Nathan looked at him blankly.

"It's how they're teaching math these days."

"It looks confusing," Nathan said bluntly.

"It is. I don't understand it at all." Joel hung his head and played with the edge of the paper with his fingers. "All the other kids laugh at me because I can't figure it out. We didn't do it this way at my old school."

"Math can be fun," Nathan told Joel.

That brought the little boy's eyes flying back up to his. He looked as though someone had just hit him. "Fun?" He shook his head. "I don't think so."

"Sure it is. There's all sorts of things you can do with math."

"Whatever," Joel mumbled.

Nathan held out his hand, palm up. "I'll show you. Can I use your pencil?"

Joel handed it over, but looked up at him skeptically.

In his comfort zone now, Nathan turned the worksheet over to the blank back side and jotted down some numbers. "Okay, so you know that math uses a base ten, right?"

"Base ten?" Joel asked.

"Yeah. Can you count to one hundred by tens?"

"Of course. That's baby stuff." Then he proceeded to do just that, showing Nathan that he indeed could do as he'd asked.

"Right, so that's base ten. There are ten ones in the number ten. And ten tens in the number one hundred." He pointed down at the number eleven he'd written on the paper. "What's this?"

"Eleven," Joel answered immediately.

"No," Nathan countered. "It's a ten and a one. The first number shows how many tens there are, and the second shows how many ones. So what's this number?" He pointed to another number he'd put on the page.

"Two tens and four ones. Twenty-four," Joel said, confusion still in his eyes, but he was catching on fast.

"Exactly. And this one?"

"Three tens and seven ones."

"Great!" Nathan enthused. "Okay, now for a hard one. What about this one?" He wrote another number on the page.

"Five tens and nine ones," Joel said immediately.

"What if I add another one to it, what do I have?" Nathan asked.

"Sixty . . . er . . . I mean six tens."

"Perfect. So what is the first number again? How many . . ."

"Tens!" Joel answered excitedly.

"And the second number?"

"Ones!"

"Good. And you said you weren't good at math," Nathan told the boy, able to see his self-esteem rise right in front of him. "Okay, moving on to harder stuff. If I write these down and ask you to add them together, how do you do it?" Nathan wrote the number ten and the number thirty-two down.

Joel began talking about subtracting numbers from the thirty-two and adding them to the ten and then adding another number back to the thirty-two, and that was where Nathan interrupted him. "Forget the core stuff. Look at it in relation to what we just talked about. Tens and ones."

Joel cocked his head and looked intently down at the paper. Then he looked up at the man sitting next to him and said hesitantly, "The first number is one ten and zero ones. The second is three tens and two ones."

"Right," Nathan praised. "So add them together and what do you get?"

"Four tens and two ones."

"And?" Nathan asked with a smile.

"Forty-two?"

"Are you asking or telling me that's the answer?"

Joel looked down at the paper again, then back up at Nathan. "Telling. Forty-two."

"Exactamundo!" Nathan exclaimed.

"That . . . that was easy," Joel said, looking completely shocked. "It can't be that easy."

"It is. Let's do another." Nathan quickly wrote another two numbers on the page.

As soon as the pencil lead left the page, Joel said, "Seven tens and three ones and then two tens and four ones. So that makes nine tens and seven ones. Ninety-seven!" His voice had risen as he'd spoken, as if he'd found out the meaning of life.

"Exactly right," Nathan told him. "How about some more?"

He and Joel continued practicing adding up numbers, and Joel got faster and faster at doing the math in his head. Nathan then turned the paper over and handed the pencil back to Joel. "Now try your homework problems."

Without a word, Joel bent to the page and quickly began to complete the problems he had left. When he was finished, he looked up at Nathan with a concerned look in his eye.

"What is it, Joel?"

"I'm not doing it the way I'm supposed to."

"But you understand it. And you're getting the right answers."

Joel nodded, but still looked concerned.

Nathan leaned against the cushion on the back of the couch and told Joel something he'd learned early in his school career. "You're right, Joel, you're not doing it the way you're supposed to. You're skipping all the steps your teacher wants you to show. But here's the thing . . . you're getting it, right?"

He nodded, but stayed silent.

"You have a choice to make then. You keep doing it the way that makes sense to you, and the way that is faster for you, or you try to do it the way the teacher wants you to. The choice is yours. But if you choose to do it the way that makes sense to you, you're gonna lose points. The teacher is gonna use her red pen and put slashes and *x*'s and tell you that you didn't show your work. You might get a *C* instead of an *A*. On the other hand, if you try to do it the way she wants, it'll take longer. You might confuse yourself more. You might get lots of smileys on your paper, and you might even get an *A*. Although you might run out of time because you can't get through all the problems. Would you rather get the *C* and understand what you've done, or get the *A* and just go through the motions?"

Joel looked up at him as if it was a trick question. "But Bailey wants me to get *A*s."

"I'm sure she does," Nathan said immediately. "Do you know why?"

"Because that means I'm successful?"

"And do you think you'd be more successful if you did it the way you understood or the way you were told to do it?"

Joel bit his lip, but didn't answer.

Nathan could tell he was thinking really hard, so he continued. "Do you think Bailey would rather you truly understand the material and learn it, or just go through the motions?"

"Learn it," Joel said immediately.

"And would you be happier if you knew what you were doing or if you were just doing what you were told?"

"If I knew what I was doing."

"So here's the hard part of the question," Nathan said, sitting up and looking Joel right in the eyes. "Can you live with being a *C* student in math and knowing you truly understand it, or being an *A* student and only half knowing it?"

"But I want to get *A*s," Joel protested.

"Why?" Nathan returned.

"Well . . . because that means I'm smart."

"Does it?"

Nathan saw the moment his point got through to the boy. He shook his head slowly.

"Right. So you do what you need to do to pass, and that's important, Joel. Don't go your own way so much that you're failing your classes, because that would just be stupid. But stop trying to please others, and make sure you're doing what's best for *you*. That you're learning the way *you* need to learn. It's perfectly okay to be a *C* math student rather than an *A* student."

"What grade did you get in math?" Joel asked with a small smile.

Nathan leaned toward him and whispered, "*C* minus. I was a bit too hardheaded and went my own way a bit too much."

Joel laughed. The sound was carefree and loud in the room.

"I . . . uh . . . have the estimate on your car," Bailey said from across the small space.

Nathan looked up and saw her leaning against the door frame as if she'd been there awhile. He felt himself blush. He'd been so engrossed in helping Joel and making his point that he hadn't even realized she'd come back into the room.

He turned his eyes to Clayson, and the older man was sitting at the desk, grinning at him as well. *Damn.*

"Oh, great."

"It's the connections. Your battery was low on juice too, so I recommend you get a new one. The engine is actually in astonishingly good shape. It might look like a piece of crap, but I've got to say, you've taken care of it remarkably well."

Nathan so wanted to make a comment about taking care of a woman under the hood so she'd purr for a lifetime, but he refrained. "Go ahead and put a new battery in, and do what you need to about the connections."

Bailey held out her hand. "If you give me your forms, I'll write the estimate down and you can make sure it's not too much."

Nathan shook his head. "It's fine. It needs to be done, so it doesn't matter what the cost is. Go for it."

"All right. Joel? You're okay in here while I finish up?"

The boy looked up at his sister as if she'd said the stupidest thing ever. "Duh. I'm okay in here every day. Why would today be any different?"

Bailey flushed, but merely nodded and backed out of the room.

When she was gone, Nathan said nonchalantly and with no heat, "That was rude."

"What?" Joel asked in confusion.

"What you just said to your sister." Nathan could see Joel was trying to come up with a reply, so he went on quickly. "Think about it from her perspective. She's worried about you. She left you in here with me, someone neither of you knows. She wanted to make sure you were feeling okay about that and weren't too uncomfortable. If you were, then she probably would've invited you to come out and watch her work. That would've gotten you out of this office, and away from me. But instead you were rude and dismissed her concerns as stupid. And trust me, having someone to watch your back like your sister does is anything but stupid."

Joel opened his mouth to respond, and Nathan could tell he was going to back-talk him, so he held up his hand, stopping the boy from saying something he'd regret. "I don't know you, and I don't yet know your sister, but it's obvious she loves you very much. You're upset with her because you had to move and change schools. You had to give up your friends and everything that was familiar. It's tough starting a new school and making new friends, but it's just as hard on your sister. She worries about you, and she only wants the best for you. I'm not saying you aren't allowed to feel the way you feel, but it might be good if you thought about what other people are feeling when they say something to you."

Nathan could see the conflict in Joel's eyes.

"I'll say I'm sorry later," Joel finally said in a quiet voice.

"I'm sure she'd appreciate that," Nathan told the boy, then moved on, changing the subject. "So . . . you're in what, the fourth grade? How old are you?"

"Nine. Well, ten next weekend," Joel said with a smile, sitting up straighter.

"Ten. Wow. Double digits. You have a party?"

With his question, the boy deflated as if he was a balloon that had been popped with a pin. "Yeah."

"You don't sound excited," Nathan observed.

"It's stupid. I wanted to go to Chuck E. Cheese's, but Bailey won't let me. We have to go to a stupid park and ride bikes and eat chips and junk."

Nathan suspected money was a factor in why he couldn't have his party at the expensive kids' restaurant. "Your friends from school coming?"

Joel shrugged, but didn't answer. Instead, he bent back over his worksheet and pretended to start working on it again.

Clarity struck Nathan. Joel was the new kid in a new school. A party in a local park probably wasn't enough incentive to get his classmates to go. Kids were cruel, he knew that firsthand from his upbringing.

"Can I come?"

Joel's head whipped up. "What?"

"Can I come?" Nathan repeated. "I mean, we're friends now, aren't we?"

"Well, uh . . . yeah, I guess. You really want to?"

"I wouldn't have asked if I didn't. But I should warn you . . ." Nathan let his voice trail off temptingly.

"Warn me about what?" Joel asked.

"That I'm the nerd in my family. My brothers are the cool ones. And my sister-in-law and my almost-sister-in-law are so beautiful it'll make your head spin."

Joel's brown eyes were wide in his small face. "I don't think you're a nerd," he said. And it was a nice thing to say. Maybe the boy really was taking his earlier words to heart.

Nathan laughed. "I am, but I'm totally okay with that. Just wait until you meet Logan and Blake. You'll see for yourself. Logan owns a motorcycle. And my other brother, Blake, has this vibe going . . . like if you mess with him, you'll regret it. Oh, don't get me wrong, they're totally good guys, but when you meet them, you'll see what I mean."

"Are they gonna come too?" Joel asked in an awed voice, as if he'd never dreamed adults would want to come to his birthday party.

"Well, I'll have to run it by your sister, make sure it's okay, but yeah, they'd love to come. Any friend of mine is a friend of theirs."

"Cool," Joel breathed. "I'll go ask Bail right now!"

Without waiting for Nathan to agree, he jumped up and ran for the door that led out to the garage bays.

After the door slammed behind him, Clayson spoke up for the first time.

"You'll do."

"Pardon?" Nathan asked, looking up at the man.

"I wasn't so sure about you when you came in here. I knew that you'd gotten to our Bailey, but in my eyes no one was good enough for her. But after sitting here, watching you with Joel and hearing what you said . . . you're not only good enough for her, you're exactly what she needs."

Nathan stood up and carried the clipboard over to the man. "I don't know about that. I'm not sure she'd ever look twice at a man like me if she wasn't in the precarious situation she's in now. But I'm not an idiot. If she'll have me, I'm all hers."

"Her precarious situation?" Clayson asked with one eyebrow raised.

Nathan considered the man for a long moment before replying, "You and I both know a woman like her, with her skills, doesn't move to the outskirts of Castle Rock and bury herself in work if something isn't amiss."

"And you know what's amiss." It wasn't a question.

Nathan didn't answer, but continued to hold eye contact with Clayson.

"Right," Clayson said. "On another note, I'm glad you called Joel on his attitude. He's full of it. Takes his frustrations out on his sister more often than not. I know he's just a kid, and I have no idea what his life was like before they got here, but it ain't right. She takes it and doesn't call him on it. I figure she feels guilty for something. Don't know what."

"I'll see what I can do to have him check that," Nathan told the older man.

"As I said, you'll do," was his response.

The door to the small office swung open and hit the wall behind it with a loud bang. "She said okay!" Joel cried out excitedly.

Nathan looked pointedly at the door, then back at the boy.

Joel took the hint, looked sheepish for a moment, and said, "Sorry, Clayson. I forgot about the door. I didn't mean to bang it."

"It's all right," Clayson said, then murmured for Nathan's ears only, "Yup, you'll definitely do."

Nathan's lips quirked up in a half smile, but he ignored the older man and turned to Joel. "Cool. So next Saturday? What time and what park?"

"Ten. And the park that's near here."

"Phillip S. Miller Park," Clayson told Nathan.

"I know where that is. I'll be there."

"Promise?" Joel asked.

Nathan saw something in the boy's eyes. He'd been let down before. More than once. He squatted down in front of Joel and looked straight in his eyes. "Yeah, I promise. I can't make that promise for my brothers, because I don't know their schedule, but mark my words. I'll be there."

Joel nodded. "Cool."

"Cool," Nathan echoed. "Want to practice more on that base-ten math stuff? I can give you some harder ones and see if you can figure them out. Then you can try subtracting."

"Yeah. I wanna try."

Nathan jotted down a few more problems on the back of Joel's worksheet. He kept one eye on the door and one on the boy in front of him. He liked Joel. He seemed like a smart kid, but he really, really wanted to talk to Bailey. He hoped she'd give him a chance.

Not because he wanted to keep her safe.

Not because of her brother.

But because he wanted to get to know *her*.

Chapter Six

"Thanks for helping him with his homework," Bailey told Nathan as they stood in the doorway of the garage.

Joel was playing catch with a football with Clayson. He'd taken the boy outside as she'd completed the paperwork and payment with Nathan.

"You're welcome," Nathan said easily.

Bailey knew his eyes were on her, and not on her brother and boss, but she refused to turn her head and look at him. He made her nervous in a good way, not nervous in a is-he-gonna-hurt-me kind of way, which was a nice change.

"Thanks for letting me come to his party next week."

She looked over at him at that. "Are you kidding? You made his day."

One side of Nathan's lips quirked up.

"What? What's funny?" she said defensively. If he was laughing at Joel, she'd—

"I'm usually the last choice when it comes to the Anderson brothers," he said without one hint of pity.

Bailey wrinkled her brow. "What's that supposed to mean? Is there something wrong with you?"

He shrugged. "Depends on who you ask."

"I'm asking you."

Nathan put both arms out to his sides with his palms up. "What you see is what you get. I'm too slender to be considered a threat, although I do know a bit of judo, which has helped me more than once in tense situations at work. I like numbers. A lot. I prefer to hang out at home rather than go to the gym and work out. Crowds make me break out in hives, and I have a sweet tooth like you wouldn't believe. While I like a good steak, I'm hopeless when it comes to cooking meat evenly on the grill." His tone was even, as if he honestly didn't care how others saw him.

"So?" Bailey asked in confusion.

"So? I'm a nerd, Bailey. A geek. Dork. Dweeb. Goober. Whatever name you prefer. I love *Star Wars* and can recite all the lines. I get excited about doing profit-and-loss sheets. You've seen my car—it's definitely not cool. When you meet my brothers, you'll wonder how in the world I'm even related to them, much less how we're triplets."

She blinked at him in shock. "You're a triplet?"

"Yup."

"Cool," she mumbled, but thought back to what he'd been saying before she'd been distracted. She felt the wall she'd been keeping up to protect herself crumble a bit. It was true. Nathan wasn't exactly the Terminator. The black slacks he was wearing were wrinkled and looked like they hadn't ever been ironed. He was wearing a polo shirt with all but one button fastened. His hair was mussed, as if he'd run his hand through it several times. His skin was more on the pale side than tan, and if she'd passed him on the street and didn't know anything about him, she probably *would've* labeled him as a nerd.

But after listening to him help her brother with his math homework, and definitely after Joel had apologized to her for his tone right before he'd asked if Nathan and his brothers could come to his birthday party—and she knew it had to do with something Nathan had said to him—she couldn't give a shit if he was nerdy.

In fact, nerdy sounded heavenly. She'd had enough of unchecked testosterone and men who thought they were God's gift to women. Lord knew the Inca Boyz certainly didn't give a crap about math, or learning, or treating the women and girls who hung around the club with an ounce of respect. Yes, a nerd, Nathan, sounded like a man she'd like to get to know better.

Bailey put a hand on Nathan's bicep and said honestly, "You're a good man, Nathan."

He shrugged, and Bailey dropped her hand, awkwardly shoving her fingers into the pockets of the overalls she was wearing.

"I'm okay with who I am. I wasn't trying to manipulate you in any way," he said.

"I didn't think you were."

"So you're okay with me coming to Joel's party next weekend?"

"I already said I was," Bailey said.

"What about dinner tomorrow night?"

Whoa. What? "Uh . . . dinner?"

He looked away from her for the first time, and Bailey realized with a sudden clarity that Nathan was nervous. She could see the pulse beating heavily in his throat, and he was shifting from foot to foot as if he couldn't stay still.

"Yeah. Dinner. Or lunch. Or whatever," Nathan told her, obviously backpedaling slightly now that she hadn't immediately said yes.

"I don't have a babysitter," she said quietly, not saying no, but not exactly saying yes either.

Nathan turned to look at her again, the hope clear in his eyes. "Do you think Clayson might agree?"

Bailey hesitated for a fraction of a second. No matter what this man thought of himself, she knew to the marrow of her bones that he was a good person. She didn't know what he did for a living, although he'd said that he had to use judo, which concerned her a little. Other than that, she only knew that he was good at math, apparently had two brothers, and he'd been wonderful with her brother. The kind of role model she wanted Joel to have, not someone like Donovan.

But she was . . . Bailey. Ex-girlfriend of Donovan and Inca Boyz whore. She was in no way good enough for the man standing in front of her looking so hopeful. But she had no idea how to explain that to him. She had a feeling he wouldn't agree, but she knew exactly who and what she was.

But she could use a friend. And Joel could use a male role model who was as good as Nathan. If nothing else, she needed to say yes for her brother's sake.

She nodded. "I'll see if maybe he or one of the other guys can come over for a few hours."

The smile that crept over Nathan's face was blinding. He huffed out a breath that confirmed to her just how nervous he'd been, and told her, "Great. If you give me your number, I'll call with the details about where we're going tomorrow."

She immediately rattled off her digits and watched as Nathan punched it into his cell.

Her ringtone sounded and then stopped after one ring.

Bailey pulled her phone out of her pocket. It was one of those pay-as-you-go phones she'd gotten from Walmart. It was cheap, especially since the only people who ever called her were Clayson and Joel's school, and no one from her old life knew the number.

"So you know my number too," he explained, putting his phone back into his own pocket. "Anything you don't like to eat?" he asked quietly.

Bailey shook her head. "I'm not picky."

"Bail!" Joel shouted. "Catch!"

She turned to look at her brother and would've gotten beaned in the face with the football if Nathan hadn't immediately reached out a long arm and snagged the ball in the palm of his hand. It was seriously a catch worthy of being replayed hundreds of times on social media as he snatched the ball out of the air and kept it from smashing into her.

"Joel!" she scolded. "How many times do I have to tell you not to do that? I wasn't ready!"

"You could've hurt her, buddy," Nathan said in a gentle voice. "Lucky I was here," he said, but for her ears only. "Go long, Joel!" he ordered loudly, then after the boy ran a few paces, he threw a perfect pass that landed directly into Joel's arms, allowing him to catch it easily.

"Thought you said you were a nerd," Bailey muttered. "Nerds can't catch *or* throw footballs where I come from."

He chuckled. "With two badass brothers, I was bound to pick up a thing or two," he replied wryly, then looked at his watch. "It's getting late. I should let you two go." He caught her eyes again with an intense gaze that Bailey felt down to her toes.

"Thank you for agreeing to go out with me. I can't promise not to do anything dorky tomorrow night, but I'll try to keep it to a minimum . . . at least for our first date. Gotta make a good impression."

"I think you've already done that," Bailey told him honestly.

He took a step, but didn't look away from her. "I'll see you tomorrow, Bailey."

"See ya," she responded quietly.

He took another two steps away, then turned and headed for his car, waving and calling goodbye to Joel and Clayson as he went.

She grinned. Yup, he was kind of a nerd. Most men she'd been around would've done a manly chin lift or merely lifted their wrist to say goodbye. Not Nathan. He held up his hand and waved at her brother as if he was standing on the deck of the *Titanic* and waving at the adoring masses as the massive ship pulled out of port.

Joel ate it up, waving back just as enthusiastically.

As soon as Nathan was out of sight, Joel headed for the Chevelle.

"Have a good chat?" Clayson asked as he strode up to Bailey with the keys to the shop in his hand, ready to lock up.

She eyed the older man. "Yeaaaaah?" The word was drawn out in question.

He smirked. "Good."

"Clayson Davis . . . what are you up to? Are you trying to set me up?"

Her boss merely shrugged as he turned to face her, putting the keys in his pocket. "Look. You've been here a few months. You're a hard worker. I never have to ask you to do anything twice, you're always on time, unless you're busy with something to do with your brother. I just think it's time you did something for yourself for once."

"And you think Nathan is"—she brought her hands up and made air quotes—"doing something for myself?"

"Don't get cheeky, woman," Clayson said gruffly, although his eyes twinkled. He pointed down the street where Nathan's car had disappeared. "That is a good man. He'll take care of both you and Joel."

Bailey put her hands on her hips, irritated now. "We don't need to be taken care of."

"You don't *need* to, no," Clayson agreed without getting bent out of shape at her tone. "You've more than done a good job of that all by yourself. But sometimes it's nice to have someone willing to step up when stepping up needs doing."

Bailey shook her head and gave up. Clayson would think what he wanted to think no matter what she said. But secretly she was relieved the older man approved of Nathan. She wasn't going to get into a relationship with him, or any man, but it *would* be nice to have a friend. "Don't go getting ideas," she warned him.

"You seein' him . . . besides at your brother's party?" he asked with uncanny insight.

Bailey felt herself blush, but nodded and said, "Tomorrow night. It's only dinner."

"Man works fast," Clayson observed.

"Bail! I'm starved. Let's go!" Joel yelled out the window, clearly done with hanging at her workplace.

"Keep your pants on!" Bailey shouted back. "I'm comin'!"

Clayson put his hand on her shoulder, and she turned and looked back at the man she respected almost as much as she'd respected her pa.

His face was completely serious as he told her, "Give him a chance. I don't know what happened to put those walls up behind your eyes, but the Andersons are good people, no matter what some people in this town say."

"What do they say?" Bailey whispered.

"Nothing but nasty gossip," Clayson returned immediately. "You're an adult, and you can make your own decisions about them. But I'll tell ya this. You don't have to worry about Nathan or his brothers. They're loyal as can be, and I have a feeling the man who just left would rather pull out his own fingernails with a pair of pliers than hurt you."

"Ew, gross," Bailey said, wrinkling her nose in disgust.

"All I'm sayin' is if you let down your guard and take the time to relax for a second, I think you'll find just what you need in Nathan Anderson."

"You're being awfully secretive, and it's making me nervous."

"Don't be," he said immediately and squeezed her shoulder reassuringly. "I have a feeling from this day forward, your life is gonna get better."

"It can't get worse," Bailey mumbled.

"Don't bet on it," Clayson returned. "Shit can always get worse."

"That's true. Hey, you think one of the guys will come over and look after Joel for a few hours for me tomorrow night?"

"I'll call and ask them for you. If they can't, I will."

"Thanks, Clayson. Seriously," Bailey said. She didn't ask for much from anyone, but with the quick way her boss answered, she knew he wasn't put out in the least.

"Go on," he told her. "Get home and feed that boy. Have a good weekend, and I'll see you on Monday. I want all the details about your date."

Bailey chuckled. "You're worse than a girl."

He shrugged. "Old men need to get their jollies where they can."

"Whatever," she returned. "See you on Monday. Have a good weekend yourself."

"Plan to. Mrs. Davis texted me and told me she got a new nightie."

Bailey threw her hands up to her ears and covered them as she walked away from Clayson. "TMI, God! I don't want to know that!" But she was smiling as she said it. Secretly, she thought Clayson and his wife were as cute together as they could be. The fact that they still had a healthy sex life was awesome . . . even if she didn't want to hear about it.

When she heard him chuckle, she took a hand off her ear, held it over her head, and waggled it at him. When she reached her car, she looked back and caught his chin lift. Clayson might be in his mid- to late fifties, but he was definitely *not* a nerd, as his goodbye clearly indicated.

Chapter Seven

The next morning while Joel played in his room on his video-game console, Bailey lay in bed, dozing. She wasn't asleep, but wasn't really awake either. They'd watched a movie until late last night, and after Joel had gone to bed, she'd lain awake for several hours . . . thoughts of Nathan and what secrets he might be hiding running through her head, keeping her from falling asleep.

Her phone rang, scaring her to death. Bailey reached over, snatched it off the bedside table, and clicked it on.

"Hello?"

"Hi, Bailey. It's Nathan."

"Hey."

"Did I wake you up?"

"No, not really."

"Not really?" Nathan asked, laughter in his voice.

"I'm in bed, but I wasn't sleeping."

Bailey would've sworn Nathan's voice lowered, but she could've been imagining it. "I didn't mean to bother you. I can call back later."

"No, it's fine. I was just thinking about getting up and showering anyway."

"I hope you haven't changed your mind about tonight," Nathan said.

Bailey had changed her mind. About a hundred times. She vacillated between deciding she'd go and tell him that she could only be friends with him, to telling him flat out that it wasn't a good idea. She opened her mouth to tell him the latter when he spoke.

"I really hope you haven't," he said earnestly. "First, because you're the most interesting woman I've met in a really long time. There's something about you that makes me almost desperate to get to know you better."

When he paused, Bailey asked, "And second?"

He sighed. "And second, because I have something I need to talk to you about."

Bailey furrowed her brow at his answer. "What?"

"Have dinner with me tonight, and I'll tell you."

How did he know exactly what to say to get her to agree? Her curiosity had always gotten her in trouble. Her pa had been a master at teasing her to get her to cooperate. "Tell me now," she demanded.

"No. After dinner."

"You know you're just pissing me off."

He had the nerve to chuckle, but didn't say anything else.

Bailey scooted up on her mattress until her back rested against the wall. She held the phone to her ear and laid her forehead on her upturned knees. She suddenly had the feeling that Nathan knew exactly who she was and everything about what and who she was hiding from. If that was the case, she'd be smart to pack Joel up into her Chevelle and leave town, but she really didn't want to. Not only was Joel's party next week, but she actually liked her job. The men she worked with. Living outside Castle Rock.

She must've paused too long, because Nathan said softly. "You're safe here."

How in the hell he could read her mind, she had no idea, but she lifted her head and said, "Okay."

"Give me your address, and I'll pick you up around five."

Bailey hesitated for a moment, then gave him her address. A part of her wanted to keep it a secret, but it wasn't as if she'd tried to hide it. Joel's school had their address, as did Clayson. It would probably be an easy matter to find it if someone really wanted to. And she had a feeling Nathan really wanted to.

"Where are we going?" she asked, wanting to know so she could dress appropriately.

"Scarpetti's."

Bailey gasped. She'd thought he'd say something like Applebee's or the Rockyard American Grill & Brewing Company or something. Not the newest Italian place in Castle Rock. It had started out as any other Italian place, but the owner had somehow managed to lure renowned chef Cameron Grimbaldi back to Colorado from Italy to spend two months training the executive chef.

Almost overnight the small restaurant had become the most popular place to eat, with patrons coming from Denver, Boulder, and Colorado Springs to experience Chef Grimbaldi's creations.

"But they require reservations to be made weeks in advance," Bailey protested.

"My brothers and I have an in with them," Nathan said, not explaining further.

"It's awfully fancy," Bailey tried again.

"I can't promise I know the correct fork to use for which course, but I won't embarrass you."

Bailey shook her head in frustration. "It's not you I'm worried about, Nathan. I don't exactly fit in at a place like that."

"Why?"

"My tattoos?" Bailey told him in a tone that clearly stated he should've known why.

"They don't bother me or any of my friends. Remind me to introduce you to one of the owners of the gym in town sometime. Felicity has arm sleeves too, but they aren't as beautiful as yours."

Aren't as beautiful as yours. Wow. "It's expensive," Bailey murmured, letting the tattoo thing go, yet still protesting. "We can just go to Cracker Barrel or something."

"It's our first date. I want to go somewhere memorable. Treat you right."

"Okay. Fine." It was silly to keep protesting. It was obvious Nathan had made up his mind and that he really did want to take her there. If she was being honest with herself, she'd been curious about the restaurant ever since Clayson talked about it after taking his wife there for their anniversary dinner. She loved Italian food, and now that she'd given in, she couldn't wait to taste the delicious creations the chef was known for.

"I'll be at your place around five. You got someone to watch Joel?"

"Yeah. Clayson called earlier and said Duke, a guy from work, could do it."

"Good. Call if something comes up. Okay?"

"I will."

"Go take your shower, Bailey. I'll see you later."

"Bye."

He hung up without saying anything else. Bailey hugged her knees for a moment, lost in the pleasure coursing through her at the anticipation of her first real date in what seemed like forever. Then another thought struck her. *Shit!* What was she going to wear?

She jumped out of bed and hurried to her closet. It wasn't hard to look through the few clothes she had and to know she had nothing that would be appropriate for dinner at Scarpetti's.

"Joel!" she shouted, wrenching open her bedroom door.

"What?" his muffled voice returned.

"We need to go to town as soon as I've showered."

"Okay!" he hollered back, and Bailey relaxed. It looked like her brother was in a good mood, which was a pleasant surprise. Sometimes all he wanted to do was hang out at home and play his games, but she refused to leave him there alone . . . just in case.

He didn't particularly like tagging after her as she did errands, especially when she went clothes shopping at the thrift shop, but it couldn't be helped. Hopefully one of the two secondhand stores in town would have an appropriate outfit in her size.

Nathan sat back in his office chair and sighed in relief. He'd thought that Bailey would back out, but was thrilled she hadn't. It was obvious she wanted to, but her curiosity about what he wanted to talk to her about, and the lure of Scarpetti's, was enough to make her agree.

After he'd driven home the night before, he'd made the decision to tell her everything. That he knew who she was, about his family's connection to the gang, and most important, that Donovan was out of jail and probably looking for her.

She might decide not to have anything to do with him after dinner, but he hoped he could convince her that he and his brothers would do everything they could to keep Joel and her safe. He hoped that the added protection for her brother would convince her not to tell him to go to hell and skip town.

It was certainly a possibility.

The chance that she'd hate him by the end of the night was another reason why he wanted to pick Bailey up, so she'd have no choice but to let him take her home at the end of the night.

"You think this is the right thing?" Blake asked.

He and Logan were in the office early because they were headed up to Boulder for a job. Nathan had told them his plan for the night with Bailey, and they weren't exactly excited about it.

"I won't lie to her. She needs to know," Nathan said firmly.

"She might run," Logan observed.

"She might," Nathan agreed, "but she might not. I just need to convince her that it's in her best interest to work with us and to trust me . . . us."

"We can meet you guys when we get home tonight," Blake suggested.

Nathan clenched his teeth together, his jaw flexing with the force. He hated that his brothers didn't think he could handle Bailey. He might not be Mr. Suave, but their lack of confidence in him stung.

As if he knew exactly what his brother was thinking, Logan said softly, "It's not that we don't think you have the ability to get her to open up to you, to trust you. It's just that she grew up around the Inca Boyz. She's probably a master at manipulation and doesn't trust easily. And face it, you're nothing like Donovan."

Nathan knew what his brother meant, but it still hurt. "You're right. I'm nothing like him. I'm a good man who treats women as if they're more than a piece of ass. Otherwise, I'm fully aware of my shortcomings when it comes to the opposite sex."

"I didn't mean—"

"It's fine," Nathan said, interrupting Logan. "I know what you meant. And you're right. But there's something between us. She'll listen to me. Trust me."

"We do," Blake told him. "Let us know tomorrow what you need from us."

The support was a bit late, but still welcome. "I will. Oh, and her brother, Joel, is having a birthday party next weekend at Phillip S. Miller Park. I got the feeling he wasn't sure many of his classmates would show up, so I asked if you guys could come. He was keen on the idea. And Grace and Alexis are also invited."

"It depends if Grace has had our babies or not, but if possible, we'll be there."

"I'm sure Alexis would love it," Blake said. "How old is he?"

"Ten."

"I'll talk to Grace," Logan told his brother. "If he won't have many of his kids from his school there, I'm sure she could talk to Felicity and see if she might invite some of the patrons from Rock Hard Gym as well. If it wouldn't be an imposition."

Nathan thought about it for a moment before nodding. "Yeah, I think that'd be great. If they've got bikes, Rollerblades, or a hoverboard or something, tell 'em to bring 'em."

Logan nodded. "Will do. Whether or not me and Grace can be there, we'll make sure there are some kids who'll show up."

"Appreciate it," Nathan said, nodding at his brother.

"Of course. It's tough being a new kid in town. How many birthdays did we spend with just the three of us?"

All three men chuckled.

"How about all of them? Mom was too cheap to let us have a party," Blake said. "Oh, speaking of which, I found a journal of Mom's in all the crap left in the house. Actually, Alexis found it when she was cleaning out the office to get ready for the construction to begin in there. There's still a ton of paperwork I need to go through, lots of Dad's papers, but when Alexis flipped through the pages of Mom's journal, she found something interesting."

"A journal?" Logan asked, leaning back and putting his hands on his head. He looked relaxed, but it was obvious to his brothers that he was anything but.

"Yeah. You know how we always wondered why she was so bitter and mean?" Blake asked.

Logan and Nathan nodded.

"I haven't read all of it, but I think self-preservation was part of it."

"What do you mean?" Nathan asked.

"I don't know for sure, and I could be wrong, but the journal is from when she was a teenager. Apparently her dad regularly beat both her mom and her."

The silence in the office was heavy and oppressive as Blake's words sunk in. The brothers had never met their grandparents, and perhaps this was why.

"Seriously?" Logan asked. "She knew firsthand what it was like to be afraid of her father, and yet she turned out to be exactly like him?"

"Dad wouldn't have hit her," Nathan said in a low tone.

"I agree, but from what she wrote in her journal, her father literally beat her every day of her life from the time she could remember to the time he died of a heart attack when she was seventeen. By then, she'd learned that having the upper hand was the only way to keep herself safe."

"I'll be in the truck," Logan said flatly to Blake, then walked out of the office, the door closing behind him with a loud click.

Nathan looked at Blake after their brother left. "It makes sense in a warped way."

Blake nodded. "Unfortunately, a lot of children who grow up in abusive households become abusers themselves. It's the only thing they know. The only kind of relationship they understand."

Nathan nodded. He knew the statistics as well as his brothers did. "But it's more unusual for a woman to become the abuser. She's typically more likely to become a battered woman. We've seen that over and over in the last year we've run Ace Security."

"But it's not unheard of," Blake said.

"You ever wonder why dad never left her?" Nathan asked.

"Dad took his marriage vows very seriously. He might not have liked Mom, but once he married her, that was it," Blake insisted. "Besides, he had us. He wouldn't have left us with her."

Nathan wasn't sure he completely agreed with his brother. About their dad not wanting to leave them with their mom, yes. But not about the marriage vows. Their dad could've fought for custody. Nathan knew he would've said whatever needed to be said to get away from Rose

Anderson. They were quiet for a moment before Nathan said, "It sucks that she couldn't see Dad for what he was—a good, gentle man."

"And it sucks more that she saw her own sons as a possible future threat and treated us accordingly."

Nathan nodded. "Give him some time," he said, referring to Logan. "It's going to be hard for him to see her as a victim when he took the brunt of her abuse growing up."

"Yeah," Blake said, years of hurt and confusion evident in his voice.

"I'll call tomorrow and bring you up to date on Bailey's situation."

"All right." Blake paused for a moment. "You want a copy of the journal?"

Nathan was tempted to say no, but he knew himself. Eventually he'd get curious and want to know for himself what their mom went through to make her the woman she'd become . . . an abuser and murderer. "Yeah. And if you find anything else interesting in Dad's papers, I'd love to see those too. No rush, though."

"Got it."

"Don't forget to ask Alexis about next Saturday," Nathan told him.

"Will do. Later, Bro."

"Later."

Nathan stared at the door long after Blake had left, lost in thought, then finally pulled himself together and turned to his computer. Their monthly taxes were due, and he needed to send off their 401(k) contribution to their financial planner and pay some bills.

His mind whirling with not only the bombshell Blake had dropped, but what he was going to tell Bailey that night, Nathan got to work.

Chapter Eight

"You're gonna be good for Duke tonight, right?" Bailey asked Joel as she smoothed a lock of hair behind her ear for the tenth time that night. She'd found a perfect little black dress at the second thrift shop she'd visited that afternoon, thank God. It had long sleeves and it was relatively modest. It had a scoop neck in the front and back and hugged her torso before flaring out into a cute flouncy skirt that hit her right at her knees. It wasn't exactly her style, but since her options were limited, and it hid all her gang tattoos she stupidly had inked on her skin, it was exactly what she needed.

She'd showered and shaved her legs, then took the time to blow-dry and style her thick black hair. It was easier to keep it up in a ponytail and out of her face day to day, but for tonight, she wanted to look her best for Nathan.

She'd gone a little heavy on her makeup since she assumed the lighting at Scarpetti's would be dim, and the overall result was that Bailey felt better about herself than she had in a long time. She felt feminine and pretty. And even though she'd decided she'd tell Nathan she could only be friends, that she didn't want anything more, a part of her hoped he'd appreciate the effort she put into getting ready for the night anyway.

"Bail, of course I am. All we're gonna do is play my *This Is War* game, and hang out."

Bailey chewed her lip. "I'm not sure that game is appropriate for someone your age. Isn't it all like . . . killing and stuff?"

Her brother rolled his eyes. "It's just a game, Bail. It's not real. Relax."

Relax. Yeah, right. "Fine. But bedtime is nine."

"Bailey! Come on! It's Saturday!"

"Oh, all right," she relented. "Eleven, but no later."

"Cool!" Joel enthused.

"And call me if anything happens. If anyone comes by."

"No one is gonna come by," Joel said, rolling his eyes. "In the months we've lived here, not one person has stopped by without you knowing about it beforehand."

He was right, but it didn't mean that Donovan or one of his gang couldn't show up. In fact, with every day that went by, Bailey had the feeling it was becoming more and more likely. She had no idea how long her ex would be in jail, but surely it was nearing the time for him to be released. She made a mental note to go to the library in Castle Rock and see what she could find out online. "Fine. I won't be too late. I'll probably be home before eleven anyway."

"Whatever," Joel said, clearly not concerned one way or another what his sister did.

The sound of a car pulling into the gravel driveway made both of them turn toward the door.

"He's here!" Joel enthused, jumping up from the couch and racing for the door.

"Don't open it without checking first!" Bailey reminded him sternly.

Showing he'd heard her, Joel stood on tiptoe and peered through the peephole Clayson had installed for her, then unlocked the dead bolt, the chain, and the lock on the door, and threw it open. He disappeared out the door, and Bailey followed behind her brother at a more leisurely pace. She grabbed the black handbag she'd picked up that day at the thrift shop, and stood in the doorway.

Joel was waiting impatiently for Nathan next to the driver's-side door. The second Nathan climbed out, Joel was chattering away.

Bailey saw his eyes flick from her brother to her, then stick as if physically unable to look away from her.

The expression on his face showed his appreciation for the effort she'd put into dressing. She saw his eyes sweep her from head to toe, before coming back up to concentrate on her face. Her entire body tingled, merely from one look. That had never happened before, and Bailey wasn't sure what to do with it.

She vaguely heard Joel talking about his video game and how the latest *This Is War* game was the best yet—involving an intense opening scene where all the players parachuted from a plane and how if they didn't steer themselves correctly, they ended up getting hit by a flying bird and crashing to the ground.

But Bailey only had eyes for the man walking toward her. She wasn't the only one who had put in extra effort in choosing an outfit for the night. Nathan's normally messy hair had been tamed, and he was wearing a pair of black slacks, a white button-down shirt, a black sports jacket, and of all things, a pink tie. It should've looked weird against the severity of his outfit, but instead it lightened it up just enough to look more casual than formal.

He walked right up to her and leaned over. For a moment Bailey thought he was going to kiss her on the lips, but at the last minute he turned his head a fraction of an inch, and she felt his lips brush against her cheek.

"You look beautiful, Bailey," he said in a low, earnest voice.

"So do you," she returned automatically. And it wasn't a lie. He cleaned up well. She saw no sign of the nerd he professed to being in the man standing in front of her. His dark eyes sparkled with an intensity she couldn't remember seeing in any man's eyes before.

Putting a hand on her stomach to try to calm the fluttery sensation in her belly, Bailey turned to her brother. "Joel, will you run in and grab Ma's necklace?"

"Sure!" he said immediately and headed for the small house.

"It's in the box under my sink," Bailey called out.

"Got it!"

When she and Nathan were alone, Bailey wasn't sure what to say. She wasn't used to this. When she'd gone out with Donovan, she always met him at his place, and he never bothered to dress up, or try to impress her. More often than not, he'd drag her into his bedroom, fuck her, then tell her to get busy making them something to eat. Not exactly romantic.

She bit her lip as Nathan's eyes wandered down her body again, pausing at her chest, then again at her legs. She'd dug out a pair of heels from her life in Denver, and she had to admit they did fantastic things to her calves.

Nervously, she ran her free hand down the side of the skirt. "Do I look okay?"

"Yeah. You look more than okay," Nathan said softly, his eyes coming up to meet hers. "Way too pretty for the likes of me."

Bailey's lips curled up into a small smile, and she shook her head. "I think we both look good. We clean up well."

It was his turn to smile. "Yeah, I agree."

Joel reappeared with the necklace in his hand. "Here ya go, Bail."

Bailey reached for the jewelry, but Nathan beat her to it. He picked it up off Joel's hand and held it up in front of him, examining it.

"It was my ma's. Pa gave it to me when I turned sixteen. He said he gave it to her on their first wedding anniversary. It's not real or anything, but he said she wore it every day after that, even the day she died. Pink was her favorite color."

Nathan didn't say anything, but Bailey saw his eyes go soft as he looked from the large stone dangling at the end of the chain to her.

"May I?" he asked, holding the necklace up.

In response, Bailey nodded and ducked her head.

Nathan carefully lifted the long, slender gold chain over her head. After it lay against her body, he surprised her by moving his hands to her hair and gently pulling it out from under the chain.

Goose bumps raced down Bailey's arms at the feel of his fingertips against her nape. It was a fleeting touch, not a sexual one, but she felt it between her legs all the same.

He brought one finger down, tracing the length of the chain down the front of her body until he came to the stone. He picked it up, brushing the backs of his fingers against the curve of her breast in the process, and held it in the palm of his hand.

"It's beautiful."

"Pa said it's pink coral."

The necklace wasn't fancy. Merely a large, rounded piece of coral hanging from a simple gold clasp. But it was the only thing Bailey had of her mother's. She didn't remember the woman; she'd died when Bailey was still a toddler. The car she'd been in had been hit head-on after she'd dropped Bailey off at a babysitter's house, killing her instantly.

Nathan took a step closer to her, and Bailey's eyes came up to his. He was still looking down at the stone in his hand, and she swore she could feel the heat from his body seep into hers as he stood in front of her.

"We match perfectly," he said in awe.

Bailey looked down then. He was holding her necklace in one hand and his tie in the other. They were side by side, and amazingly, were exactly the same color.

"I wasn't sure they would, but when I saw your tie, I remembered the necklace and thought it might be nice if we both had some pink on," Bailey said quietly.

His eyes came up at that, but he didn't step away from her. He licked his lips and Bailey saw a sheen of moisture glistening on his lips where his tongue had touched them. Another shiver went through her as all the carnal things he could do with his mouth ran through her brain.

"I don't usually wear pink, but when I was trying to decide what to wear tonight, something told me this would be perfect."

"It is," Bailey told him quietly.

"Look! Here comes Duke!" Joel cried out excitedly, breaking the spell between the two adults standing nearby.

Bailey cleared her throat and took a step back at the same time Nathan let her necklace fall out of his grasp. But it was a moment before he took his eyes from it, his gaze lingering on how it nestled between her breasts.

He took a deep breath as if trying to ground himself before stepping back another pace and bringing his eyes back up to her face. Bailey caught a glimpse of the erection in his pants before he shifted, tugging the bottom of his sports jacket down nervously.

"Thank you for agreeing to come out with me tonight, Bailey," Nathan said, his eyes intense as they looked into her own.

"Thanks for asking," Bailey responded.

They turned at the same time when they heard Duke greeting Joel enthusiastically. The other man was her age, but Bailey felt so much older than he was. He was a good guy, funny, but he lacked the maturity that she craved in a man. He'd asked her out when she first started working at Clayson's Auto Body, but she'd turned him down. Not only because she sensed he was only looking for a good time, but also because she wasn't nearly ready to get into a relationship . . . if she ever would be.

"Hey, Bailey," Duke said as he sauntered up to them, "lookin' good."

"Thanks. Duke, this is Nathan. Nathan, Duke."

The two men shook hands, and Bailey continued. "We're just going to dinner in town, so we'll be nearby in case anything happens. You have my number, right?"

"Relax. Nothing's gonna happen. You go and have a good time. Me 'n Joel will be hangin' out playin' games. Right, bud?"

"Right! And Bail said I could stay up till eleven!" Joel was quick to point out and make clear.

"Awesome!" Duke looked at his watch. "That means we have six hours of *This Is War* to play. Let's get on that, yeah?"

"Yeah!" Joel practically screeched. Six uninterrupted hours of video games was obviously his idea of heaven.

After the little boy had run back inside, Bailey murmured, "Thanks for doing this, Duke. I appreciate it."

"No problem. You're taking my shift Monday, so it all works out."

It wasn't often that she needed a babysitter, but when she did, Duke was happy to let her take one of his shifts in lieu of money, something she appreciated, as she didn't have much extra cash lying around. She didn't mind giving up her days off in return for the other man's time.

"I don't expect trouble, but make sure you keep the door locked . . . just in case," she told Duke, well aware of Nathan's eyes on her.

Duke stopped midstride on his way into her house and turned back to Bailey. "Somethin' I need to know about?" he asked quietly, but with a seriousness that she'd never heard from him before.

She shook her head. "No. Just being cautious."

Duke nodded, but it was obvious he wasn't entirely convinced. "Try not to worry. I'll make sure he eats something, takes breaks so his eyes don't cross, and is in bed by eleven. Don't rush back for our sakes."

"Thanks. Again, I appreciate it."

"Anytime you need me to look after him, I'm happy to do it, and not because you're takin' my shift. You work too hard, Bailey, and deserve a day off during the week just as much as anyone. From here on out, you need to do somethin', let me or any of the other guys know. We'll watch him for you for free."

"I can't ask—"

"You ain't askin'. I'm tellin'. It's what friends do, Bailey. You'd do the same for us."

Bailey felt the tears at the back of her throat, but forced them down. The last thing she wanted was for her makeup to run down her face if she started bawling. "You know I would."

"Damn straight. Go on. Have a good time. Don't worry about us."

"Okay. I'll see you later."

"Bye." Bailey turned back to Nathan, and squeaked in surprise when she found him standing next to her. *Right* next to her. Close enough that their shoulders were almost touching. Close enough that to a bystander, it would look like they were more than casual acquaintances, which she supposed was his plan. His eyes were on Duke's back as the other man entered her house, then closed the door behind him.

The thought that Nathan wanted Duke to know of his interest, and protection, made the tingles between her legs start up again, then Nathan's hand came up and rested on her lower back. It was a light touch, his fingertips barely brushing the material of her dress.

Instead of making her feel warm and fuzzy inside, all good thoughts fled at his touch. His fingers were resting right over where the word *whore* was inked on her skin. Once again, revulsion closed over her like donning a cloak at the memory of who she was and what she'd done.

She couldn't forget that she was Donovan's whore. That she belonged to the gang, body and soul. She wouldn't drag anyone into that life, especially not Nathan. He was too good. Too . . . nice.

Taking a side step away from him, making his hand fall away from her body, she chirped too brightly, "Ready?"

His head cocked and his gaze pierced hers, as if he could read her mind simply by looking into her eyes. But he merely nodded and held out his hand toward Marilyn. "It's not your classic car, but she'll get us where we need to go," he said.

"It's fine, Nathan. It's not a big deal."

She practically ran to the passenger side of his car, trying to make sure he wouldn't touch her again. She couldn't bear for him to touch her again. She opened the door herself and slid inside before Nathan could help her. He shut the door behind her, walked calmly around the front bumper, and climbed into the driver's seat.

Without a word, he started the engine, which turned over immediately with no issues, and headed down her driveway to Minter Lane. Her house was located down a fairly long dirt road off Wolfensberger Road—a main thoroughfare that led into the city of Castle Rock. She was far enough away to feel secure, but close enough that if she needed something, she could easily get there. Joel's school was small for the area, but nearby and convenient. When he started middle school, he'd be bused down into Castle Rock, but for now she was content for them to live, learn, and work in close proximity.

Not liking the uncomfortable silence, and knowing it was because of her actions, Bailey asked, "So, how did you manage to get reservations at Scarpetti's?"

Nathan looked over at her for a quick moment before turning his eyes back to the road. He was a careful driver, keeping both hands on the steering wheel and making sure there was plenty of room before pulling out onto Wolfensberger Road. He drove the speed limit and even used his turn signal when there was no one around to see it.

"The business my brothers and I started is a couple of stores down from the restaurant. When they first opened, we gave them a lot of business. We were single and worked long hours. It was easier to walk down the street than to go home and make ourselves something to eat. It wasn't a hardship. Even without the fancy famous chef, the food was excellent. When the owner found out what we did for a living, she declared that anytime we wanted to eat there, we'd have a table." He shrugged. "We don't take advantage of that now that they have more business than they can handle some days, but not once when we've inquired if a table would be available for us, no matter the size of our party, have they not fit us in."

It made sense to Bailey. Loyalty was important. She had a feeling that for Nathan and his brothers, it was everything. "And what do you and your brothers do?"

He looked over at her then, with a look she had no hope of interpreting.

"I was planning on telling you all about myself tonight after we ate," he said before putting his attention back on the road.

Bailey didn't know how to take that. But the closer they got to Castle Rock, the more nervous she got. What did she know about the man sitting next to her except that he drove an older car that he'd named, that he could get reservations at a restaurant it was impossible to get reservations at, and her little brother loved him even after only meeting him once? Oh, and Clayson seemed to approve of him.

It wasn't much. No, it was nothing.

She'd opened herself up for a world of hurt if she'd misread the situation.

"You're safe with me, Bailey. Stop thinking so much over there," Nathan said easily into the silence. "I don't like secrets, or lies. After tonight you'll know everything about me. It might make you hate me. It might piss you off. But I swear on my father's grave, you're safe with me. As is Joel. I would never do anything to put you in danger, or to hurt you."

His words were fervent and heartfelt. So heartfelt, Bailey felt the tears well up in her throat for the second time that night. She'd been on her own for so long, she'd forgotten how it felt to trust someone else. To feel like she had someone to lean on. While she wasn't one hundred percent sure Nathan would fall into that category, she had a feeling that after tonight, she'd never feel the same again.

"Okay," she whispered. Not sure what else to say.

"Okay," Nathan echoed.

The rest of the drive was silent as both were lost in their thoughts about what the night would bring.

Chapter Nine

Nathan held open the door to Scarpetti's and let out a calming breath. It didn't work. He'd thought he and Bailey were really connecting, but the second he touched her back, she pulled away from him. Mentally and physically.

It drove him crazy, but he wasn't dumb. He'd bide his time. She was bound to have some demons to work through, especially after being involved with Donovan and the Inca Boyz. Besides, after she heard him out later that night, she probably wouldn't want anything to do with him anymore anyway.

He vowed to wait until after they ate to bring up any business. He wanted one dinner with her, free of him being who he was and her being who she thought she was. He wanted it to be just the two of them. Nathan and Bailey. But first he needed to bring her back to where they'd been standing in front of her house, admiring each other.

They were greeted by Francesca herself. She'd obviously been on the lookout for him as she came rushing out from the back of the restaurant, her arms open, a stream of Italian coming from her mouth. Nathan awkwardly received her hug, patting her shoulder once or twice in return.

She was a small, round woman who obviously had no problem sampling the rich Italian pasta made in her restaurant. She was wearing a black dress with an apron thrown over it. The protective garment had flour stains on it, and she wore sturdy, comfortable shoes on her feet. Nathan had never seen her in a bad mood, and her laughter was contagious. Not only did he love the food they served, he honestly enjoyed Francesca's sunny outlook on life. It was a good balance to what he did and saw every day.

"It's so good to see you, Nathan! As usual, you are welcome. And who is this *bellissima* woman?"

Nathan reached out and took Bailey's hand in his, careful this time not to touch her anywhere else. He linked his fingers with hers and pulled her so she was standing next to him. "Francesca, this is Bailey. Bailey, Francesca. The owner of Scarpetti's and the person who has put Castle Rock on the map."

"Oh, pooh," she said, blushing and obviously pleased by the compliment. She brushed off a smudge of flour she'd left on Nathan's jacket when she'd hugged him as she spoke to Bailey. "I'm so glad you came tonight with Nathan. He's a lonely boy. Always eating by himself and ordering food to eat at his desk late at night. All work and no play makes him a dull boy!"

Bailey looked up at him, and Nathan knew he was blushing. *Dammit.* He'd never had a real mother, not one who treated him as a mother should treat her son, but he imagined this was what it would feel like to be embarrassed by a mom.

The older woman laughed. A deep, hearty laugh that made several patrons turn and look at them, obviously wondering who they were and why they warranted such special treatment from the owner.

"Come on then. Let's get you seated," Francesca ordered, grabbing Nathan's free hand and tugging. "I put you in the couple's corner. You'll be left alone except for the delivery of your food and refills of your drinks." She turned to Nathan as she continued to lead them through the crowded restaurant. "Will you try our wine tonight since it's a special occasion?"

"You know I don't enjoy wine, Francesca," Nathan said lightly. "But Bailey might like a glass. Bailey?" He turned to her. Bailey's eyes were wide as she walked quietly by his side. She was taking in as much of the opulent decor as she could while they were towed to their table.

"A glass of wine would be lovely," she said.

"Eccellente!" Francesca cried in excitement. "You will allow me to choose one that best fits your meal?"

Nathan squeezed her hand in reassurance, and she finally said, "Yes, please. Thank you."

Francesca stopped in front of a small table in the back corner of the restaurant. It was obvious why she'd dubbed it the "couple's corner." It was located away from the kitchen, and even the other tables were a slight distance away, giving the small alcove a feeling of intimacy the other tables didn't have.

The booth was rounded, allowing the diners to sit side by side, rather than across from each other. The high-backed velvet-covered seat curled around the table, which would effectively seal them off from their surroundings. The round table had no decoration except for a single long-stemmed red rose in a thin, high vase. The tablecloth was white, and the black napkins stood out in stark contrast.

"Here we are! I'll be back with menus. Make yourself comfortable," Francesca said, waving her hand before rushing away.

Still holding Bailey's hand, Nathan gestured to the booth. "Ladies first."

She smiled at him and let go of his hand so she could scoot into the seat. Nathan followed close behind her. They sat close, but not too close. He could feel her body heat next to his leg, and glanced down, immediately regretting it.

Bailey's dress had slid up her thighs as she'd sat down, and he saw glimpses of her creamy white flesh as she situated herself before tugging the skirt down as far as she could. He swallowed hard, trying to think about anything but how soft the skin of her thighs would be.

Before he could open his mouth to say something, Francesca was back with the menus. She brandished them and held them open in front of each of them before going on and on about the specials for the night and what the famous celebrity chef was making for the evening.

Seeing that Bailey was completely overwhelmed, Nathan put his hand on hers and asked, "May I order for us both? Do you mind?"

She sighed in relief and quickly nodded. "Please do. I'm so out of my league, I don't even know what half this stuff means," she whispered, clearly embarrassed.

"To tell you the truth, neither do I," Nathan told her in an equally quiet voice. "After the first time I came here, I had to go online and look it all up so the next time I was here I didn't end up with something slimy and squirmy instead of creamy, cheesy pasta."

She smiled at him, and Nathan made a vow to do whatever he could to always keep a smile like that on her face.

He turned to Francesca. "We'll start with the *plin*, then for the main course, *tajarin* for me and *tagliata* for the lady, and we'll share a *cioccolato* for desert . . . à la mode, please."

"Your Italian is still awful, but you have exquisite taste in food," Francesca told him with a wink. She turned to Bailey. "Would you like black summer truffles with your *tagliata*?"

Nathan squeezed her hand when she looked at him in confusion, and answered, "Yes, please, Francesca. That would be wonderful."

"I will be right back with drinks," the older woman told them, then gave them a slight bow and left.

Bailey looked up at him with a grin. "Can I ask what you just ordered for us?"

Thrilled that she hadn't pulled her hand out from under his, Nathan said, "Everything is a lot fancier than I'll describe it, but in a nutshell we're starting with *plin*, which is a homemade ravioli with cheese and spices. It's to die for. Then I'm having the house-made noodles with meat sauce, you're having grilled sirloin with mushrooms, asparagus, and potatoes, and for dessert we're sharing a hazelnut flourless chocolate cake with fruit sauce and ice cream on the side."

She looked at him for a beat before asking, "Why don't they just call it ravioli, pasta, steak, and cake?"

Nathan chuckled. "I have no idea. That's why I did my research after eating here the first time. I ended up ordering artichoke flan, belly sausage, and chocolate-dipped oranges. Wasn't my favorite."

Bailey giggled, and Nathan thought it was the sweetest sound he'd ever heard. It actually made the stress and worry melt off her face.

"Oh my God, you didn't?"

Nathan held up his free hand in a pseudo–Boy Scout salute. "Not lying. I did. Francesca just laughed in my face every time she brought something new out to me. She offered to bring me something different, but I refused, because that would be wasteful. She usually still offers to choose something for me every time I come."

"Why didn't she tonight?"

Nathan shrugged. "Maybe because she knew I wanted to impress you. Are you impressed?"

"I am," Bailey told him, still smiling.

"I don't know anything about wines, though, but I'm sure she'll bring something perfect to go with what I ordered for you."

"You don't drink?"

"No."

"Not at all?"

"Not at all," Nathan confirmed. "But before you think it's because I'm an alcoholic or that I have something against people who do, it's only because I don't like the taste. I can drink some hard alcohol, if it's disguised in something. But drinking beer or wine has just never been high on my list of things to do. Besides the taste, I don't like feeling out of control."

He could see Bailey's mind whirling with that, but she merely nodded and said, "Makes sense. I'm not a huge drinker, but I've done my share."

"Most people have," Nathan said easily. He finally moved his hand from atop hers—reluctantly—and leaned on his elbows on the table in front of him, keeping his head turned toward Bailey. "Tell me about yourself."

She shrugged, and he saw a slight pink sheen move up into her cheeks. She mimicked his position, leaning her own elbows on the table. "Not much to know, really."

"I doubt that," he said with a small snort.

"I'm twenty-four. Grew up in Denver. My ma died when I was young, and I was raised by my pa. He died when I was twenty, and I got custody of Joel. I moved down here to Castle Rock to get him out of the city. The end."

Nothing she said was a lie, but she was sure leaving a lot out. Nathan let it go because he knew a lot of what she was leaving out. "How'd you get interested in working on cars?"

"My pa. It's what he did. I started helping him when I was about Joel's age." She shrugged. "I liked it and was good at it. It was about the only thing I was good at."

Nathan immediately shook his head. "Now *that* I don't believe."

"It's true. My grades weren't great. I got in trouble all the time in high school for ditching or sleeping in class. I hung out with . . . not good people." She looked away from him and fiddled with the edge of the napkin in front of her. "If it wasn't for Joel, I'd probably still be in Denver and doing the same bad shit I've done my entire life."

Nathan couldn't stand the hopelessness in her tone. He reached up, put a finger under her chin, and gently turned her to face him.

"My brothers and I are triplets, and my mom never loved us. She was threatened by us, even when we were kids. She never tucked us in, never packed lunches for us. The only thing she did was teach me the most effective way to hit someone and make it hurt. When I left home at eighteen, I was scared to death. I didn't want to go. Like a typical victim of abuse, that's all I knew. I had no idea how to exist on my own. My brothers made it clear they were going their own way, and the Army wasn't for me. I liked numbers, so I managed to get an academic scholarship and went to a community college. Then after I graduated, I got an accountant job in St. Louis. All I did was work, then go home to my apartment. By myself. It wasn't until I came home for my dad's funeral and Logan suggested we start our own company that I began to feel like myself again. My brothers filled a hole inside of me. I'm more comfortable with them around. Braver. If it wasn't for Logan, I'd still be hiding from the world in St. Louis. Don't sell yourself short, Bailey. It's not what you've done that defines you, but what's in here."

He moved his hand to rest on the upper swell of her breast, careful not to overstep his bounds.

"What if there's nothing good in there?" Bailey whispered, her eyes so incredibly sad it made Nathan want to pull her into his lap, cuddle her, and tell her he wouldn't let anything ever hurt her again. He controlled the urge, barely.

"There's good in there, Bailey. I've seen it."

"You just met me," she protested.

"Exactly. And I've *seen* it. Bailey, you were the only person who stopped to help me when I was obviously in need in that parking lot. My hood was up, and I was standing in front of it like an idiot. No one stopped to see if they could call someone for me, or to even ask if I was okay. Except you. Your brother loves you, is terrified of letting you down. He wants to please you so much. It was plain to see in the shop yesterday. And the fact that he's a good kid, polite, for the most part, and minds you, tells me you're strict, but loving with him. So yeah, you have good inside you."

He dropped his palm from her chest to the hand that was still fiddling with her napkin, trying to reassure her in some way.

"You don't know what I've done," she said, still protesting.

"I dare you to point out one person out in this restaurant who hasn't done something they've regretted," Nathan said firmly.

Bailey turned her head from his and looked around them at the people sitting in the booths and tables, wearing fancy clothes and smiling and laughing.

"Life is hard, Bailey, I think you know that. But it's how you keep on going when it gets you down that matters. Some of us learn adversity at a young age, for others it takes longer, but it's my firm belief that adversity makes us better humans. We learn from our mistakes, and other people's too. We might trip once, or twice, or even a hundred times, but eventually we figure out how to pick up our feet when we walk."

She licked her lips, and one side of her mouth quirked up. "You're awfully philosophical, Nathan."

He felt himself blush now, and tried to control it. He didn't smile back at her, wanting her to understand in an elemental way what he was saying before he had to break the news that he knew all about her and why she was in Castle Rock. "I've tripped more than my fair share, Bailey. You've got a lot on your plate, and I can respect that. But you should know that I don't care about your past. I mean, I do because it's made you into the beautiful woman sitting across from me, but if you think something you've done, or haven't done, is going to make me not want to be with you, please put it from your mind." He didn't take his eyes from her, willing her to understand. "I'll move at your pace, pixie. We can hang out and watch movies, I'll play video games with Joel, even though I suck at them, and he'll kick my ass. I'll help him with his homework and make sure he has lots of people to help him celebrate his birthday. All I'm asking is that you give me a chance."

"Nathan, I—"

He picked up her hand and brought it to his lips, lightly kissing her knuckles before putting it palm down on his thigh and holding it there with his own warm hand. "At least give me tonight before you shoot me down. Get to know me as I'll get to know you. By the end of the night, you'll know all my secrets. You might not like them, but as I told you before, I won't lie to you."

"That doesn't exactly fill me with confidence," Bailey stated.

"I know. All I'm saying is that I like the woman who is sitting in front of me. You're the first person I've ever opened up to like this because you're the first person I've ever really wanted to know the real me."

Bailey chewed on her lower lip for a moment and opened her mouth to speak, but Francesca beat her to it. The woman had come up to their table with two glasses in her hand. A red wine for Bailey and a water for Nathan.

"Boring water for you, my friend," she said with a kind smile and winking at Bailey. "And for the lady, a nice red wine. Nebbiolo by Roberto Voerzio. Two thousand and ten. I think you'll enjoy it." She placed it in front of Bailey and stood by their table, waiting.

When Bailey didn't reach for her glass, Nathan leaned over and whispered, "She's waiting for you to taste it. To make sure you like it."

"Oh," she exclaimed, the pink in her cheeks returning. She reached out with her free hand, since Nathan wouldn't let go of the one still resting on his thigh, and sipped the light-red wine. She looked up at Francesca in surprise and murmured, "It smells a little like roses. Am I imagining that?"

If possible, Francesca's smile widened. She said something in Italian before clasping both hands together in front of her. "You are not wrong, little one. It should pair well with both the appetizer and your main dish." She then turned to Nathan and said in a mock-stern voice, "This one's a keeper, young man," before nodding and then whirling away, quickly stepping back into the kitchen.

Nathan couldn't keep the chuckle back at the look on Bailey's face, relieved when she smiled back at him.

"You certainly know some unusual people," was her only comment.

He squeezed her hand in return.

Soon after, their food began to arrive. They spent the next hour and a half talking, and laughing, and getting to know each other. Bailey drank another glass of wine, and she ate with abandon, loving everything put in front of her.

Finally, after they'd devoured the flourless dessert, she leaned back, putting both hands on her tummy, and exclaimed, "I'm stuffed. I couldn't eat another bite. It was delicious. I don't know what fancy food is supposed to taste like, but I understand why this place is so popular. That chef is a miracle worker."

Nathan leaned back against the comfortable red booth and told her quietly, "Don't tell anyone, but the items I picked out for us tonight weren't Chef Grimbaldi's dishes. They're Francesca's specialties."

"Really?"

"Really."

"Why in the world did she invite the famous chef guy to come in for two months when her cooking is so good then?"

"Marketing. What better way to get people to try out the new restaurant in town than to tell them a famous chef will be cooking here? Once she's got 'em in the door, they'll hopefully keep coming back even when he's gone."

"She's a freaking genius," Bailey said with a firm nod. "Seriously. That was delicious. I know I can't afford it, but I'll be sure to tell Clayson that he needs to continue to bring his wife here."

Nathan didn't comment on the not-affording-it statement. If it was up to him, she wouldn't have to worry about money again. Not when she was with him. But she wasn't with him, and he still had to get through the hard part of the night. The part where she'd probably end up really pissed off at him and not wanting to see him again.

"You ready to hear about what I do?" he asked quietly, suddenly wanting to get it out of the way.

She looked at him, the light in her eyes dying when she saw how serious he was.

She nodded.

Nathan took a deep breath and got to it.

Chapter Ten

Bailey had no idea what Nathan was going to tell her, but it was obvious it was something important. She'd enjoyed the night immensely and was having a hard time remembering exactly what she was and why she didn't want to get involved with him, or any man, ever again.

"You know my name is Nathan Anderson." He paused.

She nodded, but didn't speak.

"My brothers are Logan and Blake. We came back to Castle Rock a year ago after our mother murdered our father." He ignored her gasp and continued. "I told you earlier how abusive she was. Well, she wasn't just abusive to me and my brothers. We left home when we graduated from high school, and when she didn't have us around anymore to bully, things got worse for my dad. She shot him. Then shot herself. We'll probably never know what she was thinking because she didn't leave a note or anything."

"I'm so sorry," Bailey said, putting her hand over his where it was resting on the table. She felt horrible for what he'd gone through, but was happy he was back home with his brothers. It was obvious he loved them.

"Thanks. We came home for his funeral and decided that we wanted to help people who were in abusive relationships, or who needed protection from an ex, so we started our own business."

Bailey pulled her hand back and put it in her lap, twisting her hands together. She was getting a bad feeling about this. "What kind of business?"

"Ace Security. We provide security for men and women when they go to court, we dabble in investigations, and we've done some surveillance work as well."

The food she'd eaten was threatening to come back up, but Bailey kept her mouth shut and waited for Nathan to continue. He did so, somewhat reluctantly, it seemed.

"Logan got together with a girl he knew in high school, Grace. Her parents used to own an architectural firm here in Castle Rock. It was right here in this space, in fact. Francesca bought it when the firm went under."

"Why'd it go under?" Bailey asked.

"Grace's parents were Margaret and Walter Mason."

Bailey jerked at hearing the names, and her eyes got wide. *Oh shit.*

"I see you recognize their names," Nathan said, his tone hard to read. "They hired the Inca Boyz to take lurid photos of Grace with Bradford Grant. They were both drugged and unconscious when the pictures were taken. The Masons were hoping to use the photos to blackmail Bradford's parents."

"You know who I am," Bailey whispered. She was terrified, embarrassed, and freaked out all at the same time.

"I know who you are," Nathan confirmed. "But please, listen to the rest of my story?"

Bailey nodded. She couldn't move anyway. If she tried to stand up, her legs wouldn't hold her. She knew it. The last person she should've offered to help was Nathan Anderson.

"I'm assuming you left Denver around the time the thing happened with Grace and Bradford?"

She nodded again, then said quietly, "I didn't like what Donovan was doing. It was one thing to hold up convenience stores, drink, and do drugs. It was another thing altogether to take money to hurt and kill people . . . and blackmail them. I didn't want anything to do with it."

Nathan nodded. The compassionate look in his eyes was killing her. Why was he looking at her like that? He should hate her. Shouldn't want anything to do with her. But there he was, watching her, making sure she was all right before he continued. *God.*

She rushed on, wanting to get the conversation over with. "When Donovan came home that day, he was high on the rush of what they'd done. Kept talking about how much fun it was. How he'd wanted to keep the pictures, but the woman who'd hired him had paid him extra to mail the camera back to her."

Nathan nodded slowly. "Yeah. It's one of the reasons why they had enough to charge him. He put his return address on the envelope."

Bailey chuckled, but it wasn't a humorous sound. "He's not that smart." And he wasn't, but he *had* been smart enough to manipulate her for years. To make her feel as if he was the only person who cared about her. To make her think he loved Joel like a son. Except her brother had been there when Donovan and his brothers had gotten back from taking the pictures of Grace and Bradford. They'd bragged about how good it felt to feel her naked body against them. How they wanted to take her while she'd been unconscious. The only reason they hadn't was because Bradford started making noises like he was waking up, and they'd run out of time.

It had sickened her. She knew Donovan and his brothers and friends weren't exactly upstanding citizens, but not caring that they were talking about raping an unconscious woman in front of a nine-year-old kid, *her* nine-year-old kid, had been too much.

"Why'd you decide to leave, Bailey?"

It was as if he could read her mind. "You don't know?"

"The only thing I knew about you before you came up to me in that parking lot was that your name was Bailey and you were Donovan's ex-girlfriend. And that no one knew where you were."

Well, that was something, she supposed. Nathan didn't say anything, giving her the time to think through what, if anything, she wanted to tell him. And him giving her that time, not pushing her, or rushing to fill the awkward silence between them, gave her the courage to tell him. Why not?

"Because they were laughing and saying how powerful they felt being able to do anything they wanted to both Bradford and Grace while they couldn't do anything about it," she whispered. She felt dirty just talking about it. Knowing she'd spent most of her life around the evil that was the Inca Boyz. The tattoo on her lower back itched, as if reminding her just what she was. Contaminated.

"And they were doing it in front of Joel," she continued, her voice cracking with emotion. "They didn't care that he was listening. It was as if they wanted him to hear. Wanted to deaden his emotions. Make him see that women were nothing but trash, to be used however a man wanted to, whenever he wanted to. I had to go."

"I'm proud of you, Bailey," Nathan said quietly.

Bailey's eyes whipped up to his in shock. "What?"

"I'm proud of you. It couldn't have been easy to simply pack up and move with no job, no idea where you'd end up. Knowing that leaving like that would piss off not only Donovan, but likely the gang too. And to do it with a nine-year-old in tow only made it harder."

"I didn't want him to end up in some sleazy hotel room, raping an unconscious woman and thinking it was fun."

"Do you want to know the rest of the story?" Nathan asked, not commenting on what she'd just told him.

Bailey nodded. She didn't, not really. But she knew she needed to so she could decide if she should pack up and leave tonight, or if she had more time.

"You know Donovan went to jail, as did Grace's parents. Grace and my brother got married, and will be having their twin sons any day now. Alexis, who is Bradford's sister, started working for Ace Security. She and Blake were investigating the Inca Boyz, trying to get more information on them and their new moneymaking scheme. It turns out that Alexis went to school with one of the women who hung around the club. Kelly White."

Bailey gasped. God. Kelly was a bitch. A couple of years older than she was, and someone who'd always hated her. Especially because she wanted Donovan for herself. Well, it wasn't that she wanted *Donovan* per se, but she'd always wanted the power that would come with dating the president of the gang. And she hated Bailey because *she* had that power.

"You know Kelly?" Nathan asked.

Bailey only heard curiosity in his voice. Not scorn or disdain. He was either a really good actor, or completely insane.

"Yeah. She's . . . not the nicest person."

Nathan let out a huff of laughter. "That's one way to describe her, I guess. Anyway, Alexis met with her to try to find out more information on the gang. One thing turned into another and she ended up at a party at Damian's house."

"Jesus," Bailey breathed. "Is she okay?" She knew exactly what the parties at Damian's were like. Inca Boyz parties were more like fuck-fests, with the gang members passing the women who hung around the gang among each other. They had contests about who could screw the most women in one night. They didn't care about who they fucked or if the chick enjoyed it. It was all about them getting off. And the last party she'd been at, Bailey had been dismayed to see so many girls who were obviously way younger than eighteen. But again, that didn't faze the Inca Boyz. They treated them just like they did any other chick who showed up—like they were there only for them to screw.

"She's okay," Nathan reassured her quickly. "Somewhere in the midst of her trying to collect information on the gang, Damian and Dominic figured out who she was, Kelly lured her into a trap, and they, along with a guy named Chuck, took her up into the mountains, beat the hell out of her, and were going to leave her there for a couple of days before going back up there and killing her."

Bailey knew she was going to be sick. Without another word, she grabbed her purse, scooted out of the booth, and headed for the front door. Ignoring anything but the glass door and the dim but fresh air beyond it, she didn't see Nathan wave at Francesca, didn't hear the older woman's cheerful goodbye, and barely even noticed Nathan's presence at her side as she threw open the door to the restaurant and stepped out into the dark evening. She blindly turned right, not knowing where she was going, but Nathan took her arm in his grasp and turned her the other way.

"There's a small park this way."

She didn't say a word, but allowed Nathan to steer her to a bench in a small park nearby. She collapsed on it and huddled over, her arms tight around her belly, her head resting on her knees.

"Alexis is fine. Blake and Logan made it to her in time. The others . . . not so much."

Bailey's head came up at that. She could just make out Nathan's face as he sat straight next to her. His hand was still around her arm. She could feel his warmth seeping into her bones as if he was an actual heat source. His thumb was brushing back and forth against her, making her wish that she could feel it against her skin instead of only through the material of her sleeve.

"Not so much?" she asked shakily, still not convinced the delicious meal she'd eaten wasn't going to end up on the grass at her feet.

"All four are dead."

Bailey blinked. "All of them?"

Nathan nodded. "Between Blake and the cops, they were all killed."

Bailey's head spun. Donovan's brothers were dead. And Kelly. And even the awful Chuck. He'd asked Donovan if he could have her once, and of course Donovan had agreed, as long as he could watch. It had been awful. Donovan had held her down while Chuck had taken her from behind.

"I'm not sorry," she said, her hatred easy to hear.

Nathan didn't comment on that, but only asked bizarrely, "You ready to hear more?"

"There's more?"

"There's more," Nathan confirmed grimly.

"I'm ready," Bailey told him, not sure she was.

"Kelly ranted and raved about how when Donovan got out of jail, he'd be looking for you. That he'd remove your tattoos with a blowtorch, and she'd be his girlfriend once you were out of the picture."

Bailey shivered and put her head back down on her knees. When a guy tried to leave the gang, they'd either be forced back in, or they'd be allowed to leave *if* any of their tattoos that represented the gang were obliterated. Donovan had bragged often enough about burning them off with a hot piece of metal, or cutting them out.

She thought about her tattoos. She had a lot of them. From the gang logo on her arms to the initials *IB*, and of course the words Donovan had forced her to get on her back. Oh yeah, she was as good as dead. If Donovan and his gang tried to remove every trace of the Inca Boyz from her skin, she'd never survive it.

"He was released from jail last week," Nathan said, as if his previous words weren't enough to push her over the edge.

Bailey stood without thought and started walking.

Nathan caught up to her within steps and pulled her to a halt. "Where are you going?"

"I've got to go," she mumbled.

Nathan stepped in front of her and took both her shoulders in his hands. "Where, Bailey?"

"Away. He's gonna find me. I need to get Joel, and we need to leave." Bailey knew she wasn't making sense, but she was completely freaked. Why hadn't she gone to the library to check to see if Donovan was still in jail, as she'd planned? She'd gotten complacent, thinking she was in the clear. But with everything that had happened, she knew without a doubt that Donovan would want revenge. Against the Andersons, who had killed his brothers, and against her. He'd hurt Joel just because he knew that would hurt her. There was no way she'd put her brother through that.

"Listen to me, pixie. Take a deep breath and listen, okay?"

There was that nickname again. Bailey took a deep breath as he'd demanded, but closed her eyes, refusing to look at him.

"We've got eyes on him. He's too busy trying to assert his leadership over what remains of his gang to do anything else at the moment."

"He's going to find me," Bailey said morosely, her entire body sagging in defeat.

"You're right. He is."

Nathan's words surprised her so much, her eyes popped open and she stared up at him. "Is that supposed to make me feel better?" she snapped.

"Would you rather I lie and tell you that you're safe here, that he'll never find you, and you never have to worry about him or the Inca Boyz again?"

When he put it that way, Bailey grimaced. "No."

"Come and sit back down. My brothers have a plan."

Bailey looked up at Nathan. Really looked at him for the first time since he'd started telling her about who he was and that he knew who *she* was. He looked about as devastated as she felt. His lips were pulled down into a frown, and his brow was furrowed with deep worry lines. He'd loosened his tie and had undone the top button of his white shirt. His sports jacket lay back on the bench they'd been sitting on, and he was breathing hard.

She nodded. It was a minuscule movement of her head, but he saw it.

He paused for just a moment, as if making sure she was really okay and wouldn't bolt the second he let go of her shoulders, then he took a step back and held out an arm, indicating the way back to the bench.

She slowly trudged over to it and sat. A shiver rolled through her body at the implications of what Nathan had told her. Immediately she felt Nathan spreading his jacket over her shoulders. The warmth from his body was still in the material, and it seeped into her skin.

"What's the plan?"

"We tell Clayson and the other guys at the shop what's going on." He held up a hand to forestall the protest he could obviously see in her eyes. "Not everything, just that an ex-boyfriend of yours is trouble, and if he shows up, they should immediately call the cops."

"What else?" Bailey asked, not convinced. Donovan wasn't completely stupid. It wasn't as if he would waltz into her workplace and drag her off. He'd be sneakier about it.

"We know someone who can put in an alarm at your place. Nothing fancy, but enough to give you time to call for help. And, pixie, I know you won't like this, but Joel needs to know."

"No!" Bailey exclaimed immediately. "No way. I've tried to shelter him from this as much as possible."

"Have you talked to him about anything at all?"

"No. And I won't. I don't want to talk to him about the Inca Boyz or anything about it."

"But you told me yourself that Donovan was bragging about fucking an unconscious woman right in front of him. He's almost ten, Bailey. He's not stupid. He knows more than you think he does."

Bailey turned away from Nathan and took a deep breath, which did nothing to stem the tears welling in her eyes. Everything she'd done, she'd done for Joel. She never wanted to see him look at her in disgust. And he would if he knew what she'd done. What Donovan had done.

"Look at me, pixie."

She didn't. The swing set in the small park wavered in front of her as the tears filled her eyes, then spilled over.

Nathan didn't make her look at him. Instead, he wrapped an arm around her shoulders and pulled her into his side. He said reasonably, "I'm not trying to upset you. But I think Joel is probably confused. Donovan told him that women were trash, and could be treated as such. But he loves you, and isn't sure what he should think. I'm not saying you should tell him all the details, but enough so that he can be on the lookout. So that he'd tell you if he sees Donovan. If the man really wants to get his hands on Joel, he'll probably try to sweet-talk him first."

Bailey licked her lips, tasting the salt from her tears. Thankful she didn't have to look at Nathan, she said in a shaky voice, "I can't lose my brother."

"And you won't. I swear. Do you want me to do it? I can talk to him and answer any questions he might have."

Bailey's body tensed. "Why would you do that? You just met me. You don't know me or my brother. And your family has been so hurt by Donovan and the Inca Boyz. I was a part of that. I don't understand."

She felt Nathan take a deep breath next to her, then let it out slowly. Because he was sitting so close, his hot breath wafted over her upper chest, making her nipples tighten inappropriately.

"You intrigued me since I first found out about you. I wondered what kind of person you were. What made you hang around the gang in the first place. More importantly, what made you leave."

"And now you know I ran because I was scared," Bailey said in a defeated tone.

"No," Nathan countered. "You ran because of love. You loved your brother more than anything else and ran to protect him. There's nothing you could've done that would endear you to me more, Bailey. Don't you get it? Logan and Blake are my life. I was nothing without them, and I'd do anything to protect them. I'd kill for them, if it came down to it. Your love for your brother is something I see and feel every day. Every time I see Logan saunter into Ace Security. Each time I hear Blake talk to Alexis on the phone. I think I'm almost as proud as Logan is for his sons to be born."

Bailey knew Nathan wasn't lying. He was laying himself bare to her. And she had a feeling that he *did* understand.

"I wasn't strong enough when we were younger to protect either of them. I was the nerdy geek who went through life just trying to get by. They were tough and strong and not afraid of anything. I was Joel, pixie. He was me. That you want to stand in front of him and protect him from Donovan and any harm that might come his way makes me care about you all the more."

More tears fell from her eyes, but Bailey didn't move an inch. She sat stock-still in Nathan's embrace, soaking up his warmth, his goodness. She didn't deserve it, but God, it felt good.

"I said it at dinner, and I'll say it again. I don't care about your past, Bailey. What matters to me is when push came to shove, you chose your family. I'm not the most experienced man when it comes to relationships, but if I had my choice of any woman in the world, I'd choose you. I want someone who will stand by my side as fiercely as you've stood by your brother's. I want to help Joel become a man who will treasure his sister and appreciate all she's done for him."

Bailey squeezed her eyes shut and inhaled a huge breath through her nose. She never imagined a man like Nathan, a *good* man, being able to interpret anything she'd done while involved with Donovan in a positive way. She wanted to believe him. But was afraid to. He had to stop. "Please stop talking," Bailey begged.

In response, Nathan's arm tightened around her. "I don't know what's going to happen in the future, except that eventually Donovan's gonna come looking for you. Let me be next to you when that happens. Let Logan and Blake be there. Alexis and Grace, and probably Felicity too. You're not alone anymore, Bailey. Let us in."

Bailey said not a word, merely let the tears fall from her eyes. They sat together on the bench for a long time. The mountain air got chilly, but Nathan didn't budge. Finally, when her legs were almost frozen, and she was all cried out, Bailey asked in a toneless voice, "Take me home?"

Out of the corner of her eye, she saw Nathan nod, and then he was standing. Without asking, he took her hand in his and led the way back to his car, his jacket still resting on her shoulders. She tried to remove it and hand it back, but he merely shook his head and guided her arms into the sleeves, helping her wear it instead of it being draped over her shoulders.

He closed her door and made his way around the front of the car. The drive back to her house was done in silence, although Nathan had grabbed her hand the second he'd gotten the vehicle started and hadn't let go.

After arriving back home, Bailey didn't wait for him to come around and open her door. She got out and started walking for her door before he could get to her. Nathan was way too good of a man to hang around her. She'd contaminate him if he did.

Not surprised, she didn't even startle when he grabbed her hand and walked next to her until they reached her front door.

Keeping her voice low so Duke wouldn't hear her if he was still awake, Bailey said, "Thank you for dinner."

"You're welcome. Can I call you tomorrow?"

"I need time to think, Nathan."

"Okay, but can I call you tomorrow?"

Bailey sighed in exasperation. "No. I need time to think," she repeated.

"And you can have it. But I still want to talk to you."

"I don't want to talk to you, though. Why aren't you getting the hint?" she complained testily, wanting nothing more than to put on a pair of sweats, get under her covers, and cry.

"I'll call. You don't have to answer, but you should know me or my brothers will be around. Checking on you. Making sure you're okay."

"You sure you're not keeping tabs on Donovan's whore so she doesn't slip away and make it impossible to use her for bait?"

A look of shock and horror registered on Nathan's face, and he took a step back as if she'd physically hit him. Bailey felt remorse for her harsh words. "Nathan, I—"

"We are *not* using you for bait," Nathan said slowly. "I would probably still be looking for you if you hadn't come up to me in that parking lot. I'm ninety-nine percent sure Donovan has no idea where you are, and he sure as hell won't find out from me or my brothers." He looked at the ground then, running a hand through his hair before taking another step backward.

It might as well have been a mile.

He finally looked up at her, his voice devoid of any of the passion and excitement that had been present all night. He'd retreated behind a shell, and Bailey suddenly wanted the slightly nervous geek back. Not this remote stranger.

"I'll talk to my brothers. We'll make sure you're safe, and I'll get the security guy to call you to set up a time to install the alarm."

He held up a hand when she opened her mouth to protest.

"It won't cost you a dime. Trust me, we want Donovan taken down, and you or Joel getting hurt isn't a part of that plan." He shrugged. "It's a tax write-off anyway, so it's no big deal."

That hurt. Bailey tried again, even though she didn't know what she was going to say. "I didn't—"

"I'm glad you know everything now. You can do what you need to in order to keep yourself safe. I can't keep you from running, but you're a hell of a lot safer here in Castle Rock with Ace Security looking over your shoulder than you would be anywhere else. Remember that."

And without giving her a chance to say anything else, Nathan turned around and stalked back to his car. He didn't look back once, merely got into his car and drove off. Leaving her standing in front of her door, shaking with cold, and something else.

Bailey looked down at her feet. She was ashamed of herself. Nathan had been nicer to her than anyone had been in her entire life. He hadn't pushed her for anything. Had treated her as if she was precious to him. He hadn't demanded a kiss or more. Hadn't even seemed to expect it.

Anytime Donovan took her out to eat, even if it was only to McDonald's, he always told her she "owed" him. More often than not, her repayment was taking his dick down her throat. She didn't even want to think about what he'd made her do after he'd "given" Joel the game console.

But Nathan wasn't like that. She knew without a doubt he'd never force her to do anything. He'd offered to talk to Joel for her. He'd told her how he felt about his brothers, about growing up, about how his mom abused him.

She'd been a bitch, and he didn't deserve it.

The door opened behind her, and Duke walked out. "Have fun?" he asked in a low voice.

Bailey nodded, simply because it was expected.

"Good."

She kept her face turned away from him so he wouldn't see the tear marks. "Was Joel good?"

"Of course. He's a good kid. He kicked my ass in *This Is War* and went to bed around ten thirty."

"Thanks for looking after him for me," Bailey said tonelessly.

"You're welcome." Duke paused for a moment before saying, "If you need me or any of the guys to kick that guy's ass . . . we will."

She chuckled then, realizing in a sudden rush that Duke wasn't just saying that. He meant it. Somehow she'd gone from having no real friends, to having not only Clayson and the others at the auto body shop, but having Nathan, Blake, and Logan Anderson at her back too. Her head spun.

"Thanks. But not necessary."

"Okay, but all you gotta do is say the word," Duke insisted, then let it drop. "I'll see you on Tuesday, Bailey."

"See you, Duke."

She watched as he strode to his car and pulled away.

Looking up at the sky as if it would hold all the answers she needed, Bailey took a deep breath. She stood that way for several moments before heading inside and closing the door behind her. After making sure all three locks were engaged, she kicked off her shoes, then wandered down the hall.

She peeked in on Joel, finding him fast asleep and snoring slightly. She stripped off Nathan's jacket, then her dress and underwear. She pulled a pair of sweats up her legs and grabbed the extra-large T-shirt she liked to sleep in. She padded back out into the hall and into the bathroom to brush her teeth and wash her face.

Then once more she entered her bedroom. Before lying down, she grabbed Nathan's jacket and put it up to her face. Inhaling deeply, she pulled Nathan's scent into her nostrils. The slightly sweet smell of his shaving lotion, or deodorant, or soap wasn't overwhelming. It was just right. Somehow she knew he wouldn't bother with cologne, or the fancy man-scent spray that was so popular nowadays. He simply wouldn't think that it would do any good. That a woman wouldn't be attracted to him, regardless of the way he smelled.

Without thought, Bailey snuggled into her covers, with Nathan's jacket still held to her face.

She'd hurt him.

She hadn't meant to, but she'd done it all the same.

But she did need time.

Time to figure out what the hell she was going to do.

She needed to make sure she and her brother were safe, try to explain to Joel that the man he'd come to love when in Denver was actually a thug and a criminal, and figure out how in the hell she'd come to care for Nathan after knowing him two days.

Bailey fell asleep with the scent of Nathan in her lungs, and not having any answers to what she was going to do next.

Chapter Eleven

Six days. That's how long it had been since Nathan had heard Bailey's voice. He'd done as she asked, and given her space.

Logan had arranged for a local company to go to her house and install a basic alarm. Nathan had wanted the expensive one with all the bells and whistles, but he also didn't want to make Bailey uncomfortable. He hated that he'd thrown the "tax write-off" excuse at her because it wasn't true, not in the least. He was footing the bill personally. But after a conference call with the technician, he'd agreed that with Joel in the house, and it being as small as it was, the basic alarm would work.

One thing Nathan insisted on was that if the alarm was tripped, a call would go out to the cops, and they'd immediately be sent to her property. If Donovan tried to get to either Bailey or Joel at their house, it would be a lot harder to get away with it with the cops breathing down his neck.

He'd also called Clayson and explained in as little detail as possible what was going on with Bailey and what he and his other employees needed to be on the lookout for. Clayson promised that they'd keep their eye on both her and Joel and would walk her to her car after work. The older man also said he'd try to convince Bailey that she needed to stop walking to work. It simply wasn't safe, all things considered.

Nathan didn't like not talking to Bailey herself, especially after it had taken him so long to find her, but her accusation had sliced through him as easily as a warm knife through butter. The fact that she thought for one second he would use her as bait, killed. But what cut him to ribbons even more was that she thought of herself as Donovan's whore.

Bailey Hampton was *no one's* whore.

He wasn't an idiot. He knew what kind of life she must've led hanging out with the Inca Boyz. She'd been with them since she was a teenager, so that meant she'd spent seven or eight years hanging with the gang before she'd gotten out.

He'd done plenty of research on the Inca Boyz and gangs in general. On an intellectual level, he knew what happened behind closed doors within the gang. He'd seen the video Alexis had taken when she went to an Inca Boyz party. The women were expected to have sex with whoever wanted it, whenever they wanted it. He hated that Bailey had been a part of that.

Not because of the actual sex, but because she deserved more than that. She deserved to be worshipped. To be told every day of her life how beautiful she was. How smart. How absolutely amazing she was. But he knew without a doubt, Donovan didn't tell her those things. Didn't treat her as she deserved to be treated.

He wanted so badly to give her the life she deserved. And to do that, he had to do everything in his power to make sure she was safe.

To make sure she had the freedom to choose who she wanted to spend the rest of her life with.

To make sure Joel didn't get sucked into the gang lifestyle.

So he hadn't called.

He hadn't stopped by her work or home.

And he'd left the surveillance of her to his brothers and Alexis.

They'd reported that she seemed to be a night owl, with the lights in her small home on late into the evening.

That she did nothing but go to work, pick up her brother, and go home.

She was lying low, being safe and smart.

But still, Nathan wanted to hear her voice. Make sure she was okay mentally as well as physically.

But he stayed away and concentrated on Donovan. He and Alexis checked the Inca Boyz Facebook account every day. There hadn't been one new post. But the more Alexis learned from her newfound hacking skills, the more certain Nathan became that Donovan wasn't going to let Bailey go without a fight.

Donovan's dad had been a drunk who stayed home and drank while his wife worked twelve-hour days to put food on the table and tequila in his belly. Nathan would've felt sorry for the kid Donovan had been, except from the age of ten, he'd been in trouble. It started with visits to the principal's office in grade school, and then in junior high, he'd been suspended several times.

Alexis hacked into his juvie records and found that he'd been put into detention for the first time at the age of fourteen for holding up a convenience store with a pair of seventeen-year-olds from his neighborhood. After that, he was in and out of jail for various violent offenses until he turned eighteen.

He'd gotten better at hiding his illegal activities from the cops when he was officially an adult, but he was still very much on law enforcement's radar. He'd never done any hard time in jail, until the incident with Grace. Every time he was charged, witnesses had recanted, or victims had refused to press charges. But his long list of suspected crimes included sex with a minor, solicitation, and assault with a deadly weapon.

But it was an interview with a prostitute that had solidified that Donovan would come for Bailey and Joel. The woman had been found unconscious in an alley in Denver. The alleged victim had been taken to the hospital, and a detective had taken her statement:

> "When he was raping me, he kept telling me that it was my duty to take whatever he gave me. That

> women were only good for one thing. He said that the world would be a better place if boys were taught from a young age that women were deceitful and needed to be kept in their place. I thought he was going to kill me. His voice was cold; he had no remorse whatsoever that he was hurting me. In fact, I think he enjoyed it. When he was done, he started to beat me. Calling me by the wrong name and saying that I was his to do what he wanted with."

The detective asked the alleged victim what name he called her. Her response:

> "Bailey. I tried to tell him that I wasn't her, but he didn't care. Just kept saying over and over that he'd teach me to run from him. That he'd show my brother what it meant to be a man."

The woman had disappeared after being released, and Donovan had never been charged with her rape and assault. Nathan hadn't visibly reacted when Alexis had unearthed the statement, but every muscle had tightened. Donovan wanted Bailey back. And he'd do whatever it took to get her and her brother under his thumb again. And Nathan knew without a doubt that she wouldn't have another chance to escape if the gang member got his hands on her. Not alive anyway.

Detective Ross Peterson, from the Denver Gang Task Force, had been communicating with Nathan and his brothers on a regular basis as well, letting them know what was happening inside the gang now that Donovan was back.

And what was happening was a bunch of nothing, at least outwardly. With his brothers dead, Donovan was trying to get back control of his minions. Apparently the group did a lot of sitting around and drinking. But that didn't mean they weren't planning on revenge, or that Bailey, hell, or Alexis and Grace, were safe.

The Inca Boyz had to be pissed at everything that had happened over the last months. Their gang was basically in disarray as a result. If Donovan was smart, which he doubted, he'd be watching the Andersons. And Nathan's interest in Bailey could lead him right to her.

It was just one more reason he should stay away from her . . . but he couldn't. If nothing else, Bailey needed a friend. And he'd be there for her even if she didn't want anything to do with him. He'd realized that he'd pushed Bailey too hard. Of course she didn't want to jump into a relationship. He needed to be her friend before he could be anything else. And he could. He had lots of practice being friends with women. In the past, most of the women he'd had an interest in didn't see him as anything other than a good buddy. Yeah, unfortunately, he'd had lots of practice hiding his feelings and being nothing more than a friend.

Glancing at his watch, Nathan pushed back from the counter in his kitchen and stood. It was time to stop feeling sorry for himself and head out to the park, and Joel's party. He'd promised he'd be there, and be there he would.

Grace had done an excellent job of corralling people to attend. She'd spoken with her best friend, Felicity, who'd gotten at least four families from her gym to come. She'd even convinced Cole, the co-owner of the gym, to show up.

Alexis and Blake were picking up pizza and soft drinks, Grace had arranged for Felicity to get decorations, and Nathan told his brothers that he'd be in charge of the presents.

He'd had no idea what kind of toys ten-year-old boys played with, but it was easy to get ideas from the Internet, and combined with his love of *Star Wars* . . . it was a no-brainer.

Nathan had packed his car the night before, so after finishing his coffee, he placed his mug in the sink and headed out.

He arrived at the park around nine and was pleased to see Felicity already there. She had all the decorations, so he jogged over to her car to help her unpack. They brought the ten bags up to the pavilion Bailey had rented.

It wasn't hard to find out which one was reserved for Nathan's party. All he'd done was call up the park office and inquire about the party on Saturday, and the secretary on the other end of the phone told him without quibble. It was a little disheartening she'd shared the information so readily, especially with Donovan on the loose.

"Hey, Nathan. I got all the things you asked for," Felicity told him, her head buried in one of the bags she was digging around in. "There was a ton of Pokémon stuff, but I couldn't do it." She turned to him then, one hand on her hip, the other gesticulating wildly as she spoke. "Some of those things are just creepy. Fat, squat, yellow bug things. Ew. So I went with something easy. Legos and Star Wars, like you requested." She held her hand up as if Nathan voiced a protest.

He simply looked on with amusement.

"I know, I know, they don't really go together, but when I was standing in the toy aisle and looking at Legos, there were a ton of different sets with Star Wars. A woman was there with her son, who looked around ten, so I asked her. She said her son was obsessed with both. I figured if *you* still liked Star Wars, I couldn't go wrong with combining that with Legos." Felicity shrugged. "So I went with it."

"All this is great, Felicity. Thank you. I'm sure he'll love it," Nathan told her.

Felicity stopped fiddling with the bags and decorations and pinned him with a look. Her eyes narrowed, and she tilted her head as she said, "You're going to an awful lot of trouble for a woman you didn't know until a week ago."

Of course Grace had been talking to her.

Nathan started arranging the presents he'd brought on one of the tables in the shelter. "Joel's a good kid. I like him." He knew full well it didn't answer her implied question.

"And?"

Nathan sighed and looked at Felicity. She was wearing a white tank top that made the colorful tattoos on her arms stand out in stark contrast. In that way she reminded him of Bailey. They looked similar, with their tattooed arms and height, but that was where the similarities ended.

Nathan didn't know Felicity's history; she hadn't grown up in the area, but she was around his age, maybe a year or two older. Despite Bailey's time with the Inca Boyz gang, she still had a look of innocence about her. Felicity had lost her innocence long ago. There were flashes of deep pain in her eyes that she couldn't hide. She didn't make friends easily—Grace and Felicity's partner, Cole, were the exceptions. She worked hard and was at the gym more often than not.

He studied Felicity for a long moment. For some reason he had a feeling she and Bailey would get along really well, and not just because they both had tattoos. There was something about Felicity that made him want to take her in his arms and let her know that everything would be okay. She'd never allow it, but he had that same feeling about Bailey. He was a good judge of character, and the pain that sometimes showed up in Felicity's eyes matched Bailey's. Yeah, they probably had a lot more in common than anyone knew.

He sighed and answered her earlier question. "And I like them both, okay?" he told her in a low voice. "But she wants nothing to do with me, or any man. I can't blame her. So I'm just helping out a friend."

Felicity held his eyes for a long moment before she nodded and changed the subject. "You think Grace is ever going to have those babies?"

Nathan smiled, thinking about his unborn nephews. "I'm hoping she holds off another week. That's the date I picked for the bet."

Felicity laughed. "I don't care when she has them. I just can't wait to hold them and squeeze their chubby cheeks. I'm ready to get on with my godmother duties."

Nathan turned to one of the bags of decorations as he remembered how happy Felicity had been when Grace had asked her to be the babies' godmother. At the time, Felicity didn't have any idea what a godmother did, but she was tickled pink to have been asked anyway. As far as she was concerned, it meant that she was allowed to spoil the babies rotten.

The two continued to hang banners, cover tables with the *Star Wars*–themed tablecloths, and put centerpieces on each table. Felicity had bought party favors for the children—fake light sabers and little boxes of Lego sets they could take home at the end of the day.

Nathan had ordered cupcakes instead of a full cake, figuring it'd be easier for the kids to eat. The bakery was supposed to deliver the confections in a half hour.

"Good Lord, Nathan. Did you buy out the store?" Felicity asked when she got a look at the gift table.

He eyed it. "Hmm," he murmured. "Is it too much?"

"Too much? Nathan, there have to be at least twenty presents here!" Felicity told him.

"But is it too much?" Nathan repeated.

Grace's friend eyed him for a long moment before saying, "If you're trying to impress Bailey, I'm thinking not."

Nathan's eyes whipped up to hers. "I'm not trying to impress her."

"Uh-huh. You can deny it all you want, but it's easy to see how much you like her."

When Nathan stiffened, she said quickly, "It's a good thing."

"It's too much," was his response, and he reached for the gifts, piling three into his arms. "I'll go and put them in my car. I'm sure I can return them."

Felicity put her hand on his arm, stopping him. "Nathan, it's fine. Put them down." After he did, she said softly, "Caring about her, and

Joel, isn't a bad thing. I would've done anything to have a man like you in my life when I was Bailey's age."

Nathan looked down into Felicity's eyes. The pain that was usually banked was suddenly not. The sincerity and agony was clear to see. "What happened to you?" Nathan whispered, wanting to help her. He hated to see anyone hurting, but especially a woman who was close to not only him, but the rest of his family as well.

His question shook her out of whatever memories had taken over, and she blinked, her eyes showing nothing but polite interest again.

Damn. He'd almost gotten in there.

"I'm good. Anyway, all this is great. Joel is gonna be so happy." Felicity turned away from him then and fiddled with one of the centerpieces.

"Hey, guys!" a feminine voice said from nearby.

Nathan turned to see Alexis walking up from the parking area to the shelter. She was carrying three two-liter bottles of Coke. "There are about twenty more of these in the car if you want to help."

Felicity jumped at the chance to escape from Nathan's piercing gaze, calling out a greeting to Alexis and hurrying for the car and the drinks.

Forty minutes later, Nathan looked at his watch nervously. It was ten o'clock and there was no sign of either Bailey or Joel. The cupcakes had been delivered and looked like perfect fluffy confections, weirdly reminding him of Bailey herself—a work of art on the outside and soft and squishy on the inside. Sappy, but true.

Logan and Grace were there, Grace sitting in a camping chair his brother had brought. He'd assisted her into it, then warned her that she wasn't to move an inch. She looked uncomfortable, and Nathan hoped he lost the bet and she had her babies sooner rather than later. She looked like she was about to pop. But hopefully she'd wait until after the party.

Three of the four families had arrived, and there were six kids running around already playing with their toy light sabers. There were bikes and skateboards strewn about the area, and one of the families had brought a corn-hole game as well.

All they needed was the birthday boy.

Nathan walked down to the parking lot, pulled out his phone, and dialed Bailey's number.

It rang twice before she answered.

"Hello?"

"Hi. It's Nathan. Everything okay?"

"Uh . . . hi, Nathan." She paused. "Why are you calling?"

"It's Saturday. I'm at the park for Joel's party."

"Oh yeah, well, we canceled it. He doesn't want to have one."

"Can I talk to him?"

"I don't think that's a good idea. He's not in a good mood."

"Bailey. I'm here at the park with my brothers, their women, and about a dozen other people. We're all here to wish Joel a happy birthday."

"Oh my God," she whispered. "I'm so sorry. I should've called you."

"Don't be sorry," Nathan told her in a gentle voice. "Let me talk to Joel."

"Okay, but I warned you," Bailey said, sounding unsure.

He heard her walking, then a tap on a door. "Joel? Honey? Nathan is on the phone and wants to talk to you."

Joel said something that Nathan couldn't hear because it was muffled; then he heard a door open, the hinges creaking loudly.

"He said it wouldn't take long. Here," Bailey told her brother, obviously holding out the phone to him.

"Bitch, I told you not to bother me."

Nathan inhaled at Joel's words. They were disrespectful and hurtful. He clenched his teeth, hoping the boy took the phone from his sister.

Finally, in what was most likely a battle of wills, with Bailey standing firm and holding the phone out, Joel huffed, "Fine." And took the phone.

"What?" he barked into the receiver.

"Hello, Joel. Happy birthday," Nathan said calmly.

"Whatever," Joel grumbled.

"So . . . you decided you didn't want a party?"

"They're stupid. For babies. No one was coming anyway."

Nathan heard the pain in Joel's voice. "Really? Hmm, that's weird. Because I'm here at the park, and there are a ton of people here. There's a present table, which is sagging because of all the gifts, kids running around, enough soft drinks for a kick-butt burping contest, and Star Wars light sabers for everyone."

Joel was silent for a moment, and Nathan could just picture him sitting on his bed with his mouth gaping open. "Really?" he finally asked.

"Really. Me and my brothers were looking forward to seeing you, but if you don't want to come . . ." He let his voice trail off, not feeling guilty in the least for manipulating the young boy.

"Your brothers are there too?"

"Yup. I told you we'd be here. And we are. I keep my promises."

Nathan heard Joel's fast footsteps; then he was telling his sister, "I changed my mind. I wanna go. Can we leave now?"

"Is Nathan still on the phone?" Bailey said in the background.

"Oh yeah, here, you talk to him. I gotta find my shoes!" Joel said.

There was a crash and muffled noises coming from the phone, before Bailey was there. "Sorry. I dropped the phone. I take it you heard that he changed his mind?"

"Yeah, I got that."

"What did you say to him?"

"Just that I was here waiting for him."

Bailey's voice got soft. "Thank you, Nathan. Seriously. I think he found out this week that none of his classmates were going to be there, and he got depressed about it. I can't blame him. I wouldn't want to go to a party if no one showed up."

"Just hurry up and get here, Bailey," Nathan said softly. "I'm here, and we can throw the football around or something." He purposely didn't tell her about the small army of people who were waiting on them.

"Okay. It won't take long. I can hear him tearing around in his room."

"See you soon, pixie."

"Yeah. Okay. See you in a bit."

Nathan clicked off his phone and stared down at it for a long moment. He didn't know why he kept calling Bailey *pixie* . . . except that it seemed to fit. One of the first things he'd noticed about her was her height. Next to him, she seemed small and delicate. *Pixie* just seemed to fit. Besides, she hadn't complained about the nickname, which made him hope she didn't truly mind.

Twenty minutes later, he was still standing near the parking lot, pacing, when he saw her classic Chevelle pull in. He gestured her over to a space in front that he'd saved just for her. Nathan could see both her and Joel's wide eyes as they caught sight of the number of people milling about and the decorated shelter. Black-and-blue streamers were blowing gently in the wind, and the banner, which stated **May the Force Be with You: Happy Birthday**, was flapping around as if waving hello.

Bailey turned off the engine, and she and Joel stepped out of the car. The little boy ran up to Nathan and threw his arms around his waist.

Nathan took a step back in surprise, but then locked his legs and put his arms tentatively around Joel's shoulders. "Hey, buddy."

"Is this all for me?"

"Of course. Do you see any other birthday boy around here?"

"No!" Joel tilted his head back so he could see Nathan's eyes. "Who are all these people?"

"Why don't we go up and I'll introduce you to everyone, and you can get on gettin' your party on."

"Okay!" Joel said happily, stepping away from Nathan. He turned to his sister. "Bail, look!"

"I see, honey," Bailey told Joel before bringing her eyes up to Nathan's. They were sparkling with tears, but she merely said, "Hey."

"Hey," Nathan returned, wanting to take her into his arms, but instead he put his hands into his pockets. He reminded himself that she didn't want anything from him. The only reason she was here was because of her brother and wanting to make him happy.

She looked good, though. She was wearing a pair of skinny jeans and sneakers. She had on a turquoise top with a long-sleeve cardigan over it. It covered the tattoos on her arms, and as he observed her, she hugged herself around the waist as if giving herself comfort. He hated that. He wanted to be the one comforting her. More, he wanted to be by her side supporting her so she didn't *need* comforting.

"Come on, you two," he said abruptly, "let's go introduce you. And, Bailey, you can take a load off while your brother plays."

He held out a hand indicating they should go ahead of him. Joel ran up the concrete walkway, and Bailey followed at a more sedate pace.

"You didn't need to go to all this trouble," she said softly once Joel was out of earshot.

"It wasn't trouble, pixie," Nathan told her. "It was fun."

She eyed him sideways at that. "I doubt that."

"You did the hard part of reserving the shelter. All I did was get a few decorations and arrange for the food," Nathan said, stretching the truth just a tad.

"Bail! Look at all the presents!" Joel yelled from the top of the walk.

They didn't stop walking, but Bailey looked over at Nathan. "Presents? It's too much, Nathan."

"No. It's not. Now hush and enjoy," Nathan admonished.

When he got to the shelter, he brought Bailey and Joel around to everyone and introduced them. He noticed Bailey was extremely reticent around both Grace and Alexis, but she seemed to click with Felicity, which didn't surprise Nathan at all.

Felicity's tattoos seemed to be a good icebreaker, and soon the two of them were sitting at a picnic table quietly chatting.

Nathan stood with Logan and watched Joel greet the kids who were there, and then immediately start playing with them as if he'd known them forever.

"He seems like a good kid," Logan observed, coming up beside his brother.

"He is," Nathan returned immediately.

"No side effects from living in the shadow of the Inca Boyz?"

"I didn't say that."

Logan looked at Nathan for a long moment before turning his head to check on his wife, then back to Joel. "You'll help him through it."

Nathan couldn't help the skeptical look he aimed at his brother.

"You will," Logan insisted. "Out of all of us, you're the most patient. The one least likely to lose it if he back-talks Bailey. The one who can stay calm in the midst of chaos. I admire that about you."

Nathan swallowed hard. When he was little, he'd felt like the brother the others had to look out for. He hated that feeling and, as a result, had done what he could to look after others, especially women and kids, who were being bullied or picked on. He'd tried really hard not to be a burden to his brothers since they'd started Ace Security. He might not be as strong as they were, but he'd held his own in a few fights. But to hear his brother tell him flat out, without hesitation, that he believed in him and admired him, made him feel good. It wasn't that he thought Logan or Blake didn't love him, but hearing those two words—*you will*—meant the world to him. "Thanks," was all he said, though.

"You're welcome. Heard any more about Donovan or the Incas?"

Nathan shook his head and tried to get his head straight again. "No, but I'm sure it's just a matter of time. The more we do things like this," he said, using his head to indicate the party around them, "the quicker he'll find out about Bailey and make his move. She accused me of using her for bait, and that's the last thing I want to do."

"So you want to pull back? Leave her alone?" Logan asked.

"Honestly? No. But I should."

"Fuck that," his brother said quietly. "Look at her. Look at Joel. They wouldn't have had this if it wasn't for you. You want to deny him this? Her?"

Nathan glanced over at Bailey and saw her throw her head back and laugh at something Felicity said. She looked so carefree it made his heart hurt, knowing she probably hadn't had that in a long time. He then looked at Joel. The boy was chasing a little girl, being careful not to get too close to her or to run too fast, so she wouldn't get hurt. He looked back at his brother. "I'm not like you and Blake. I have no idea how to keep them safe. I'm afraid she'll get hurt by association. I can fight Donovan, but I probably can't fend him off in a prolonged one-on-one fight."

"You know exactly how to keep them safe," Logan countered. "You're underestimating yourself. I've seen you take down perps bigger and stronger than you. You use your brain, find their weakness, and even use their strength against them. Do the same with Donovan. Out of all of us, you're the best man for that job. You've always been the smartest one. Remember in high school when we wanted to go to homecoming, but Mom wouldn't let us go?"

Nathan nodded.

"Me and Blake were all pissed about it, but not you. You brought her a beer from the fridge as soon as we got home Friday night and kept bringing them to her one after another. Even though you knew she'd get meaner with every drink and knock you around, you still did it. What was it . . . around the eighteenth one when she finally passed out?"

"Something like that," Nathan murmured, remembering the incident as if it was yesterday.

"Dad told us he'd leave the back door open and told us to have a good time. We went to homecoming, and it was lame as hell, but dammit, we went. You had a black eye, I had a bruised wrist from blocking one of her blows with the bat, but we were there. We would've missed it if it hadn't been for you. Underhanded, but smart."

"Well, you guys always took blows for me. I figured none of us would get to go if we were all black and blue."

"True," his brother told him, then clapped him on the back before heading back to check on Grace and make sure she was comfortable.

Nathan thought about Logan's words for a long moment. He was right. He'd studied judo and had learned that by keeping things simple and understanding the forces of balance, power, and movement, even a man a hundred pounds lighter than his opponent could still win in a hand-to-hand fight. But Nathan had a feeling Donovan wouldn't play fair. He was the kind of man who would bring a gun to a knife fight just so he could have the upper hand. So, regardless of his brother's confidence in his ability to physically subdue Donovan, Nathan had a feeling he'd be better off outsmarting him from the get-go. If he played his cards right, Donovan could be taken down before he'd even know he was being outplayed. Nathan's mind whirled with scenarios and possibilities.

Before today he'd been ready to step aside. To leave Bailey and Joel alone. To watch over them from afar. But now that he'd seen how little it took to make both Hamptons happy? He realized that he wasn't giving up without a fight. It wouldn't be easy, and it would take a lot of work on his part, but he was willing to do it.

Bailey was worth it.

Joel was worth it.

Starting today, Operation "Woo Bailey" would commence.

Chapter Twelve

Nathan sat next to Joel on a hill overlooking the shelter in the park. They watched as Felicity and Bailey scurried around cleaning up the mess that had been left behind.

"You have a good day?" Nathan asked.

"Sure did," Joel told him, smiling.

"Good. Did you thank everyone for coming?"

"I think so."

"You did?" Nathan asked, looking at the little boy with his eyebrows raised.

Joel giggled. "Everyone but you. Thanks, Nathan. I liked all my stuff."

"That was from everyone."

Joel shook his head. "No, it wasn't. I heard Blake telling Alexis that you got it all, and you wouldn't let them pay for any of it. They was kinda pissed."

"They *were* kind of pissed," Nathan corrected, then shrugged a little self-consciously, not knowing what to say.

"You know my sister will fuck you if you ask." He shrugged. "She fucks everyone. You don't have to butter her up by getting me presents."

Joel said it with the same inflection as if he were telling Nathan what he'd eaten for breakfast that morning. Nathan sucked in a breath as if he'd been punched. The words were not only offensive, but disrespectful as hell.

His voice ringing with reprimand, Nathan said in a low, harsh voice, "That was extremely offensive not only to your sister who isn't here to defend herself, but to me as well. Apologize."

Joel looked over at Nathan, surprise in his eyes. "I'm sorry," he said immediately. Then quieter, he said, "I didn't mean it in a bad way."

Nathan was confused. How in the hell could he not mean it in a bad way? "Explain," he ordered.

Joel hugged his knees and looked back down at the shelter. "Donovan says that women are only good for fucking. That when you have a woman and you train her right, like by hitting and yelling at her, she'll do whatever you tell her to do in the bedroom and out. And I saw him do it, and he was right. The women did what he wanted after he hit them. And every time he gave me something, all he'd do was look at Bailey and she'd go into his room with him. All the girls did that. Donovan said that the more guys a woman fucks, the more she's worth."

Nathan thought he was going to be sick. He knew Donovan was a bastard, but to tell a nine-year-old boy that, about his sister no less, was reprehensible.

"You met Grace and Alexis today, yeah?"

Joel nodded.

"You think either of them is going into a bedroom with anyone except my brothers? You think Logan or Blake *want* anyone else to touch them?"

The little boy looked up at him in confusion and shook his head slowly.

"You think they're hitting them?"

Again, Joel shook his head.

"Exactly. They treasure them. They wouldn't harm a hair on their heads, and they, and I, won't stand by and let anyone else hurt any woman either. Joel, a woman's worth is not because of how many people she's going into a bedroom with. It's in her heart. And how she treats others. It's in the way she looks at you as if you're the only person in her life. It's how she treats her *family*," Nathan emphasized.

Nathan nodded his head toward where Grace had been sitting all morning. "Grace is going to have Logan's children. He loves her so much, he'd kill anyone who hurt her, or his kids. The real measure of a *man*, Joel, is how well he treats those *he* loves. Be that his woman, his brother, his sister, or his friends. I hesitate to say this, because I know you hung out with Donovan and his friends a lot, but they are *not* good men, and you shouldn't take anything they told you to heart." Nathan pinned the little boy with his gaze. "You're ten now. Not a kid anymore. You have to know deep in your heart what Donovan said and did was wrong."

Joel looked down and picked at the grass with his fingers. "Right before we moved, we watched movies together."

"Who did, buddy?"

"Me and Donovan. He said he wanted to teach me how women were supposed to be treated."

Nathan's stomach rolled. "What movies?"

Joel shrugged but didn't look up. "I don't think they had titles. They were real short too. The acting was bad. Everyone was naked, and they did gross things to each other."

"Porn?" Nathan really hoped he was wrong, but in his heart knew he wasn't.

"That's what Donovan said the movies were called. I didn't really like them," Joel admitted in a small voice. "They were disgusting, and all the women did was cry when the men fucked them."

Nathan didn't think Joel really even understood exactly what the word *fuck* meant. His mind spun trying to think of the right thing to say. He felt out of his depth, but was happy Joel was talking to him about it. "Did you tell Donovan you didn't like watching?"

Joel shook his head. "No, 'cause I knew he'd get mad. He also made me smoke a weird cigarette. It made my head spin."

"Look at me, buddy," Nathan ordered.

It took a second, but Joel finally looked up and into Nathan's eyes.

"Donovan is *not* a good man, and he's wrong. Your sister, *all* women, should be treated with love and respect. What you saw is *not* normal. When two people make love, both should want to do it. If a man forces a woman to do anything, he's not a good man. The fact that Donovan forced you to watch those movies and to smoke the funny cigarette when you're not old enough to do either shows that he is not a good man."

Joel's lip started quivering, but Nathan forged on.

"Your sister loves you more than anything. She's scared of Donovan—did you know that? She did what he wanted her to because she was scared of what he'd do to her if she said no. Just like you didn't want to tell him you didn't like the movies, she felt the same way. Now she's scared Donovan will find her and hurt her and make her do more stuff she doesn't want to do. But more than that, she's scared he'll find *you*. Do you know why you moved away from Denver?"

Joel shook his head, his eyes wide as he took in what Nathan was saying.

"Because she was protecting you from Donovan." Nathan took hold of Joel's chin and held it gently. "Men who hurt women should be in jail, buddy. Locked away. That's where Donovan was because he hurt Grace. Beautiful, pretty, gentle Grace. And his friends hurt Alexis. I know you just met them today, but those women are two of the most wonderful people I've ever met. If you hear nothing else that I say, hear this."

Nathan paused and leaned down into Joel.

"Are you listening?"

Joel nodded quickly.

"A real man doesn't talk down to a woman. Not his sister, not his girlfriend, not his wife. If he's upset, he talks to her calmly and rationally. He doesn't call her a bitch, like you did today when all Bailey did was try to give you the phone to talk to me. He doesn't yell at her, and he never, *ever* hits her. I know you've been confused because of what Donovan told you and what you've seen. But you should be thanking your sister every night for getting you out of Denver and away from that sleazeball Donovan and his friends."

"I don't understand. Donovan was nice to me," Joel whispered, his little face scrunched up with confusion.

"Was he?" Nathan returned, letting go of his chin. "Think about today. About how much fun you had. How Blake helped you learn how to skateboard. How Logan got up and got you another cupcake when you dropped yours. Then think about the time you spent with Donovan and answer me honestly. Would he have done any of that for you today? Would he have let you run around with your light saber? Would he have made sure you had presents to open and kids to play with?"

Nathan could see Joel thinking. Finally, he licked his lips and said in a small voice, "No. He once told me he wanted to take me shooting. But, guns kinda scare me, and I didn't want to shoot one. He smacked me when I told him and said that I was a pussy and if I wanted to be an Inca Boy, I needed to toughen up. He also said women were weak. That if I wanted to be in his gang when I grew up that I had to make sure my sister knew I was better than her."

"Can you change a tire?" Not giving Joel a chance to respond, Nathan then asked, "Can you change the oil in your car? Can you *drive* a car? Do you earn money for groceries or rent? Would you leave all your friends and belongings if it meant your sister would be safe? Would you jump in front of a moving car for your sister? Joel, you are not better than your sister. I'm not better than her, and she's not better than Grace or Alexis. Generally, no one is 'better' than anyone else. Not because of their age, not because of the color of their skin, not because of who they love. That's not the way it works.

"With that being said, I do know without a doubt that Bailey *is* better than Donovan and his friends. She wouldn't hurt anyone the way he's hurt people. In my eyes, that's what makes one person better than another. Every time you say mean things to your sister, you make her sad. And that tells me that right now, until you see Bailey's worth, *she* is better than you. She would do anything for you. *Anything.* Don't you understand? Don't you get that Donovan *hurt* her? And she let him because it meant he'd leave *you* alone. Everything she's done in the last few years has been because of you. And you treat her like crap. Yell at her. Make her feel bad. But she doesn't stop, does she? She buys you food, gets you video games and clothes, and you continue to disrespect her. You want to be tough? Be a man and not a boy? Then open your eyes and see the love Bailey has for you. See that Donovan is nothing but a bully."

The tears in Joel's eyes spilled over and ran down his cheeks. "I—"

Nathan didn't let him continue. In a gentle tone, much different from his earlier words, he said, "If your sister looked at me with half the love she has in her eyes when she looks at you, I'd cherish her. I'd let her know every day how proud I was of her and how much I admired her. Women aren't weak, Joel. Women have to be stronger than men simply to deal with the shit they get dealt on a daily basis by men who wrongly think, like Donovan, that they're 'better' than they are. Simply because they're a man. If Bailey was mine, I'd move heaven and earth to make sure nothing ever hurt her again. In fact, even though she's not mine, I'll still do just that."

"I'm sorry, Nathan," Joel said, still sniffling. "I was just saying what Donovan did."

"I know. And I'm sorry too."

"For what?"

"I was pretty harsh with you. I shouldn't have been so blunt."

"What's blunt?"

"Straightforward. I should've gone easier on you when I explained it all."

"Did Donovan really hurt Bail?"

"Yeah, buddy. He did."

"She didn't want to fu—er . . . go into his room with him?"

"No."

"And the other girls?"

"What about them?"

"Did they want to go in the room with Donovan?"

Hating that Donovan openly cheated on Bailey, but honestly not surprised, Nathan said, "I don't know. Some probably yes, others, no."

"I'm sorry," Joel repeated, the remorse in his voice easy to hear. It was obvious this was a genuine apology. "I love Bailey. I just get so mad sometimes. I miss my friends at my old school, and I don't like being the new kid."

"Don't be sorry for something someone else did," Nathan said. "What Donovan did is on him. The best thing you can do is move on. Be friendly with the kids in your class. They just don't know you. If you act around them like you did around the kids you met today, I'm sure they'll be begging to be your friend. Think about your actions from here on out. Take responsibility for what you do. It sucks. You should be allowed to be a kid, but you need to help take care of Bailey, instead of letting her take on all the burdens. Do you help out around the house?"

Joel shook his head. "Donovan always said that it was women's work."

Nathan merely looked at him and raised his eyebrows.

"But Donovan was mean, so he was probably wrong," Joel allowed in a small voice.

"I live by myself. Who do you think cooks, cleans, does the laundry, shops, takes the trash out, dusts, and cleans the toilet?" Nathan asked.

"You," Joel stated without question.

"Exactly. You want to live with Bailey for the rest of your life?"

Joel shook his head.

"Then it's about time you started to learn how to do some of that stuff, yeah?"

"Yeah."

"And one more thing. Well, two," Nathan said gently.

Joel looked at him expectantly, his tears having dried up.

"If you *ever* see Donovan here in town, you need to tell Bailey or me and my brothers immediately."

"Why would he be here?"

"For no good reason. He's mad at Bailey for leaving him. He thinks he owns her. That she should do whatever he says. He's not happy she left."

Nathan could see Joel mulling over his words. "People can't own other people. I learned that in school. Slavery is bad. But, Nathan, even though Bailey doesn't want to, Donovan wants to take her back to his house and do . . . the things I saw in the movies . . . doesn't he?"

"Yeah. He does. And he'll hurt her, buddy. But not only that. He wants *you* back."

"He likes me that much?"

Nathan put his hand on the little boy's shoulder. "He wants to make you as bad as he is."

Joel sucked in a breath.

Nathan continued. "He wants to make you hate your sister. Wants to turn you against her. Then he'll throw that in her face to hurt her more."

"I couldn't hate Bailey," Joel protested.

"You said some pretty mean things to her today," Nathan said. "I heard you call her a bitch when she wanted you to talk to me on the phone. You telling me you weren't mad at her? That you didn't want her to hurt as much as you were hurting?"

Joel didn't respond.

"I like you, buddy. You're an amazing kid. I know all this is confusing, so this is the second thing. If you ever have any questions, I want you to ask me. You can talk to me about *anything*. I'm sure your sister wouldn't mind if you talked to her either, but sometimes it might be easier to ask another guy certain questions. You can ask me about those movies you watched, your feelings, if you're sad, your math homework, if you're missing Donovan . . . whatever it is. I won't get mad. I won't yell. The only thing I ask is that you treat your sister with respect. That's it."

"I like you too, Nathan. And thanks . . . there are some things I wouldn't mind talking to you about. Not that I don't like Bailey, but it'd be less embarrassing to talk to a guy, like you said."

"Good. Then we're friends. We had a man-to-man talk today. It wasn't easy, for you or me. We didn't yell. We didn't hit each other. And we still like each other. Right?"

"Right." Joel smiled tentatively.

Nathan reached into his back pocket and pulled out a pay-as-you-go phone and handed it to Joel as he said, "One last present."

"A phone? For me?" Joel breathed, running his hands over it.

"Yeah. And my number is programmed in. Not only that, but my brothers', Grace's, Alexis's, even Felicity's and all the guys at Clayson's. I'll warn you, though, it's not fancy. It doesn't text or play games. It's only for emergencies, or when you need to talk to me."

"Can I tell Bailey?"

Nathan hesitated. He didn't know how Bailey would take him giving her brother a phone, but he wouldn't keep from her what he'd done. "I'll tell her. You won't get in trouble for having it."

"Cool. This has been the best birthday ever," Joel said with a huge smile.

Nathan had no idea if he'd handled the conversation correctly or not. He'd probably been way too harsh with the boy, but it was about time someone told him that Donovan wasn't a good guy. It was obvious Joel was confused. Donovan had told him some pretty messed-up stuff, and had allowed him to watch porn, smoke weed, and didn't care if the boy saw him hitting women or taking them into his room to screw. It was fucked up, and Nathan was pissed.

He hoped that he'd gotten through, even just a little bit. The need to protect Bailey, even if it was from the hurtful words of her little brother, ate at him.

"Why don't you go on down there and help Felicity finish cleanup?" Nathan told Joel as he saw Bailey headed up the hill toward them. The little boy bounced up and gave him a wave as he ran down the rise toward the shelter. Nathan saw him stop momentarily and give Bailey a hug before he shot off.

He met Bailey's confused eyes as she came up toward him with his own.

One tough conversation down, one more to go.

Chapter Thirteen

"Can I sit?" Bailey asked Nathan uncertainly. She'd seen him talking with Joel and didn't like that her brother looked upset. Felicity had told her to give them some time, but finally she hadn't been able to ignore the duo anymore.

As she'd started up the hill, she saw Joel smile and put something in his pocket before he raced down the hill toward her. He'd surprised her by giving her a hug and thanking her for the great party before he'd run off again.

Bailey felt as though she'd spent the last few hours being surprised. When she and Joel had pulled up, she'd thought at first that they were in the wrong place, but then she'd seen Nathan waiting for them.

She was surprised by the number of people there.

She was surprised by the decorations.

She was surprised when twenty pizzas were delivered around lunchtime.

She was surprised by the number of gifts for Joel on the table.

She was surprised that Nathan and his brothers were friends with a woman who looked like Felicity. Full-sleeve tattoos didn't seem to be their thing, but she quickly learned that the Anderson men were three of the nicest, most nonjudgmental men she'd ever met. She'd even felt relaxed enough to take off her sweater when the temperature rose to an uncomfortable level. And not one person looked at her funny, or gave her the stink eye because of her tattoos.

Overall, the day had been wonderful, and she knew she had Nathan to thank for it. She'd spent the last week vacillating between being sorry she'd written off all men, to knowing it was the right thing to do. But she'd still hoped Nathan would call.

She shouldn't have accused him of only wanting to use her for bait. After meeting Logan and Blake, she knew without a doubt that was the last thing any of them would ever do. Their entire business focused on keeping people safe, not putting them in danger recklessly.

"Of course you can sit," Nathan told her, patting the ground next to him where Joel had been moments earlier.

She eased down beside him with her legs stretched out in front of her. She leaned back on her hands and lifted her face to the sky. There was a slight breeze, and it felt heavenly against her hot skin. She'd put her hair up in its customary ponytail, and the air felt nice against her slightly sweaty neck.

"You shouldn't have gone to all this trouble," she told Nathan without looking at him.

"Why not?"

That brought her head up, and she turned to look at him. "Why not? Well, because. You just met me and Joel last week."

"So?"

Bailey simply stared at him. He looked truly confused. He honestly saw nothing wrong with spending what had to have been hundreds of dollars on gifts and food for a kid he'd just met. "Nathan, it's just not right."

"I know where you grew up and who your friends were. And I have to say, they're all pieces of shit. I might've just met you last week, but you've been on my mind for months. And just sayin', the reality is way better than my imagination. You've been on your own for a long time, I get it. But you're not anymore. I like you. I like Joel. It was fun to shop for Legos, cars, Star Wars stuff, and nerf guns. Throwing a football with him, and seeing his eyes light up with every present he opened, was a gift for me."

"Thank you," Bailey said quietly.

"You're welcome. I'm sorry I didn't call this week."

Bailey was surprised by the change in subject, but she shrugged it off. "It's fine."

"It's not. I said I'd call, and I didn't. I was upset at what you accused me of, and I acted like a baby about it. It won't happen again."

Bailey looked at Nathan in disbelief.

"What? Why are you looking at me like that?" Nathan asked.

"I just . . . you . . ." She couldn't figure out what she wanted to say.

"You're surprised that I apologized and admitted I was wrong," Nathan stated correctly. Then he grinned at her. "I take it you aren't used to men owning up to their mistakes. Let me guess, anytime Donovan or one of the others made a mistake, they blamed you."

How in the world this man could know exactly what she was thinking and what she'd been through, Bailey had no idea, but somehow he did. She liked that he came right out and owned up to what he'd done. She didn't like that she'd upset him, but it had been her goal at the time. The fact that she'd succeeded and he'd admitted it didn't sit well with her.

"Yeah. I'm sorry for accusing you of wanting to use me for bait. It was out of line."

"Actually, it wasn't," Nathan counteracted. "You don't know me. I'd just dumped a lot of shit on you, and you were freaked."

"Still," Bailey insisted, "I'm sorry."

"Apology accepted," Nathan said immediately.

Feeling as if it needed to be said, Bailey told him, "But today, and all this"—she waved her hand toward the shelter and the remnants of the party—"doesn't mean I want to date."

She caught Nathan's wince, but his tone didn't let on that he was upset; instead, he sounded understanding and sympathetic.

"Bailey, when I do something for you or Joel, I'm doing it because I want to. Not because I want something from you. That's not how I operate. If I want something, I'll come out and ask you. You'll never be in a situation with me where you owe me a favor because of something I've done. Look, I get it, I do, and I'll respect your wishes. You're not ready to date. You need to know you can stand on your own two feet. Get your confidence back. But I hope you'll let me be your friend. And Joel's."

She looked at him. "So you want to keep watch over us?" It came out snarkier than she intended, but Nathan didn't look ruffled in the least.

"Yeah, I do. Just because you don't want a romantic relationship right now doesn't mean my feelings for you are turned off."

"I just said—"

He held up a hand to stop her.

"I know. And I respect that."

"I don't want to hurt you, Nathan."

"All due respect, it's not your problem. It's mine."

"You deserve more. Don't fall for me," Bailey warned him.

"Too late," was Nathan's whispered response. Then, in a more normal voice, he said, "But that's on me. I can be your friend, Bailey. I swear. I've had lots of practice. I'll keep my hands to myself, and I'll be good. I just want to be in your life, and Joel's, any way you'll let me."

Bailey looked down at her brother. He was laughing with Felicity, and for once, actually helping pick up trash. Somehow she knew his newfound desire to help was because of Nathan.

"What'd you say to Joel to make him willing to help pick up trash?"

For the first time, Nathan looked discomfited. He ran a hand through his hair and looked off into the distance. "He's . . . Donovan said a lot of shit to him. Shit no one has the right to say to a nine-year-old kid. He's confused. We talked about it a bit, and I told him that no matter what Donovan might've told him or what he saw, a real man doesn't talk mean to a woman."

Bailey's hands began to shake. She'd known Joel's attitude was because of Donovan, but she didn't know what to do about it. Anytime she tried to talk to her brother about it, he closed up and shut himself in his room. He probably needed to see a psychologist, but she didn't want her brother to say anything that might get the cops involved. It was selfish, but she constantly worried that the state would take Joel away from her if they knew the kind of life she'd exposed him to.

Nathan's hand closed over her own and held tight. "He expressed his disdain for any kind of woman's work, as he called it, and I told him that I lived alone and did all the so-called women's work by myself." He shrugged. "I guess it sunk in."

"I guess it did," Bailey agreed. She bit her lip and looked over at Nathan. "You're good for him. I'd love to be your friend, if nothing else because Joel needs you. But it's more than that. I like being around you, Nathan. I like the way you make me feel about myself. How you see me as more than just an Inca Boyz castoff. I'd like to be strong enough to tell you that me and Joel will be just fine on our own, but I don't think that's true. I'm too selfish. I know I'm going to end up hurting you, and that kills me, but I can't say no to your friendship."

She turned her hand around and clasped his in her own.

He brought his other hand to hers and covered their clasped hands with his. "You're not selfish, Bailey. You're cautious. There's a big difference. You don't have to worry about me pressuring you for anything more than you want to give. If all I can have is your friendship—sitting down for meals, hanging out watching movies, helping Joel with his math homework, and having your back when it comes to your past, I'll take it. With no reservations."

"Thank you," Bailey whispered and held her breath when Nathan leaned toward her. She was afraid he was going to kiss her after he'd just said he was okay with being just friends, but she should've known he wouldn't do anything to make her uncomfortable.

His lips touched her forehead in a barely there caress before he pulled back. "You should know, I'm not a text kinda guy. It takes too long. If I want to talk to you, I'll call."

"Okay."

"Oh, and one more thing. I gave Joel a phone of his own."

Bailey frowned. "He's only ten, Nathan."

"I know. That's why it's not a smartphone. It's a cheap pay-as-you-go thing that only makes calls. There's no Internet on it, and I've programmed your number, Clayson's Auto Body and all the guys who work there, the number at Ace Security, Rock Hard Gym, Logan and Grace, and Blake and Alexis's numbers into it. I want him to be able to get ahold of someone if something happens."

God, that was smart. She should've thought about it.

"I should've done that already."

Nathan shrugged. "You would've thought about it sooner or later. Come on, let's go see if they need any more help," he said nonchalantly as he stood, still holding on to her hand, forcing her to her feet as well.

They walked down the hill hand in hand, but Alexis intercepted them before they got back to the shelter. She stood in front of them awkwardly for a moment before blurting, "I'm so glad Nathan found you—or, well . . . that you found Nathan. We've been looking for you forever, and we were really worried about you. After spending time with those assholes, I have no idea how you were able to stand it for so long!"

Bailey wasn't sure what to say. But even after only spending an afternoon with Logan, Blake, and Nathan, it was obvious that Donovan and the rest of the Inca Boyz didn't come close to being in their league.

"Uh . . ."

"And Kelly! Ugh! I know we were friends once upon a time, but what a bitch. Seriously!" Alexis continued to rant. "I'm really, really sorry if you thought she was your friend, but she wanted Donovan bad, and was pissed he was with you."

"We weren't friends," Bailey said quickly. "I knew she didn't like me."

"Girlfriend, she *really* didn't like you," Alexis said, and Bailey couldn't help but smile at the other woman. Even though Alexis seemed really young and naive, for some reason Bailey couldn't help but like her.

"Alexis, are you scaring away Nathan's friend?" Blake said as he came up behind his girlfriend, putting his arms around her. She immediately brought her hands up, clasped his forearms, and tilted her head back.

"Of course not. I just wanted her to know how happy I was that she was here with us and not up in Denver with those assholes."

Blake turned dancing eyes to Bailey. "What she really means to say is how happy she is to meet you and that you're safe."

"Blake," she protested immediately, eyes narrowing. "I *did* say that!"

They all laughed. Bailey had thought it would be weird to meet Alexis, considering she almost died at the hands of the gang. But the other woman made things not awkward at all, and she didn't seem to hold any resentment toward Bailey, which was a huge relief.

"Thank you for being concerned about me," Bailey told the couple in front of her, her sincerity sounding clearly in her words.

"After spending time with them, I'd worry about any woman or child in their circle. I sure hope the kids who were hanging around at the one party I attended have moved on," Alexis said.

Bailey didn't think they had. She didn't know who Alexis was talking about, but especially now that Donovan was back, the girls were probably spending more time with whoever was left in the gang to try to get closer to him. Just as she'd done when she was in high school. She shivered in revulsion, wishing she could turn back time. Wished she'd listened to her pa when he'd tried to tell her Donovan was bad news.

As if he could read her thoughts, Nathan moved to put his arm around her shoulders and stated firmly, "Bailey needs to get going. It's been a long day, and I'm sure she has stuff to do."

"Right," Alexis said. "But I need your number," she said without artifice. "I need to be able to get ahold of you to let you know when Grace goes into labor so you can join us at the hospital."

Bailey startled at the other woman's plain statement. She'd spent quite a bit of time talking with Grace, apologizing for Donovan's role in what happened to her. She knew she wasn't responsible for it, but since she had been dating Donovan at the time, she kinda thought she should've been able to talk him out of it. Grace refused to accept her apology, saying Bailey had nothing to do with it, and changed the subject to how much she wanted the babies out of her body once and for all. Bailey didn't think she'd ever be invited into their inner circle and to the hospital when Grace did give birth.

"Sure," she stammered and recited it to Alexis, who whipped out her phone and keyed in the number.

"I'm sending a text, so you'll know it's me," she said definitively. "And I hope Nathan told you that he's text-averse."

Bailey looked up at Nathan in time to see him roll his eyes at the other woman.

"He did," Bailey confirmed.

"It's ridiculous. It's so much easier to send a text than call, but he refuses."

"I just like hearing your voice," Nathan told Alexis with a smirk.

This time, Alexis rolled her eyes. "Whatever. You do not. You just like to be a pain. You ready to go, Blake?"

"Sure. You say 'bye to Joel?"

"Yup. He's checking out the new *This Is War* game Nathan got him. I should warn you, Bailey, he's been jonesing to play it all afternoon."

"Got it. He's been good today, so he's earned some game time," Bailey told her honestly.

Blake gave his brother a chin lift and asked, "See you tomorrow?"

"Yeah. Ten?"

"That's the plan," Blake confirmed before shifting Alexis in his hold until his arm was over her shoulder, much as Nathan's was over Bailey's body, and the two walked toward the parking lot.

Bailey watched as Alexis wrapped her one arm around Blake's waist and the other around his stomach and held on as they walked. It was cute and snuggly, and if asked, she would've sworn a man who looked like Blake never would've stood for it. Although her experiences with men and women were obviously warped. If she'd tried to show any kind of display of affection to Donovan in public, even holding his hand, he would've smacked the shit out of her and said that she was ruining his "street cred." Whatever that was.

She thought about that as Nathan led them the rest of the way to the shelter. He still had his arm around her shoulder, and didn't seem to care one bit about how it looked or what anyone else might think.

"Bail!" Joel enthused when she got within earshot. "This game is so *cool*! It's got a team-player mode where you can go online and play with five other people and you're a team of Delta Force operatives and you have to go to Iraq and rescue a hostage guy who is another Delta and is hurt. His arm gets blown off and you have to figure out how to make sure he doesn't bleed to death and rescue him and not get shot and find your way out of the country all at the same time. I can't *wait* to play it!"

"Well, you're gonna have to wait until we get home," Bailey told him with a laugh. "Think you can last that long?"

"I guess," he answered sulkily.

"How about taking a box down to the car?" Bailey suggested.

Joel opened his mouth to respond, but Nathan beat him to it.

"Why don't you sit and relax for a second, Bailey, while us men do the heavy lifting?" Nathan suggested, steering her to a picnic table.

"Oh, but I—"

"Sit, Bailey," he insisted, interrupting whatever protest she was going to say. "We've got this. Right, Joel?"

Joel paused a moment, clearly torn between examining the rest of his presents and doing manual labor, but his desire to impress Nathan won out. He nodded. "Yeah, we got this. You worked hard today, Bailey. Thank you."

Bailey stared at her brother in surprise. He'd already thanked her, but it had been in passing. He sounded honestly sincere with his thanks this time. "You're welcome. But I think Nathan did most of the work."

The man blew off her words. "Nonsense. You made sure everyone was happy, handed out napkins, made sure everyone got a cupcake, rented the shelter, volunteered to be Darth Vader and be attacked by light sabers . . . you did the hard stuff," Nathan said with a smile.

So Bailey sat. And watched her little brother, who never voluntarily did any kind of manual labor without being asked fourteen times and then threatened. And then he usually complained while he did it.

But not today. He and Nathan carried four boxes of presents to the back of her Chevelle, and made three runs to Nathan's car to fill it with all the trash bags. They even walked around the shelter grounds, making sure there was no stray trash on the ground. Bailey heard Nathan tell Joel that it was the polite and right thing to do to make sure they left the area better than they found it.

Finally, the shelter was spick-and-span, and it was time to go.

The three walked down to the parking lot. Nathan put his hand on Joel's shoulder and knelt down in front of him. "I told your sister about the phone, so you don't have to hide it from her."

Joel looked up at her then. "Are you mad?"

"No, not at all. You're old enough to have the responsibility of it, and it's a good idea."

"In case Donovan finds us." It wasn't a question.

Bailey sucked in a breath. Nathan had said they'd talked about Donovan, but she wasn't expecting this.

"Right," she choked out.

"You're not with him anymore, right?" Joel insisted.

"No, Joel. I'm not with him anymore, and I don't want to see him again. He's not happy I left him, and I'm afraid he might come looking for me. And you."

"To make you go into his room with him," Joel said solemnly, nodding his head. "I'll make sure I call Nathan or someone if he shows up."

"Happy birthday, buddy," Nathan said, squeezing his shoulder. "Go on and get in the car while I say 'bye to your sister."

"Okay," Joel said, oblivious to the bomb he'd just dropped on his sister.

The second he was in the seat and the door shut behind him, Nathan took Bailey's hand and led her around to the back of the car where he stopped and turned her so her back was to the car and she was looking up at him. "Breathe, Bailey," he ordered.

"Did he mean what I think he meant?" she asked in a choked voice.

"Yeah. He did. But, Bailey," Nathan said, putting both hands on her shoulders and leaning down so he could look her in the eye, "he loves you and is happy you don't have to do anything you don't want to do anymore."

She closed her eyes. "God, I've done a horrible job in raising him."

"No, you haven't," Nathan said sternly. "Look at me."

She did.

His dark eyes glittered with intensity. "You got out. You got him out. You have to go forward. You can't go back. Live for today and tomorrow, not yesterday. Okay?"

She nodded. It made sense. As much as Bailey wished she could turn back time, she couldn't. She hated that Joel knew sort of what went on behind Donovan's bedroom door, but he was safe now, away from Donovan, and she'd do whatever it took to keep him that way.

"You're right. Thank you for talking to him and giving him the phone. It makes me feel better."

"You're welcome. I'll call you tomorrow."

"Why?" The question popped out before Bailey could stop herself. It sounded extremely rude even though she didn't really mean it to be.

"Because we're friends. And friends call each other to chat," he said solemnly.

Bailey chuckled. "Are we gonna go and get our nails done too?" she joked.

Nathan smiled, and Bailey noticed for the first time how it lit up his face. Butterflies swam in her stomach, and she reminded herself that she only wanted to be friends with the fascinating man in front of her. Friends only.

"No, but that doesn't mean I won't take *you* if you want to go. Go on. Get home. Call me if you get scared or anything feels weird. I'm always only a phone call away."

Strangely, that made her feel safer. It was silly, she lived quite a bit away from Castle Rock and presumably wherever Nathan lived, but the reassurance that she could always call him made her feel not so alone.

"Okay. Thanks."

"You're welcome. Thanks for sharing Joel's birthday with me and my family."

She shook her head, ready to tell him once more that *she* should be thanking *him*, when she saw the serious light in his eye. He wasn't just saying that. He was honestly appreciative of being able to spend time with Joel and her.

"It was our pleasure," she said, standing on tiptoe and kissing Nathan's cheek. Her lips tingled where she touched his slightly scratchy skin. Without another word she backed away, raised a hand to give him a half wave, and climbed into her car.

Chapter Fourteen

Bailey's phone rang the next morning, and she groaned as she turned over to try to see her clock. She and Joel had stayed up way too late looking at all his presents—the boy had been way too pumped up on sugar, soda, and excitement to go to sleep.

But because of Nathan and his brothers, she felt somewhat safe in her little home. The alarm system meant she didn't have to search the house before allowing Joel inside. When she was inside and the alarm was set, she could pretend that everything in her life was normal. That she wasn't waiting for her ex-boyfriend to find her, possibly kill her, and take Joel away forever, turning him into a rapist, killer, and thug.

She squinted her eyes and saw that it was 5:41 a.m. Feeling more alert, because anyone calling her this early could *not* be good, Bailey grabbed her cell and clicked it on.

"Hello?" The word came out croaky and rough, letting whoever was on the other end know without a doubt they'd woken her up. Why people always tried to pretend they hadn't been asleep when they answered a phone was something Bailey had never understood. The other person was the one being rude and calling way too early or late, so why would *she* pretend not to have been asleep so the other person didn't feel bad?

"Bailey! It's Alexis! Grace is in labor! You gotta come to the hospital."

"Now?" Bailey asked incredulously.

"Yes! Now!" Alexis insisted, sounding excited and panicked at the same time.

"But babies generally take a while to be born," Bailey pointed out.

"I know, but Grace apparently started having contractions this afternoon at the party, but didn't tell Logan. Then he got called out on an emergency job. He got back around ten and found Grace doubled over in pain."

"Why didn't she call you? Or Blake or Nathan?" Bailey asked, now up from the bed and looking for her jeans.

"She said she didn't want to bother anyone and that she figured Logan would be back sooner than he was. Anyway, she's been at the hospital all night, and Logan just called us. The doc says she could have them any second now. So get your butt down to the hospital!" Alexis finished on an almost yell.

Feeling the urgency herself now, even though she really didn't know Grace or Alexis that well, Bailey tugged on her jeans as she told Alexis, "Okay, okay. I need to get Joel up, but I'll be there as soon as I can."

"I'm so excited, I just can't stand it," Alexis told her. "Hurry. See you soon!" Then she hung up.

Bailey stood in her dark room and stared at her phone for a moment. She was half-tempted to go back to bed, but knew if she did, Alexis would probably just keep calling her. And besides . . . she really did want to see the babies. Grace and Alexis obviously didn't harbor any ill will toward her because of her association with the Inca Boyz and Donovan, and if they didn't care about her history, Bailey would try not to either.

She missed having girlfriends, and Grace and Alexis seemed like the kind of women she'd like to get to know . . . not to mention Felicity. She had been surprised at the number of tattoos the other woman had. But the more she spoke with her, the more Bailey realized that Felicity's eyes hid something terrible. It was the same look Bailey saw when she looked at herself in the mirror. But Felicity was smiling and going through her life as best she could. Bailey wanted to get to know her better. Wanted to get to know Grace and Alexis better too.

So she whipped off her sleep shirt and grabbed the bra she'd dropped on the floor the night before. She opened her dresser and pulled out a long-sleeve fitted T-shirt. She wasn't quite ready to parade her tattoos to Castle Rock just yet, no matter how hard she was trying not to care.

Knowing the hard part was ahead of her, Bailey went to Joel's room and opened the door. She could see him lying on his back, both arms over his head, sleeping the sleep of the dead.

"Joel?"

He didn't move.

"Joel?" She tried again, louder.

When he again didn't even stir, she went into his room and touched his shoulder. "Joel, you need to get up."

He groaned that time.

Bailey shook him and spoke louder. "Joel! I need you to get up. We need to go to the hospital. Grace is having her babies."

He finally rolled over and glared at her between slit eyes. "Don't wanna. I don't give a shit about babies."

Damn. Looked like grumpy, disrespectful Joel was back. "Please? Logan, Blake, and Nathan will be there." She hated bribing her brother with the presence of the men he so obviously looked up to. She'd prefer that he did as she asked without giving her grief, but she'd use what she had if it meant they could get going faster.

"Women are only good for fucking, having babies, and cleaning house," Joel muttered as he rolled over and swung his legs over the side of the bed away from her.

Bailey took a step back in shock. *God.* She'd thought leaving her brother with Donovan would be okay, but he'd obviously picked up some of the fucked-up beliefs of the gang in the short time she'd let him hang out with them. The thought depressed her. She was the worst sister in the world. If Joel turned out to be a gangbanger, it would be all her fault.

She didn't reprimand him though; for the moment it was enough that he was getting up. "I'll get us some breakfast while you get ready," she said softly, backing out of the room, not giving him a chance to berate her further.

For just a moment, Bailey leaned against the wall outside her brother's room. She closed her eyes and imagined what her life might be like four years from now. A ten-year-old Joel who bitched at her was one thing. A teenager who treated her like she was back in the midst of the Inca Boyz was another altogether. She wouldn't do it. Not again. Now that she'd gotten out, she didn't want to go back.

She needed to do something about Joel, but she was at a loss as to what she could do. Deciding to think about it another time, she made her way to the kitchen to get both Joel and herself something to eat before they headed out.

Within thirty minutes they were making their way into the emergency room at the Castle Rock hospital. As soon as they entered, Bailey saw Nathan, Blake, and Alexis sitting on some chairs in the corner.

Alexis came rushing up to her, exclaiming, "It's about time you got here! The last time Logan came out, he said that it was only a matter of time!"

Next, Blake wandered up to his girlfriend, put his arm around her chest, and hauled her into him. "Relax, Alexis. Jeez, you're more worked up than Logan is—and that's saying something!"

He then turned to Bailey and Joel. "Hey. We're glad you could come down."

"Thanks for calling. I know I just met you guys, but I'm really excited."

Alexis opened her mouth to answer, but Joel beat her to it.

"This is stupid," he exclaimed grumpily. "Who cares about babies anyway."

The moment the words were out of his mouth, Nathan was there. "Good morning, Joel. It's good to see you too."

The boy's eyes came up guiltily, and he stared at Nathan for a beat, but he just grunted.

"I know you're tired and not used to getting up this early, but you wanna try that again?"

It was a question, but it wasn't. Bailey held her breath. She was embarrassed that Joel was acting the way he was, and even more so that it had been Nathan who had reprimanded him, and not her.

"Morning," Joel said only fractionally less grumpily.

"Better, but still disrespectful," Nathan warned, not looking away from the boy. "You forget about our conversation yesterday already?"

Joel heaved a huge sigh, then bit his lip and looked at the floor. "Good morning," he said with a lot less attitude than anything he'd said since being woken up that morning.

"Good morning, Joel," Blake echoed, as did Alexis.

Nathan put his hand on Joel's shoulder and said, "Happy day after your birthday. I'm sorry you had to get up so early, but we're all really excited about Grace's babies. I get that you're a bit young to feel the baby love, and that's okay. Why don't you go over there and have a seat. I brought my iPad if you'd like to play a game while we wait."

That got Joel's eyes up from the floor. He looked up at Nathan. "Cool. Thanks."

"You're welcome." Before the boy could make his way over to the chairs, Nathan leaned down, whispered something into his ear, then stood up and warned, "No more disrespect, Joel. Yeah?"

He nodded and sucked both lips in.

"Go on then," Nathan told him, squeezing his shoulder once and dropping his arm.

The adults all watched as Joel walked across the waiting room to the chairs Nathan indicated and pulled the electronic device into his lap. He was quickly engrossed in whatever game he was playing.

"What'd you say to him?" Blake asked.

Nathan shrugged. "Just the password to my iPad."

He turned to Bailey then. His eyes were intense, and she tried to read the emotions she saw in them . . . with no luck. In some ways Nathan was an open book; in others he was a complete mystery.

The four adults made their way over to the seats, and Alexis said, "You know what the best part of this is?"

"What?" Blake asked, his hand resting lightly on Alexis's lower back as they walked.

Bailey couldn't take her eyes off the man's hand. The tattoo on her own back tingled and itched. She could feel Nathan walking just behind her, and she imagined him putting his hand on her skin. Then she imagined the look of disgust on his face when he saw her naked for the first time as he realized what the tattoo branded on her skin meant. That she was contaminated by the stench of the Inca Boyz. Would forever be. She walked a little faster so there wasn't any chance he'd be tempted to touch her like his brother was touching Alexis.

"That this means I won the bet," Alexis crowed, looking up at Blake with an evil smile on her face.

Nathan chuckled as Blake rolled his eyes.

"I'd say I was upset, but there's no way I'd want Grace to have to go another week before she had those babies," Nathan said. "This is one bet I'm happy to lose."

"I had already lost," Blake said with no remorse in his voice. "What are you gonna spend your money on?"

Alexis pretended to think it over before declaring, "Girls night out as soon as Grace is able. Me, Bailey, Grace, and Felicity will go to the Hideaway Bar and Grill and chill."

Blake raised an eyebrow at his girlfriend as they settled into their seats. "You honestly want to go and get drunk after what happened"—he paused and glanced over at Joel, who was engrossed in his game, then continued—"the last couple of times you drank?"

Alexis grimaced, then shook her head. "We're not going to do shots until we're sick, Blake," she admonished. "We're gonna be civilized women and have some wine, some finger food, and gossip. Then when we're all gossiped out, we'll call you guys, and you can join us."

"I like that plan," Blake said, leaning into his girlfriend and nuzzling the side of her neck, while his hand disappeared behind her back in the chair.

For some reason their display of affection embarrassed Bailey, and she looked away, right into Nathan's eyes, which were devouring her as if she was a meal and he hadn't eaten for days.

She knew he'd said that he would be her friend, but the look he was giving her wasn't any kind of look she'd ever received from any friend before. Or from Donovan either. It wasn't lust, it was . . . affection. As if simply her being in his sight satisfied him on an elemental level.

Then he blinked, and the look disappeared as if it hadn't been there at all. He smiled and joked, "I'm not sure I'd have much gossip to add, but I wouldn't turn down an invitation to hang with all the pretty people in this town."

Bailey frowned at him, not liking his self-deprecating humor in the least. But before she could say anything, Blake asked Bailey where she worked.

For the next forty minutes or so, the adults chatted while Joel ignored them all, engrossed in the iPad in his lap. Finally, when Bailey thought Alexis was gonna burst with anticipation, Logan appeared in the doorway.

"Everyone's happy and healthy," he announced with his arms raised above his head as if he was king of the hospital and everyone sitting around morosely were his subjects.

His brothers jumped up, as did Bailey and Alexis, and rushed over to him, congratulating him and asking about Grace.

"She's good. For a while they thought they were going to have to take her in for a C-section, but she was finally able to push through it, and our sons were born. They're small, but generally healthy. They'll be put in the neonatal intensive care unit for a while to make sure their lungs and insides are all working properly, but the doctor says he thinks they look good. If they show no signs of any problems, we can probably take them home within the week."

Blake clapped his brother on the back, and Nathan simply beamed at him.

Alexis hopped around excitedly as if not sure who she needed to hug or what she needed to say.

Bailey simply stood there and soaked in the love that was emanating from the Anderson brothers. It was easy to see how much the three men loved each other, and the fact that there were two more humans to welcome into their inner circle and shower with affection was simply icing on the cake.

"So, don't keep us waiting. What'd you name 'em?" Blake asked.

"Well, we had a few names in mind, but Grace wanted to wait until we saw our sons before making the final decision." Logan paused dramatically before continuing. "The oldest will be Ace Blake Anderson, and the second will be Nate Bradley. We wanted to name them after the men in our lives who mean the most to us."

Bailey would've missed it if she hadn't been looking right at Nathan when he heard his nephews' names for the first time. Disbelief, shock, and so much love it hurt to see it. His eyes filled with tears, and he immediately shut them, trying to hold back his emotion.

Without thought, Bailey's hand went to his back, and she laid her palm on his arm. Supporting him, congratulating him, and telling him without words that she understood his emotions.

Blake grabbed his brother and gave him a bear hug. The two men pounded each other on the back and laughed with joy. Alexis was next, hugging her almost brother-in-law tightly. Then it was Nathan's turn.

"You named your son after me?" he asked, hesitantly. "Are you sure you wanna do that? He'll probably end up a math geek like me if you do."

Logan looked his brother in the eyes and said sincerely, “I would be proud as fuck if my son was half the man you are, Nathan. I know you think you’re the odd man out, that you’re somehow lacking in some way because you don’t have the build we do. But, Bro, what you don’t realize is how everyone you meet admires and looks up to you.”

“Shut up,” Nathan choked out, then grabbed his brother. They stood still for a long moment, holding each other. Blake wrapped an arm around Nathan’s shoulders, and the three Anderson brothers—the men no one in Castle Rock thought would amount to anything, the men who appointed themselves protectors of the abused and neglected men and women of the area—unashamedly celebrated their love and the creation of a new generation of Anderson men.

Bailey wiped a tear off her cheek, embarrassed until she looked over at Alexis and saw her doing the same thing. The two women grinned at each other and waited for the brothers to compose themselves.

Nathan finally pulled away from Logan and said in a slightly shaky voice, “Looks like I need to go shopping for a newborn Star Wars T-shirt for my namesake.”

Everyone laughed, and Logan wrapped his arm around Nathan’s shoulders. “Want to see your nephews?”

Both Blake and Nathan said “Yes!” at the same time.

“I’ll wait here with Joel,” Bailey said quietly to Nathan when he looked at her expectantly.

“He’ll be okay, come with us,” he requested quietly.

Bailey shook her head. “No, you guys go. I’m sure I’ll see them soon enough.”

“Come on, Bro. Wait until you see Nate. He’s an inch taller than Ace. He’s definitely gonna look just like you,” Logan said easily.

“Are you sure?” Nathan asked Bailey, his eyes going from her to the doorway that led into the depths of the hospital and his nephews.

“I’m sure. Go. We’ll be here when you get back,” Bailey assured him.

Forty-five minutes later, Nathan emerged through the doors. Joel hadn't said much, but hadn't been rude to her either, which Bailey thought was an improvement over earlier that morning.

Nathan made a beeline for Bailey, and she stood up in alarm. He looked serious, not happy and carefree as he had before he'd gone back to see the babies.

"Is everything all—"

He cut her off by wrapping his arms around her waist and spinning her around in circles.

"Nathan! Put me down!" Bailey exclaimed, laughing.

When he finally stopped and let her down far enough so her feet could touch the gray tiles, he looked down at her and said softly, "Thank you for being here. For sharing this with me."

Bailey bit her lip, and instead of protesting that she still wasn't sure exactly why she was there and why she'd been included, merely said, "You're welcome. Are they cute?"

"Are they cute?" Nathan echoed incredulously. Instead of answering, he pulled out his cell phone and pulled up the photos.

They were adorable. But what made Bailey's heart stop was the picture of Nathan holding one of the babies, most likely his namesake, Nate. He was sitting in a chair cradling the tiny baby. There were tubes coming out of the baby's nose, probably oxygen, but it was the looks on both of their faces that made Bailey want to cry.

Nate's eyes were open and he was staring up at his uncle as if he could really see him. And Nathan was looking down at the baby with the most incredible look of awe on his face. Like he couldn't believe the baby was really there.

The Anderson brothers might not have grown up with their mother's love and affection, but they still had it in spades to give out. The lump in Bailey's throat continued to grow as she saw picture after picture of the brothers and the babies. She pointed to one and told Nathan, "Frame that."

Logan was standing with a baby in each of his arms, and Nathan and Blake were standing on either side of him. Each had an arm around Logan's shoulder, and one hand under the baby closest to them. Nate and Ace were sleeping, but all three brothers had huge smiles on their faces. It was easy to see the family resemblance among the three men in the photo, and their love for each other was front and center. It was an awesome photo. One that should be on the wall in each man's home.

"I will," Nathan reassured her. "You ready to go? I'll walk you out."

Bailey nodded. It was still early, since their day had started at the crack of dawn. They didn't have plans that day, but knowing her brother and the way his moods were, she needed to get him home so he could take a nap, and hopefully lose the attitude that seemed to still be hanging around him, like a cloud hovers around a mountaintop.

"Come on, Joel. Time to go," Bailey told him.

"But I'm in the middle of something. I'm almost to the next level," Joel complained without looking up.

"Your sister said it was time to go," Nathan reiterated. "You can play again the next time I see you."

Joel didn't respond but continued to tap on the screen as if his life depended on it.

In a quick movement, Bailey reached down for the iPad, and Joel finally moved.

His hand holding the tablet swung upward, as if trying to keep it out of his sister's grasp, and the corner caught Bailey in the face.

She spun around, her hands moving to cover her cheek. Pain radiated out from where the iPad had whacked her, and she inhaled sharply. She closed her eyes as she tried to breathe through the discomfort.

Nathan was there in a second. Standing in front of her, his large hand resting over her smaller one on her face. "Let me see," he told her in a firm yet tender tone.

"I'm okay," she protested, not wanting to move her hand just yet.

Nathan took hold of her shoulders, steered her until her back was to the row of chairs, and gently pushed until she sat. Then he knelt down in front of her and put his hands on her wrists, holding her gently.

Bailey kept her eyes closed and tried to get her equilibrium back. Joel had hit her. Granted, she didn't think he'd really meant to, but still. He'd *hit* her. Donovan used to smack her all the time, and she didn't think much about it. But being hit by her brother devastated her.

"Let me see, Bailey," Nathan repeated, pulling gently on her wrists to try to get her to move her hands away from her face.

She opened her eyes and looked into Nathan's as she let him tug her hands down. Nothing showed in his face as he gently checked to make sure nothing was broken. He probed her cheek with his thumb, pressing, but kept his touch light so he didn't hurt her.

"It's red, but it's not bleeding," Nathan told her. He ran his thumb over her cheekbone where she'd been hit. He didn't really touch her, it was more a wisp of air, but it made Bailey shiver in reaction nevertheless.

"I didn't mean it," Joel said in a soft, scared voice next to her.

Forgetting about her own injury, and only wanting to reassure her brother, Bailey said, "I know, it's okay."

"What did you mean then?" Nathan asked, still crouching in front of Bailey.

"I . . . uh . . ."

"You swung your arm up as if you were mad. Were you upset your sister was making you stop playing the game and leave?"

"Yeah, but—"

Nathan pressed. "You were mad and didn't want her to take away the iPad."

"Nathan," Bailey protested, uncomfortable with the pressure he was putting on Joel.

But Nathan didn't take his eyes from Joel. "Look at her face, Joel. It's red and will probably bruise."

Joel's eyes came up to his sister's face, then quickly fell back to his lap, where he fingered the iPad.

"Donovan always does that when he's mad," Joel said quietly. "But I really didn't mean to. For a second I thought it was you, Nathan, and you were gonna hit me for talking back."

Bailey gasped, all thoughts of the pain in her face gone. *Jesus.* She opened her mouth to reassure her brother, but Nathan beat her to it. He moved so he was squatting in front of Joel. He took his little chin in his hand and forced him to look at him. "We talked about this, buddy. I know you remember. But it's not right to ever hit a woman. Ever. Got that?"

He waited until Joel nodded before continuing. "But it's also not okay for anyone to hit a kid either. I would never hit you. *Ever*. And we already established that Donovan isn't a good person, right?"

"Right," Joel whispered.

"You have the right to be mad. I'm not saying you don't. But you *don't* have the right to strike out against anyone because of it. Or be mean to your sister. You can say what you want as long as it's respectful. Okay?"

"Okay."

"Now, are you all right?" Nathan asked, letting his fingers drop from Joel's chin.

"Me?"

"Yeah. Did you hurt your hand with the iPad when you connected with your sister's cheek?"

Joel looked down at his hand, then back up at Nathan. "Why do you care when it's Bailey who has a red mark on her face?"

Nathan smiled then. "Because I like you, buddy. And I want to make sure you're okay too."

The little boy looked up at his sister then. "I'm sorry, Bail. I won't do it again. Promise."

"Thank you," she told him honestly. "That means a lot to me. I'm sorry you saw Donovan hit me. It's not right. I shouldn't have brought you over to his house as much as I did."

"He's not nice, is he?" Joel asked tentatively.

"No, Joel. He's not nice," Bailey confirmed.

As if he were four years old again, Joel climbed awkwardly into his sister's lap, put his arms around her neck, and laid his head on her shoulder. If it hadn't been for Nathan being right there, she probably would've dropped him, as he was a heavy armful. Nathan pulled a chair over and put his knees right next to hers, helping prop Joel's butt on her lap. But he didn't say a word.

Bailey held and slightly rocked Joel for a few minutes, stroking his hair and murmuring nothing important to him. Finally, he lifted his head. "Can we go home?"

"Yeah, Joel. We can go home," Bailey told him.

Nathan helped Joel stand, then did the same to Bailey. Without a word they headed out of the busy hospital waiting room and to the parking lot. Bailey wanted to tell Nathan that he didn't need to walk them all the way to her car, that they'd be fine, but secretly she was glad. She couldn't be sure Donovan wasn't already looking for her, and having Nathan at her side made her feel safer.

It wasn't until Joel was buckled safely inside the car that Nathan spoke. "He needs to see a counselor, Bailey."

"I know," she sighed. "I'm still scared that they'll think I'm a horrible guardian and take him away, but it's obvious what he saw and what Donovan did has affected him a lot more than I'd thought."

"Grace has been seeing someone who she really likes. I'll get her name and see if she might be appropriate for Joel to talk to. And if not, we'll find someone who is, who specializes in trauma in children."

Hearing him say it out loud made it sound even more awful.

"Are you really okay?" he asked, his hand coming back up to the side of her face, his thumb once again brushing over the slight red mark on her cheek.

Bailey nodded. "I've had a lot worse."

"That doesn't make me feel any better," Nathan informed her sadly.

Raising her hand and feeling bold, Bailey rested her palm over his hand and leaned her head into his touch for a short moment before saying, "Thanks for talking with him."

"Anytime. I was serious when I told you yesterday that I wanted to be your friend, Bailey. I won't lie and tell you that I don't want more, but I'm here for you. For both of you, as long as you need me to be."

"I don't deserve you."

"Ha. It's me who doesn't deserve you," Nathan retorted, then leaned in, kissed her forehead, and took a step back. "Get home. Relax. You'll both feel better after a nap. I'll call tonight to check on you both."

"Congrats on your new namesake," Bailey told him with a smile.

He returned it. "Thanks. I still can't believe Logan named him after me."

"He loves you."

"Yeah. And I love him just as much. Go on, get home. Maybe put some ice on your face so it doesn't bruise as much. I'll talk to you later," Nathan told her, taking another step back. "Drive safe. Call if you need me."

"I will. 'Bye."

"'Bye."

Nathan waved his silly, dorky wave at Joel, who eagerly returned it, as he walked backward out of the way of her car.

Bailey watched in the rearview mirror as she drove away and was more than aware that Nathan didn't stop waving, and didn't head back into the hospital, until she was well out of sight.

She sighed. If she was ever ready to get into a relationship again, it would definitely be with a man like Nathan.

Compassionate.

Understanding.

Tender.

Loving.

And totally out of her league.

Chapter Fifteen

Two months later

Bailey took in the sight of her brother and Nathan leaning over Joel's homework. Their heads were almost touching, Joel's black hair a striking contrast against Nathan's light brown. Nathan had been a constant figure in their lives ever since Joel's birthday party. Bailey tried to think back to a day when she or Joel hadn't seen or talked to Nathan and couldn't think of more than a handful.

He'd been a perfect gentleman, a friend, just as he said he would be. He never pushed her for more, never touched her inappropriately, and somehow in the last two months, he'd become a necessity in her life. Bailey wasn't sure exactly how it'd happened, but every time she saw him, she kept waiting for him to do something that would reinforce her vow never to get involved with a guy again . . . but he didn't. In fact, it had been the opposite. Everything he'd done for her and her brother only made that vow seem silly.

He wasn't Donovan.

Not even close.

Nathan was honest to a fault, open about the information he had about Donovan and the rest of his gang, was silly, laughed a lot, and wasn't afraid to do it in front of other people. He liked sci-fi almost obsessively, and shared that with Joel. He didn't treat Joel like a baby, but neither did he share anything with him in earshot that was too mature for his years. He drove Joel to see a counselor and took him to dinner afterward. He never talked down to her and never lost his temper with Joel or her. He hung out at the shop with her friends even though he had nothing in common with them . . . and amazingly, the guys liked him. Nathan was who he was, and made no apologies for it.

He wasn't perfect. Not at all. But the things that he did that were irritating didn't even come close to being things that she couldn't live with. He tended not to rinse the dishes after eating, letting them sit in the sink and get crusty, which made them harder to get clean in the dishwasher. He left lights on all the time. They'd been to his house quite a few times, and each time every room in the house had a light on. His clothes were always wrinkled, which honestly didn't irritate her, but it showed that he wasn't perfect. He could not do more than one thing at once, like talk and watch TV, but since most men she knew were that way, Bailey didn't take too much offense to it. And Nathan was constantly changing his clothes. She could wear the same T-shirt each night for a week when she got home from work, or wear the same pair of jeans two or three days before washing them, but she'd noticed his laundry was overflowing and that he always talked about needing to change his clothes, when she thought he both smelled and looked fine.

She'd asked him about it once, and Nathan had told her how when he and his brothers were younger, they didn't have a lot of clothes, and their mom certainly didn't care what they looked or smelled like. He'd been made fun of enough that as an adult he always wanted to make sure he was clean. It about broke her heart.

All in all, Nathan was an amazing friend. But Bailey knew he still wanted more than that. She would see his eyes following her with a longing that made her stomach clench, but he didn't say anything to try to get her to change her mind about the status of their relationship. He didn't pressure her or make her feel bad about taking all he had to give to Joel and her. He gave his time, energy, and friendship freely, with no strings, just as he'd promised her.

So they were friends. Period. Every time Nathan laughed with Joel, or when she heard him yawn when she was talking on the phone with him and he'd deny he was tired, and say that talking to her was better than sleeping any day of the week, or when he'd show up at Clayson's and chat with Ozzie or Bert as if he wasn't ten times smarter than they'd ever be . . . all it did was make her walls fall away more.

And now, Nathan and Joel were laughing, *laughing*, while Joel did his math homework. Not once in the history of school could Bailey ever imagine anyone having fun while attempting to figure out mathematical problems.

But Nathan had somehow done that for Joel. Made his schoolwork fun and interesting. And she was quickly learning that her brother was smart. Really smart. She'd barely made it through high school, and she knew without a doubt Joel was going to breeze through. Oh, his grades weren't great, Mostly *B*s and *C*s, but she figured that was partly because of what Nathan had told him the very first day he'd met her brother. But Bailey couldn't be upset, because it was obvious Joel knew what he was doing. He just preferred to do it his way, rather than the "official" way.

"Okay, you want to learn something fun?" Nathan asked after they'd completed his homework, the small smile Bailey had come to love to see on his face.

"Yeah!" Joel responded enthusiastically.

"Okay. You know how to round, right?"

Joel nodded. "Yup."

"So if I said you had three dollars and forty-eight cents, what is that rounded up?" Nathan tested the little boy.

"Three fifty," Joel said immediately.

"Right. Rounding will come into play here in a little bit. But first, let's say we all go out to eat and the bill comes to twenty-two dollars, and sixty-eight cents and Bailey wants to know how much tip to leave. She tells you she wants to leave fifteen percent. How do you figure out how much that is?"

"Uh . . . ," Joel said, his face scrunched up in what could only be called utter and complete confusion.

"There's an easy way to do it. Look," Nathan said, writing the dollar amount on a piece of paper in front of him. Think back to base ten; it's the same with money. There are ten tens in one hundred. And ten dimes in a dollar. With me?"

"Uh-huh," Joel said, his eyes fixed on the paper in front of Nathan.

"Right, so when you look at this number, to find ten percent of it, all you have to do is move the decimal."

Bailey watched from the armchair she'd been sitting in reading a book, as Nathan's hand moved over the paper, drawing an arrow to show Joel what he meant.

"So what do you have?" Nathan asked Joel.

Her brother studied the paper, then looked up at his idol. "Two dollars and twenty-six cents."

"Good. So you have two dollars and twenty-six cents. That's ten percent. Now, don't think too hard . . . what's half of that?"

Joel looked down at the paper again, counted on his fingers for a moment, and tentatively said, "One dollar and thirteen cents?"

"Perfect!" Nathan exclaimed, startling both Joel and Bailey.

"So what's ten percent of twenty-two sixty-eight?" Nathan asked, pointing to the paper with the pencil again.

"Two twenty-six."

"And half of that?"

"One thirteen."

Nathan scribbled both numbers on the paper. "Now add those together."

Joel paused a beat, then said, "Three thirty-nine."

Bailey grinned. Jesus, Joel was a smart cookie.

"That's fifteen percent of twenty-two sixty-eight," Nathan said with a smile, sitting back. "You can easily round it up to three forty to make it easier to leave the tip if you want. When you want to find a percentage, it's easy to figure ten percent because all you have to do is move the decimal. Then you take half of that, and that's five percent. You add them together, and you get fifteen. That's what you would tell Bailey to leave as a tip."

Joel whipped his head around to look at his sister, and she bit her lip to keep her composure. If only she could've had a teacher like Nathan when she was younger. School might not have been quite so painful. The look in Joel's eyes was one of absolute delight. As if Nathan had showed him a secret door that led straight onto the Millennium Falcon, and he could meet Luke Skywalker.

"Bail! Did you see that?" he said breathily.

"I did. Cool," she told him, grinning.

"Yeah, cool. Do another one!" Joel demanded of Nathan.

Without a word, Nathan wrote another number on the paper in front of him. He walked through the math with Joel the same way he'd done earlier, and Joel picked it up even faster this time.

When Joel had figured out fifteen percent, Nathan asked, "What if the service was really good and Bailey wanted to leave a twenty percent tip?" he asked, his eyebrows raised in question.

Joel looked back down at the paper and chewed his lip. Several moments later he gave Nathan his answer with a confident smile.

"How'd you get that answer?" Nathan asked.

"Oh, it's not right?" Joel asked, his shoulder slumping.

"I didn't say it wasn't right, I just asked how you got to that number, buddy," Nathan reassured him.

"Well if ten percent is this," Joel said, pointing to a set of numbers on the paper, "I just doubled it."

Nathan leaned down right into Joel's space until their noses were almost touching, and whispered, "Ding, ding, ding. Exactly right! Good job!"

The smile on Joel's face could've lit up a room. "More. Give me more," he demanded.

Nathan humored him and wrote several more numbers on a piece of paper. "Start with those. I'm going to go and sit and chat with your sister since you obviously don't need me anymore."

Joel didn't even respond, lost in the joy of the numbers on the page, and leaned over the paper and started scribbling.

Bailey watched Nathan push back from the chair and ruffle her brother's hair before sauntering her way. He didn't look different from the first time she'd seen him, but for some reason she found him more attractive now than she did a couple of months ago.

His light-brown hair was messy from him running his hand through it, and he had a slight five o'clock shadow. The muscles in his arms flexed as he picked up a book from the side table where he'd dropped it earlier after he'd arrived. His long, lanky frame couldn't compare to his brothers', or to Donovan's, but somehow that appealed to her more than she ever thought it would.

Bailey had only seen him without a shirt once, and he'd obviously been embarrassed she'd seen him. He and Joel had been doing unscientific science experiments in the kitchen, combining one household item with another to see what would happen, then discussing why, and one of their concoctions had literally exploded. Not exploded as in fire and brimstone, but the liquid in the bowl had bubbled up forcefully and sprayed both Joel and Nathan. They'd laughed hysterically and declared the experiment a bust. Joel had gone to his room to change, but Nathan didn't have anything to change into at her place, and she knew it would bug him to wear the dirty, damp shirt.

So Bailey had offered him the extra-large T-shirt she usually slept in to wear until his shirt was dry. He'd accepted and closed himself in her bedroom to put the shirt on. Bailey had opened the door to tell him something—she didn't remember now what it was—and had caught him reaching for the shirt.

He had wide shoulders and a spattering of dark-brown hair on his chest. His waist was small, and he didn't have an ounce of fat on him. He didn't have a six-pack, but Bailey could still clearly see the muscles in his stomach clench as they stood frozen staring at each other.

Nathan had recovered first, flushing a dark pink and turning his back while at the same time pulling the shirt over his head. Bailey had apologized and shut the door quickly before retreating into the living room.

It was more than obvious that Nathan wasn't comfortable in his own skin, but from where Bailey was sitting, he had absolutely nothing to worry about. Oh, he didn't look like a bodybuilder, but he wasn't a beanpole either. It was getting harder and harder for her to keep her hands to herself whenever he was around, which was one reason she'd started sitting on the old, comfortable armchair instead of the small couch. It put Nathan out of reach so she didn't accidentally do something stupid, like leap on top of him and beg him to make love to her.

She'd always enjoyed sex . . . well, at least before Donovan had started taking her whenever and however he wanted with no thought whatsoever to whether or not she was turned on, or even ready for him. Sex had been exciting at first. Donovan had shown her things she didn't know were possible. He'd treated her as if he truly enjoyed her company. They'd laughed a lot in the bedroom. But the more he moved up in the gang, the rougher he got with her. As she'd gotten older, Bailey had slowly begun to realize that just because a man had sex with her didn't mean he liked or respected her.

It had been a long time for her, almost a year, since she'd been with a guy, and she was horny and frustrated. She didn't want the kind of sex Donovan had forced on her, but craved the intimate connection sex forged between two people. Craved to feel the way she used to when she was naked with a man. Being around Nathan every day wasn't helping her cravings. Neither was masturbating almost every evening either.

"Good book?" he asked quietly as he sat on the end of the couch with his own.

Bailey shrugged. "It's okay."

That was another thing. Nathan had taken Joel to the library one afternoon and had gotten him his own library card. Now, instead of playing video games every night, more often than not he was reading science-fiction graphic novels. Since Bailey was the one who took him to return the ones he'd read and get new ones, she picked up a card for herself and learned that she actually enjoyed reading now that it wasn't mandatory and that she didn't have to write an essay on everything she'd read, like she'd had to do in high school.

"Thanks for helping Joel," she said quietly. "Whenever I used to try to help him, I just confused him more. School's not my thing."

"Don't sell yourself short, Bailey," Nathan told her, his intense eyes not leaving hers. "There's more to life than knowing how to conjugate a verb or take the square root of a prime number."

"Since I have no idea how to do either of those, I'll have to take your word for it," Bailey joked.

"Don't," Nathan said, not smiling at her attempt at levity.

"Don't what?"

"Don't put yourself down. I like you exactly how you are. You don't need to have a ton of degrees on your wall or know how to calculate estimated quarterly tax or know the difference between MLA and APA formatting to be a good person."

"It's a good thing," she mumbled, looking down at the pages of the book in her hands, not seeing the words.

"Bailey."

It was just her name, but she knew it meant Nathan wanted her to look at him. She raised her eyes to his.

"Everyone has things they're good at. Just because we're good at different things doesn't mean those things are better or worse than each other."

"I know," Bailey whispered.

"Do you?"

She nodded without speaking.

"I don't think you do. Don't think I haven't noticed that you're uncomfortable around Grace and Alexis when we've hung out together."

"Grace is so ladylike," Bailey told Nathan. "She knows exactly which fork to use with which meal. She's quiet and dignified. And Alexis is outgoing, and when Blake teases her, she gives it right back to him. She's not afraid of him, or of anyone. I'm in awe of your family, Nathan. I know you've told me a hundred times, but I can't help but feel as if they're out of my league."

"How about some video-game time, buddy? I need to talk to your sister," Nathan said to Joel loudly, not taking his eyes off Bailey.

"Can I take these math problems with me and finish them first?" Joel asked.

"Of course. Make sure you clean off the table before you go, though," Nathan reminded him.

Bailey closed her eyes at the longing that swept through her. Ever since Nathan had started hanging out at her place in the evenings, he'd started acting more like a father to Joel than a friend. No, that wasn't quite right. Not a father—more of a mentor. If Joel would slip and say something inappropriate to her or in general, Nathan would clear his throat and look at Joel meaningfully, and her brother would blush and apologize.

He'd help him with his homework, and encourage him to assist in making dinner and to clean up afterward. Joel had even started helping to do things like take out the trash and carry in bags without having to be nagged to death first.

Nathan was good for him. Hell, Nathan was good for both of them. And Bailey wanted him. But she had no idea how to let him know that she'd changed her mind about them only being friends. She didn't want him to see the awful tattoo on her back, but figured if she kept the lights low, or off, and they only made love in the missionary position, she could probably get away with it.

It was scary that she was even thinking about having sex with Nathan, but the more she got to know him, the more she wanted him. She was wet even now, just thinking about him kissing her and putting his lips on her body.

Bailey watched absently as Joel gathered up his books and papers and put all but one piece of paper into his backpack. He then brought it to the front door and placed it against the wall, ready to grab in the morning.

"Good night, buddy," Nathan called as Joel headed for his room.

"Night, Nathan," he returned.

"Forty minutes," Bailey told him. "Then bed."

"Okay."

"Good night," Bailey called as he went down the short hall.

He didn't respond, and she heard the door to the bathroom shut. She looked back over at Nathan.

"Come here, Bailey," he ordered gently.

She didn't trust herself not to jump him if she was sitting next to him, especially considering she'd finally admitted to herself that she wanted him, so Bailey shook her head and said, "I'm comfortable here."

"Come here," Nathan repeated sternly.

She shivered. To look at him, you wouldn't think he could be very forceful. But Nathan had obviously picked up some alpha tendencies from his brothers, because there was no doubt if she refused, he'd simply come over to where she was, pick her up, and make her move. He would never hurt her or force her to do anything she really didn't want to do, but he had no problem encouraging her to do what he wanted in some cases. Like now.

"Fine," she grumped. She uncurled her legs, took the few steps over to the couch, and flopped down.

Without delay, he pulled her into him. He curled his arm around her shoulders and put his hand on her bent knees. It was their usual position when they sat together on the couch. Her head resting on his shoulder, arms curled up between their bodies, her legs drawn up so one rested on his thigh. It was extremely comfortable, and she'd gotten used to being with him like this. Not once had he crossed the line between friends to put pressure on her for more.

But tonight, Bailey wanted more. Oh, how she wanted more. She inhaled deeply, bringing his scent into her lungs. Clean. Fresh. And all Nathan. She hadn't realized until she'd started hanging out with him that a man's scent could be a turn-on.

Donovan hadn't cared that much about his personal grooming, because whenever he wanted sex, he didn't seduce a woman or try to entice her into his bed; he just ordered her there. He usually smelled like sweat, cigarette smoke, booze, or weed. Personal hygiene wasn't something he ever worried about.

But Nathan. *God.* Bailey took another deep breath, loving whatever aftershave he used. Bailey felt her nipples contract, and she squirmed next to him.

Without a word, Nathan reached over, grabbed the remote, and clicked on the TV. He adjusted the volume so it was loud enough to mask their conversation from Joel, but not loud enough to bother him or make him come out of his room to investigate.

God, he was so considerate. Bailey knew he'd done it without a second thought too. That made it even more awesome.

As if their conversation five minutes ago hadn't been interrupted, Nathan took up where she left off. "For the hundredth time, you are *not* out of Grace's, Alexis's, or my league, Bailey. Jesus, me and my brothers grew up getting the shit knocked out of us and were known as the white-trash Anderson boys. You want to know why Grace is so ladylike?"

Without waiting for her response, he continued. "Because her mother and father emotionally abused her. They made sure she was proper at all times—when eating, what she wore, who her friends were—she wasn't allowed to do anything without their knowledge. It was hell for her, and she didn't break free until Logan came back into her life."

Bailey inhaled and bit her lip. She hadn't known. Now she felt awful.

"And Alexis is the way she is because it *is* the way she is. Her parents are wonderful, her brother is great, and she has a naturally sunny outlook to life. That took a hit when she was almost buried alive, but Blake has helped her find herself again."

He continued relentlessly. "*You* are amazing, Bailey. You had a tough upbringing, lost your parents young. But when push came to shove, you chose your brother over yourself. I know it hasn't been easy, but you've persevered. You earned all of our everlasting gratitude when you rescued Grace and my nephews last month."

"It wasn't a big deal," Bailey whispered. "It wasn't like I was going to ignore her when she called."

"It's not a big deal to you," Nathan countered. "But when Logan heard she had a flat tire on the interstate with Ace and Nate in the car with her, and she couldn't get ahold of him . . . it's huge."

"It was just a tire change," Bailey protested.

"No. It wasn't. Logan's wife was stranded on the side of the road with cars zooming past her at eighty miles an hour. His kids were in the car, and she was scared. You dropped everything, left work early, drove twenty miles out of your way, and not only changed her tire, but followed her to the next exit and service station. You browbeat the mechanics when they tried to overcharge her to fix her flat, then you made them let you supervise putting it back on her car. It wasn't nothing."

Bailey blushed. She almost hadn't answered the phone when she'd seen it was Grace, but felt bad about trying to avoid her. When she'd heard Grace sniffling and sounding scared, she'd told Clayson she had to go and simply left. The vehicle she'd been working on was still only half-done, but it didn't matter.

Changing the tire and making sure Grace didn't get gouged was nothing for her. But the hug Grace had given her when they'd arrived back in Castle Rock had meant the world to her. And when Logan had found out what she'd done, he insisted on taking her and Joel out to eat, and every time he saw her, he thanked her again.

"And when Alexis asked if you wanted to go hiking with her, you went, even though I know it's not your thing. She blindsided you by wanting to talk about the Inca Boyz, but instead of shutting her down, you let her say what she needed to say. I don't know what you talked about, but she told Blake that she's felt lighter since your talk. That she isn't alone anymore. That while Blake could empathize with her, you *knew* what she'd been through. That's fucking amazing," Nathan said in a low, urgent voice, and Bailey knew he was feeling emotional because he didn't usually swear all that much.

"Alexis has talked to therapists for a while now, and no one has been able to help her as much as you did on that one hike. And you earned Blake's trust that day. He wasn't completely sure about you, since you were a part of the Inca Boyz for so long, but now he'd defend you to anyone who dared say anything derogatory about you."

"He would?" Bailey asked in a small voice.

"Of course. But the point I'm making here is that you are in no way out of any of our leagues. We're just people, Bailey. We all have histories, some better than others, but we're all just muddling along, trying to do the best we can at this moment. Look toward the future, not at the past."

Bailey didn't say a thing, just let his amazing words soak into her psyche. She was trying to change her beliefs, but it was hard. She'd been a second-class citizen in the eyes of the Inca Boyz, and one of their whores for so long, she wasn't sure exactly who she was outside of that.

Nathan tipped her chin up with one finger and looked down into her eyes.

The desire and want was easy to read in his eyes. She'd seen it before—of course she had—but tonight was the first time she wanted to do something about it. Bailey still wasn't sure about a lot of things in her life. Until she knew for a fact Donovan wasn't looking for her, or had forgotten about her, anyone who hung around her was in danger. She'd tried to tell Nathan that last month, and he'd merely rolled his eyes and said, "As if that would scare me away."

It should, but of course it hadn't. When she'd brought up his nephews, and how they might be in danger, he'd asked, "Do you think Logan would let anything happen to his kids?"

When he put it that way, she had to say no, but she still worried. She'd hate herself even more than she did now if Nate, Ace, Grace, Alexis, his brothers, or even Felicity got hurt because of her.

"Kiss me?" she breathed. It came out more of a question than a statement, but she'd heard Nathan say often enough in the last couple of months that they were just friends that she'd wondered if she was imagining the look in his eyes that said he wanted her.

Nathan's breathing immediately sped up, and he licked his lips, but he didn't protest. He didn't ask if she was sure. It was as if he decided to take the opportunity she'd given him before she could change her mind.

Slowly his hand moved from her chin to the side of her neck, his hand sliding into her hair, and he held her tenderly, but immobile. His eyes met hers briefly before moving down to her mouth. Then his lips were on hers. Bailey couldn't help the small whimper that escaped. It was as if she'd been struck by lightning. Goose bumps broke out on her arms, and she immediately brought her hands up from between them and clasped them around his neck.

This was no gentle get-to-know-you kiss. It was carnal and passionate. Their tongues dueled, their teeth knocked together as they licked and nipped at each other.

Moving so she was straddling his thighs, Bailey refused to let him pull away from her as the kiss continued, not that he was trying very hard. His hands went to her hips to hold her steady on top of him, and hers went into his hair and clutched him to her by the back of his neck.

The kiss continued, and Bailey inched her hips forward on his lap, pressing herself against the erection she could feel against her core. Just when she was ready to tear both their shirts over their heads so she could feel his skin against hers, his palms moved from gripping her hips and encouraging her to grind against him to her back. One high, one low.

It was the low one that made her freeze in his arms. His hand was large, and she could feel his fingers against her side as he pressed her into him. But his touch reminded her of the marks on her skin. How she shouldn't be encouraging Nathan. And why.

The second she stiffened, Nathan backed off. Resting his head on the back of the couch, he stilled completely, but didn't move either of his hands.

Bailey shifted, trying to dislodge him, but he held on.

"Why don't you like me touching you?" Nathan asked quietly, but she could see the rage in his eyes. His jaw ticked as he clenched his teeth against some extreme motion.

"I . . . I don't mind if you touch me," Bailey semi-lied. She liked when he touched her in some places, just not her lower back.

"The hell you don't. I'm not an idiot." Nathan pressed his hand on her lower back, and she stiffened even more. "Did that asshole rape you?"

Bailey sucked in a breath. God, sometimes she forgot how blunt Nathan could be.

"No, not really."

When Nathan merely raised his eyebrows at her, she relented. "Okay, there were times when I wasn't in the mood, but I went along with it, but that's not the same thing."

"The fuck it's not." He leaned into her so their noses were almost touching. "If you didn't want to, and he did it anyway, then it's rape. If he took what he wanted without making sure you were one hundred percent with him, and ready for him, it was rape."

"Nathan," Bailey breathed, not sure what she wanted to say with that one word.

He leaned back, giving her some space, then took both his hands off her body and stretched them out so they were lying on the back of the couch on either side of him.

Even though it was what she wanted—him to stop touching her back—it sucked. She immediately felt cold and awkward perched on his lap without him touching her.

As she swung her leg over his legs to sit beside him, he said in a low, rough voice, "I have never, and I *will* never, force myself on a woman. Especially you."

"I know you wouldn't, Nathan, and seriously, it's me, not you."

"Wrong. It's not you. It's that asshole. I'll leave if you need me to. I never want you to associate my touch with anything *he* did."

"Don't," Bailey said immediately, resting her hand on his arm before he could get up. "I don't want you to go."

He looked at her for a long time, making her feel like a bug under a microscope, before he said softly, "I've wanted to know what your lips tasted like since I first met you. But I haven't pushed. I waited for you to make the first move. And tonight you did. I'm still not going to push, but you have to know I want you. That this changes things between us."

Bailey nodded.

"But here's the thing. I want you to want me for who I am. Not because you feel sorry for me or some other fucked-up reason. I'm a big boy, Bailey. I can handle being with you and Joel and only being friends. It sucks, I won't lie, but I can do it. But what I *can't* handle is you letting me touch you, kiss you, make love to you, if it brings back bad memories. I can be with you without anything physical happening between us. I can wait for as long as it takes for you to feel comfortable with me. I can go as slow as you need, even if that means years. Decades. I like *you*, Bailey. I'm here right now because of the person you are inside. Not because of what you look like or because I'm hoping we'll end up in bed together. I've fallen for you. Head over heels. There isn't one thing about you I don't admire. I'm perfectly aware you and Joel have issues to work through as a result of the Inca Boyz. I don't doubt it for a second. But I'm not them. You don't have to be afraid when you're around me."

"I'm not scared when I'm with you," Bailey said immediately. "It *is* me. I just . . . he marked me, Nathan."

"Marked you."

Nathan's nostrils flared and his fists clenched at his sides. But as she'd just said, Bailey wasn't afraid of him. Not like she would've been of Donovan. Nathan didn't make a move toward her. It was obvious he was pissed off *for* her, not *at* her. As sick as it made her, Bailey loved this side of him. Made her feel as if she was a virgin princess from a kid's movie, and the handsome prince wanted to keep her safe from all the bad that was out in the world. It just sucked that he was too late.

She looked down, away from his eyes. "He branded me, Nathan. Put a tattoo on my back that I didn't want. That I hate. It's . . . awful and I'm ashamed of it. Of what I've done, of who I was."

"That fucker," Nathan swore, then took a deep breath through his nose. "I'm so sorry that happened to you. You want to talk about it?"

She shook her head. "I'd really like to forget all about it. But I can't. I feel it every time I move. It's like it's burned into my skin and it's still raw and painful like it was right after they did it."

"They?"

"Donovan and his buddies held me down. I wasn't exactly willing," Bailey said softly.

"Can I please hold you?"

It wasn't what she was expecting him to say. Bailey looked up at Nathan. She wasn't sure what she expected to see. Maybe more of the pissed-off dragon. Maybe pity. But all she saw was compassion. And caring. She needed that.

Bailey nodded and snuggled into his side, noting that Nathan was sure to keep his hands on her upper back this time as he drew her into him.

They sat like that for a long moment. And with each minute that passed, Bailey realized that she felt stronger. Nathan wasn't talking, he wasn't trying to blow off what happened to her, nor was he trying to pretend he knew what she had gone through. He was merely being there for her. Letting her work through her feelings in her own way.

After long minutes went by in silence, she said, "Donovan wasn't always an asshole. In the beginning he was nice to me. He helped me finish high school. Made me feel good about myself. I felt as if I was a part of something. The gang was fun to be around, slightly dangerous, but nothing too terrible."

Nathan hugged her, but let her talk.

"The first time he wanted sex and I told him no, he was okay with it. But when it happened again, he wasn't as happy. Eventually, sex became all about him. He didn't care about me or what I wanted at all. He began to see me as his property. Which is why I think he put that tattoo on me."

"I don't care what that asshole put on your skin," Nathan said. "What's on your back isn't who you are. But with that said, it's obvious that it hurts you. If you want, I'll hook you up with Felicity. She knows a lot of great tattoo artists who could probably get it covered for you."

She stiffened in his arms. "It's bad, Nathan. It's not like throwing a rose over it will work."

Nathan moved until he was cupping her face. He leaned forward and kissed her forehead in a touch so gentle, so loving, that tears came to Bailey's eyes. "I hate this. I'd do anything to turn back the clock and fix this for you."

"You can't. I made the decisions that led me here. I have to live with them."

"You said it yourself, pixie. Donovan wasn't always an asshole. And you were a teenager. They aren't exactly known for making the most rational of decisions. I've said it before, and I'll say it again. We all have things we wish we'd done differently. I'm so in awe of you it isn't funny."

Bailey pulled back a fraction and looked at him with her brows drawn down in confusion. "Awe? Of *me*?"

"I saw some of the women who hung out with the gang, Bailey. I saw how they were. You aren't anything like them. Not even close."

"I was," Bailey protested.

"No. You weren't. If you were, you'd still be there. At Donovan's side. You would've worked with Kelly to abduct Alexis. You would've laughed at what Donovan did to Grace. Instead, when things got to be too much, you got out. That takes guts. An inner strength made of iron."

Bailey really thought about what Nathan said, instead of blowing it off. Was he right? She thought about Kelly. The woman had been mean and manipulative. She would've done anything to be in Bailey's shoes, to be with Donovan. She wouldn't have cared who suffered in the process. If she had a brother, she probably would've used him to get what she wanted in the gang.

And she had been young. She was still only twenty-four, but she felt as if she'd lived a lifetime in the last ten years. If she could go back and tell her fourteen-year-old self one thing, it would be to stay far away from Donovan and the Inca Boyz. If she was advising a teenager today, she'd tell her the same thing. So why was she still beating herself up about her past? She was trying to do the right thing now. Get back on her feet. She wasn't a bad person.

For the first time in a really long time, Bailey felt lighter. Felt as if she could finally move on. Maybe she would get the tattoo on her back covered up. She hadn't asked for it. Didn't ask to be treated like shit.

The night had started out with her wanting more from Nathan. Wanting to be with him sexually. She wouldn't let Donovan take that from her. She wasn't ready to have sex right this second, but for the first time in a long time, she had a feeling that she'd get there. With Nathan.

They sat in each other's arms for a moment before Nathan sighed and kissed her on the forehead again. "I gotta go."

"You can stay," Bailey blurted, and almost melted at the tender look on Nathan's face.

"I appreciate that, but no. I want you to really think about this. About us. Be sure you want to be with me, pixie. I meant what I said, I can be your friend for as long as you need me to. I don't need the physical relationship between us to be with you."

"I'm sure, Nathan. You've done nothing but show me the last couple months what kind of man you are. You won't force me to do anything. You're gentle, caring, patient, hard when you need to be, but you relent just as often. You don't let Joel or anyone else disrespect me, but you don't care if someone makes fun of you or says shit to you. I like it. I like you, Nathan. I've fought it for months, but I'm done. If you want me, I'd be an idiot to continue to keep you at arm's length."

He didn't respond verbally, but slowly lowered his head to hers.

Bailey lifted her chin and met him halfway.

They spent another ten minutes kissing. And it was just as passionate as it had been before they'd stopped earlier. Bailey wasn't so far gone that she didn't notice that Nathan made sure to keep his hands away from her tattoo. He was incredibly sensitive.

He wouldn't take whatever he wanted and ignore her needs.

He'd let her tell him what felt good and how to move.

And she'd get the chance to return the favor. Show him things he'd never experienced before. God, was that a turn-on. He'd told her more than once that he didn't have a lot of experience, and she wondered if anyone had ever sucked his cock. Her mouth watered at the thought. She wanted to be his first.

Oh yeah, she wanted Nathan Anderson.

Bailey felt her libido come back to life. When she'd first fled Denver, she'd thought she'd never want to have sex again, but what she didn't realize was that all it would take was the right man to change her mind. And Nathan was the right man. She was sure of it.

It was Nathan who pulled back. Bailey had once again straddled his lap while they were kissing, and she ground herself down on his erect cock. He moaned, but smiled at her as he grabbed her ass and pulled her harder down on him.

"You're gonna have to do something about that tonight," Bailey joked, looking down at his lap briefly before smiling down into his eyes.

"Nothing I haven't done every night since I've met you," he said quietly.

Bailey's eyes opened in shock. "Really?"

"Really," he confirmed.

"Wow." Then in a softer voice, she said, "Me too. At least for the last couple weeks or so. I kinda . . . like sex . . . and you've grown on me."

The smile on his face was one she'd remember forever. Part smugness, part awe, and a lot of pleasure.

With one last squeeze of her butt cheeks, Nathan gently pushed her back a few inches. "I really do have to go, and you need to check on Joel. It's been an hour. He should be in bed."

Bailey smiled.

"What?" Nathan asked, tilting his head.

"You. You're horny as hell, but you're still thinking about my brother and what's best for him."

"I care about him, Bailey. He's a good kid."

"Yeah."

Nathan leaned forward and kissed the tip of her nose before gently pushing her all the way off his lap.

Bailey stood up and let him take her hand as he stood. He walked them both to the door and keyed in the alarm code before opening it. He squeezed her hand once more, then let go and took a step back. "I'll call you tomorrow."

He always said that, and he always had.

"Okay."

"Sleep well, pixie."

"You too."

"'Bye."

"'Bye."

Bailey watched from the doorway as Nathan walked quickly to his car and climbed in. Then just as he did every time he pulled away, he turned to her and waved enthusiastically. Dorkily. Embarrassingly. But Bailey loved it.

Chapter Sixteen

"What do we know about what Donovan has been up to recently?" Nathan asked Blake and Logan the next day at work. It was Thursday morning, and they all happened to be free that afternoon for the first time in a couple of weeks, so they wanted to update each other before heading out. Usually, Nathan and Alexis had the office to themselves while Logan and Blake were out on jobs, but today all the brothers were in Castle Rock. Alexis was spending the afternoon with Grace and the kids.

"Nothing. Which doesn't give me warm fuzzies," Logan responded.

"We might not know what he's been up to recently," Blake added, "but Alexis has discovered Donovan is *not* a good guy."

"I think we all already knew that," Nathan said.

"Right, but you haven't heard the half of it," Blake informed his brother. "First of all, Donovan is forty-two."

"What?"

"That can't be right."

Blake held up his hand to forestall any other questions from his brothers. "It is. We all know how he got started in his life of crime, but Alexis dug deeper. He's done a lot of shit he hasn't been caught at. He's killed people just because they irritated him. He's been preying on teenagers for over two decades. Bailey wasn't his first, but he did keep her around a lot longer than some of the other girls."

"Did Alexis find them and talk to them?" Logan asked.

"No. They disappeared. One day they were around, and the next they weren't. None of the gang members ever talked about them once they were gone either."

"Fuck," Nathan breathed. "Did he kill them?"

Blake shrugged. "Rumor on the dark web is that he sold them. Had his brothers set up the deals and collect the money for them."

There was silence in the office for a long moment before Nathan asked, "Sexual slavery?"

"From what Alexis has found, most likely."

Nathan thought about the tattoo on Bailey's back. He hadn't seen it, but why would Donovan do something like that if he was going to sell her as a sex slave? That didn't seem like something a future douchebag would want to look at on the slave he purchased.

As if he could read his brother's mind, Blake said, "Alexis ran into a brick wall when she was researching him, so she asked her mentor for help—you know, that retired Navy guy. He found evidence that they were setting Bailey up to take the rap for a bank robbery."

"What the fuck?" Nathan said between clenched teeth. "I thought Donovan wanted Bailey . . . he's certainly acting like it now. So why set her up? Not to mention the gang was known for holding up convenience stores, but a bank?"

Blake nodded. "It's messed up, that's for sure. Donovan wants Bailey now, but maybe it's because she ran out on him. Maybe he wanted Joel made into a true Inca Boy more than he wanted his sister. I have no idea. Anyway, there was a whole conversation that had been deleted from Donovan's computer between him and his brothers about how they would kill everyone in the bank, then take off, making sure Bailey was caught red-handed."

"How?" It was Logan who asked this time.

"They were gonna shoot her in the leg, make it so she couldn't leave with them. She'd be captured, they'd see the gang ink on her body, and throw her in jail for manslaughter."

There was so much wrong with that asinine plan, it wasn't even funny. Nathan didn't feel the least bit better about the fact that Donovan wasn't going to sell Bailey as a sex slave, but making it so she'd spend the rest of her life behind bars, knowing Donovan would be taking care of her brother and turning him into the kind of man he was, didn't sit well either.

"We need to take Donovan down," Nathan said, his temper flaring.

"I talked to Ross yesterday, and he said that he hadn't heard any intel about him in over a week. He's in the wind," Logan said, his own voice brimming with anger after hearing how much of a threat Donovan actually was.

"Is that even possible?" Blake asked. "I mean, he's basically the only thing holding that gang together now that all his officers are gone. He's been pissing the rest of the members off, and last we heard they were ready to mutiny. Think they'd off him?"

Logan shook his head. "No. There might be dissent, but I think everyone is too scared of the man to try anything."

"Has the task force heard anything from the women who are still hanging around? What about some of the high schoolers?" Nathan asked worriedly.

"Nope. No one is talking."

"Damn," Blake swore. "I'll give Alexis a heads-up . . . although she probably already knows this. She's becoming a spooky good hacker. I think Donovan is just as likely to come after her or Grace as he is Bailey."

Nathan shook his head. "I think you're wrong. I mean, yeah, Grace and Alexis need to be careful, but Grace was just a job to him." He held up his hand to stop the protest he knew would be coming from Logan. "I get it. He went to jail as a result of the job he did concerning her, but I have a feeling he'll feel as if that was just a part of doing business, and not a personal thing."

"And Alexis?" Blake asked.

Logan shrugged. "He wasn't even around when what happened with her went down. Yeah, his brothers were killed, but it wasn't like they were close. Remember Ross said Donovan threatened both Damian and Dominic that if they fucked up his gang while he was in prison, he'd kill them when he got out. But Bailey was *his*, and he had plans for her. It's got to be a blow to his ego that she got away from him. He's just the kind of asshole who thinks he owns her. And he probably wants her back to make an example of her and hurt her as badly as he feels she hurt his standing as president."

"Joel," Logan said definitively.

"Yeah. Joel. He was well on his way to molding him into one of his gang members. And honestly, the fuck of it was that he was doing a good job. It's taken two months of therapy for Joel to finally admit that he didn't like Donovan as much as he acted like he did. It's a start, but I have a feeling it'll take several years for all the mental damage he did to Bailey's brother to fully be resolved."

"We need to make a plan. That asshole is gonna show up here eventually. And with no one knowing where he is at the moment, I'm afraid it's only a matter of time."

"We can protect Bailey," Blake said.

Nathan shook his head. "No, we can't. Not unless we stick by her side twenty-four seven, and you both know that's not happening."

"Then *you* can protect her, Bro. You're over at her place more than you are your own anymore. You used to hang out here long into the night working; now you bolt before five, sometimes in the middle of the afternoon," Logan said without heat.

"You know as well as I do, if Donovan wants to get ahold of her, he will. He could snatch Joel from school and wait for Bailey to get home. Or he could waltz into her job and force her to leave with him. Hell, he could even cause a car accident like he did with you, Logan. No, in this case, the best thing to do is to prepare for him so we're all ready when he does eventually show up."

Both Blake and Logan eyed their brother, respect shining in their eyes.

"So what, an ambush?" Logan asked.

"Something like that, yeah," Nathan confirmed. "But I'll need both of you to help me. I have some ideas, but I need your security expertise, and your combat experience from the Army."

"You got it."

"Absolutely."

"And we need some sort of silent signal for each other. She lives all the way up on Wolfensberger Road. I can probably stall Donovan when he shows up, but if it takes longer than thirty minutes for either of you to get there, I don't think anything I do will matter. He'll either kill Bailey and take off with Joel, or he'll hurt one or both of them. Not to mention, I'm a wild card. We don't know how he'll react if I'm there when he shows up."

"No problem. We can set up some silent alarms that trigger both our cells. If they go off, we'll immediately contact the PD, although they should already know since the alarm you had installed is programmed to call 911 if breached."

"They'll need to be briefed in advance so they know what they'll be up against," Nathan warned.

"Already done," Blake reassured his brother. "We've been working with them closely for the last year. We've got some buddies on the force. Officers who are on the SWAT response team. They'll be ready."

Nathan breathed out a sigh of relief. "Good. So . . . shall we plan?"

"Definitely," Logan told him. "What do you have in mind?"

For the next two hours, the three brothers discussed, argued, and dismissed several different scenarios for what should happen when Donovan finally caught up with his ex-girlfriend. They were all risky, and they all depended on one thing—that the man wanted to hurt Bailey by letting her know he was taking Joel with him after he tortured and probably killed her. But that he wouldn't actually kill the little boy or Bailey the second he saw them.

When they were done, and they'd planned as much as they could, Logan stood up and walked over to Nathan. He put his hand on his shoulder and said softly, "You've got this, Bro."

"For what it's worth, I agree that I think he's gonna make his move sooner rather than later," Blake chimed in. "But there's no way that fucker is gonna get the drop on the three of us. And there's *no* way after what Grace and Alexis went through, we're gonna let Bailey suffer any more at his hands. He's done."

Nathan nodded. "Damn straight."

Logan smiled and squeezed his brother's shoulder once before stepping back, grabbing his jacket, and shrugging it on. "So . . . you break through some of those walls she's got up?"

Nathan grinned, but didn't respond.

"You did!" Blake exclaimed. "Good for you."

"She it for you?" Logan asked.

Nathan knew exactly what he meant. "Yeah. Before, she was this mysterious person who managed to escape the gang, but now that I know her? Know what she went through with them? What she escaped from? I'm in awe. She's the strongest person I know. The thing of it is, she's so amazing and doesn't have a clue. I can't measure up, but I'm hoping I can convince her to give me a shot at giving her and Joel the kind of life they should've had all along."

"You will," Blake said immediately.

Nathan's eyes went to his brother, and he raised his eyebrows in question.

"I've seen the way she looks at you. Sure, she's cautious, and I can't blame her. But you've given her space, haven't pressured her, and you're you."

"What does that mean?" Nathan asked.

"Just that it's more than obvious you wanted her, but you bided your time and earned her trust. You spent time with her and Joel, and you were yourself." He shrugged. "I'm guessing that she's had experience with plenty of assholes. But that's not you. You wouldn't hurt one hair on her head. You're more attentive to others' needs than your own most of the time."

His brother was right, and not only about guessing Bailey's background with men. Nathan used to be self-conscious about the fact he didn't want to sleep with a woman on the first date. That he wanted to get to know her before they got naked together. But with Bailey, he hadn't had that reticence. If he could've, he would've taken her home with him the first chance he had, but since that was what she expected he'd do, he'd waited. Not that it was any hardship to spend time with Joel and her.

"I'm not sure . . . ," he started, then stopped, not sure he wanted to discuss this with his brothers.

"What, bro?" Logan asked, leaning forward. "You can tell us anything."

"I don't want to disappoint her." Nathan paused, but pushed on. If he couldn't ask his brothers, who *could* he ask? "I've had sex, but I always got the impression that I wasn't doing it right. Bailey's latest experiences weren't good, and the last thing I want to do is hurt her with my inexperience. I thought maybe . . ." He blushed, but rushed on. "You guys were always popular with the girls. Can you give me some tips?"

Nathan was prepared for any kind of reaction from his brothers. Laughter. Mockery. Exasperation. But what he got was more. Much more. Respect and acceptance. They didn't laugh at him or make fun of him. Logan got up from his chair and moved it closer to Nathan's, and Blake did the same.

They then spent the next thirty minutes telling him the best places to touch Bailey that would turn her on. Where to lick and suck, and how hard. They told him what positions felt the best for women, and after she'd orgasmed, what would feel best for him. They gave him pointers on how to make himself last longer so he didn't come before her, and warned him that women sometimes got emotional after orgasming.

The conversation could've been awkward, and his brothers could've made him feel stupid for asking, but by the time they were finished, Nathan actually felt confident that he could make Bailey feel good. That he could actually make love to her and have it be memorable for all the right reasons.

"Thanks, guys," Nathan told his brothers. "I just . . . I want to make sure I don't do anything that might remind her of *him*."

"There's no way she could ever think you're anything like that asshole," Blake insisted, his eyes intense on Nathan's. "Making love is way different than having sex, and I think both you and Bailey will be making love for the first time . . . together. Trust her to let you know what feels good and what she likes. Follow her cues, and you can't go wrong."

"Besides," Logan chimed in, "if you can't ask your brothers for sex advice, who can you ask?"

Nathan chuckled. "That's what I told myself before I opened my mouth."

"Damn straight," Logan said with a smile. His phone vibrated with a text, and he looked down at it. "Grace says that I've had enough brother bonding time and it's time for me to get home."

Nathan raised an eyebrow at him.

Logan grinned, huge, before shrugging and informing them, "She got the okay from the doctor to 'resume normal activities' as she sees fit, and it seems my Grace is happy to have our marital relations resume."

Both Nathan and Blake grinned at their brother.

"Far be it from us to keep you from your wife's bed," Blake told him, standing. "And, since we have this rare day off, and Grace will be busy, I think I'll see what my girlfriend is up to tonight. She might be tired after visiting with your sons. She might need a nap."

All three men chuckled, then Logan got serious as he turned to Nathan. He put a hand on his shoulder and said low and earnestly, "Be careful. That son of a bitch is dangerous, and I don't trust him as far as I can throw him. If you even suspect he's near, trip the alarm or call us."

"I will," Nathan reassured him. "I'm not going to take Bailey's or Joel's life for granted. I want this behind her so she can move on once and for all, even if it's not with me. The last year hasn't been easy for her."

"I'll call tomorrow and let you know what, if anything, I've heard from Ross about Donovan, and just to check in. Remember what we talked about. Relax, be yourself. You're going to be great. You're an Anderson," Logan said with a serious look on his face.

Forcing himself not to blush, Nathan merely nodded at his big brother.

"Oh, and tell Bailey that Felicity and Grace were talking about how much they liked her, and Grace suggested that Felicity and Bailey go out to lunch," Logan said while getting his things together.

"That's a great idea. She hasn't had many girlfriends as far as I can tell. Thanks."

Nathan gathered up his belongings after his brothers left. In the past, he would've stayed in the office and worked, but he was anxious to see Bailey. He checked his watch. He had time to stop and get her some lunch before he stopped by the auto body shop. Then he'd pick Joel up and bring him back to his house for the afternoon, as he'd been doing for the last couple of weeks.

They'd get his homework done, Nathan would watch the boy play his new *This Is War* game, because he certainly wasn't any good at it, then they'd go and get Bailey. Nathan would make them dinner, and they'd hang out.

Then, maybe, if he was really lucky, he'd see about beginning to put some of his brothers' tips and suggestions to use. Just the thought of doing some of the things Logan and Blake talked about was enough to make him half-hard and to set his mouth to watering. It was too soon, especially after learning about how badly she'd been treated by Donovan, but he wanted to be with Bailey. Wanted to erase every bad sexual encounter she'd had with the feel of his body next to hers.

He wasn't centerfold material, but maybe if he could give her an orgasm, she'd overlook it and want more.

He could hope.

Nathan left Ace Security with conflicted emotions. He was excited to see Bailey and Joel, but nervous about their safety at the same time. He watched over his shoulder as he drove up Wolfensberger Road and couldn't help but feel like the confrontation with Donovan was coming. Sooner rather than later.

Chapter Seventeen

Bailey stared at Felicity across the table. She wasn't sure what to say to the other woman. She'd been surprised and flattered when Nathan had told her Felicity wanted to have lunch with her. But now that they were at the restaurant, she felt awkward.

"How are you?" Felicity asked, breaking the silence as they waited for their lunch to arrive.

"I'm good," Bailey said automatically.

Felicity cocked her head, then shook it. "No, really. I honestly want to know. You look better, less stressed, than at Joel's party, but I can tell you're still hanging on by a thread."

Bailey blinked. "You can?"

"Yeah." Felicity put her elbows on the table in front of her and leaned forward. "I've been there, Bailey. You can trust me."

Bailey wanted to reject the other woman's words, but for some reason she couldn't. There was something in her eyes. They were haunted, just as Bailey's were. Felicity might come across as brash and confident, but underneath her exterior shell, there was . . . something.

"You've been there?" Bailey asked after a moment.

Felicity nodded. Her voice dropped. "I thought I was alone in the world. That I'd never be safe. That no matter what decision I made, it'd be the wrong one. Unlike you, my nightmare didn't start in my teens. It was later, but ever since then I've kinda had a knack for being able to recognize a kindred soul. First Grace, now you. Anything you say will stay between us."

Bailey's mouth opened, but the waitress chose that moment to appear with their plates. "Here ya go. BLT with bacon and mayonnaise and a side of fries for you, and a cheeseburger with the sweet-potato fries for you. Anything else I can get for you ladies?"

Bailey looked down at the huge burger on her plate, and her mouth watered. With Nathan around so much, she wasn't skimping on meals as much as she once had since he insisted on paying or cooking most of the time, but the cheeseburger in front of her looked absolutely decadent.

"We're good. Thanks," Felicity told the waitress.

She gave them a perky nod, twirled on her feet, and walked away to greet the guests just seated at a nearby table.

Felicity picked up her sandwich as if she hadn't just rocked Bailey to the core.

"I'm not good enough for Nathan," Bailey blurted.

Felicity didn't react other than to put down her sandwich and wipe her mouth. "Why?"

"Why?" Bailey asked, confused.

"Yeah. Why aren't you good enough for him? What makes him so much better than you?"

"Um . . . everything?"

"Come on, Bailey. Specifics. Give it to me."

Bailey lifted her hand and counted off on her fingers as she spoke. "I've slept with just about everyone in the Inca Boyz. I almost got my brother sucked into the gang. I'm a coward who ran rather than turn in Donovan to the police. I barely graduated from high school, and Nathan is some kind of genius. Oh, and I'm not sure I can give him what he wants."

Felicity took another big bite of her sandwich and chewed. After she swallowed, she said, "Okay, let's tackle those one at a time. Your brother *isn't* in the gang, so that one is a moot point. Nathan is the least likely man I've ever met to hold your lack of a degree against you. He couldn't care less about that sort of thing. And now for the harder ones."

She reached across the table and grabbed Bailey's hand. "Sometimes the bravest thing a person can do is run. When you can't handle things on your own, and you know if you try, it'll only end up biting you in the ass and ending badly, running's the only thing you *can* do."

Bailey stared at the woman across the table from her. Felicity's black hair fell in sheets around her shoulders, and her blue eyes seemed even brighter against her pale face. For the first time in a really long time, she felt as if someone truly understood. Truly got her.

Felicity continued. "And as far as sleeping with people goes—when you first met Donovan, was he an asshole? Did he force you to have sex with him?"

Bailey shook her head, her lunch forgotten. "No. I wouldn't have gotten involved with him if he was. At least I'd like to think I wouldn't have. He was nice. Walked me home from school. Kept some of the bullies from fucking with me."

"And did you like it? Was it good?"

"Yeah," Bailey whispered.

"Do *not* be ashamed of your sexuality," Felicity ordered. "Just because you enjoyed sex doesn't make you a bad person. The double standard regarding sex in our society is disgusting. There's no reason why men are allowed to fuck anyone they want and they're considered studs, and women are labeled as sluts and whores if they do the same thing. Having a healthy sex drive is nothing to be ashamed of."

Bailey licked her lips and thought about Felicity's words. She knew she was right, but it had been so hard not to think of herself as a whore when Donovan had tattooed the words right on her skin.

"Do you think less of Nathan because he doesn't have the same experience as you?"

"No, not at all. I . . . just wish I was pure for him."

"That's bullshit," Felicity declared, sitting back in her seat with a huff. She looked around the restaurant as if to make sure no one was listening, then leaned forward again. "All being pure would mean is that sex would hurt the first time, and you wouldn't know what you liked and what you didn't. Bailey, you're going to be the expert when you're with Nathan. You have the chance to show *him* what you like. Think about that. You can help him be the kind of sexual partner you want. You want sex once a month? Great, that's what you can train him to expect. You want it twice a day? Great, show him that's what you want. You're holding all the cards. And I have a feeling in your situation, that's a good thing. Right? Have you ever been the more experienced person in bed?"

Bailey thought about it. "No."

"Right. So now you are. Big deal. But Bailey, the bottom line is that you're allowed to like sex. You're allowed to be upset about your past, but that's just it. It's in the past. Let it go. Embrace your future. You *absolutely* are good enough for Nathan. In fact, you're perfect for him. You're exactly the woman he needs. Trust me, he's a good man. One of the best. I'm just sorry there aren't any more Andersons left for me." She chuckled after the words left her mouth.

Bailey returned her smile.

"All I'm saying is that you have no reason to be ashamed of your past decisions. You were a kid. Cut yourself some slack. Let yourself be happy now. With Nathan."

Bailey had already come to the same conclusion, but hearing it from Felicity went a long way toward making it truly sink in. "You're right. I didn't ask to be raped. Just because I liked sex with Donovan didn't give him the right to pass me around to his friends. I didn't deserve what he did to me. He was wrong, not me."

Felicity's eyes got wet. "Exactly."

"Are *you* okay?" Bailey asked, alarmed at her new friend's tears.

"I'm good. I'm just so happy that you're as strong as you are. Believe me, not every woman who has been abused by her boyfriend is," Felicity said with only a small wobble in her voice.

Bailey wanted to ask Felicity who she was talking about, but was feeling pretty raw with everything they'd shared and wasn't sure how much more she could take. "So, Nathan says that you know some good tattoo artists." She gestured to Felicity's arms. "I love your ink. I've been thinking about getting some more, maybe covering up some of the gang stuff."

Felicity reached out and turned Bailey's arm over as she examined the tattoos there. After a while she said, "Most of these are pretty good. There are only a few I'd get covered if I was you. If you're serious, I do know of a couple of artists that are amazing at cover art. I could introduce you if you wanted."

Bailey took a deep breath. Then asked, "I've got one on my lower back that I'd love to change up. It's big, though. Can they work with big art?"

Felicity nodded. "Yeah. They're awesome at it. I haven't needed to get anything changed, but I've seen some before-and-after pictures in their shop, and you'd never even know the old art had been there."

"Even if it's big?"

"Even if it's big," Felicity confirmed. "I'm happy to go with you anytime, any day. All you need to do is ask, and I'm there."

"Thanks," Bailey said, then took a deep breath. "I'm starving. All this heavy talk isn't helping either. How long have you known Grace?"

And with that, the conversation lightened up. They chatted as they ate. Bailey learned more about Grace and Felicity's friendship, how the gym she co-owned with her friend Cole came about, and some of the plans they had for the future of their business.

It felt good to talk to another woman about everyday things. Bailey didn't feel as if she was in competition with Felicity for anything, as she always had with the girls who hung around the gang. She felt comfortable. For the first time in her life, Bailey felt as if she could become anyone she wanted. And what she wanted at the moment was to be a supportive friend to Felicity, Grace, and Alexis . . . and to be more than friends with Nathan Anderson.

She'd made the first move the other night, but Nathan had backed off after their intense conversation. She wanted to get back to where they'd been before she'd freaked out at his touch. She wanted to embrace her sexuality once again. She *had* enjoyed sex once upon a time, and she was ready to again. With Nathan. Now she just had to convince him she was ready.

Chapter Eighteen

"You guys want to spend the night?" Nathan asked in what he hoped was a nonchalant tone. He didn't want to move too fast with Bailey, but after their conversation the other night, and after she'd had lunch with Felicity, she seemed to have gained a lot of confidence. She'd begun to touch him more, and even had initiated an intense make-out session the other night.

Nathan wanted her. Badly. But he wanted her to be comfortable, ready for a sexual relationship more than he wanted to assuage his own needs. After what she'd been through, he didn't want to do anything that would bring back bad memories. He'd continue to let her take the lead when it came to anything sexual . . . although he'd do whatever he could to spend time with her. Including asking her and her brother to spend the night with him.

"Really?" Joel said excitedly before turning to his sister. "Please? That'd be so cool!"

Bailey frowned at both of them. "I don't know . . . it's a school night."

"I promise to go to bed right at nine," Joel pleaded. "We're over here most evenings anyway."

Bailey tried again. "We don't have any of our stuff."

"Joel can wear one of my shirts to bed," Nathan said easily. "We can stop by your house before school tomorrow so he can grab clean clothes, and I can drop you off so you can change before work."

Bailey smiled, and Nathan let out a silent breath of relief. She was caving.

"And what about toothpaste and shampoo and stuff?"

"We can run down to the pharmacy. It's close."

Bailey was silent for a moment, and Joel begged, "Please, Bail?"

"No pressure," Nathan said softly. "I know I kinda sprung it on you. But I can tell you're both tired, and I've got the room. I swear I'll get you both to work and school on time tomorrow."

Finally, Bailey nodded, not taking her eyes off Nathan. "Okay. If you're sure it's all right with you."

"It's more than all right with me," Nathan reassured her.

"Yay!" Joel shrieked. "A sleepover!"

"I don't have your game player here. You gonna be okay not playing for a night, buddy?" Nathan teased.

"Yeah. I can last one day. I'll just play tomorrow after school. I have my new book from the library, and you said you were gonna show me math that didn't have base ten."

Nathan grinned at Joel. He loved the little boy's curious mind. Loved that he wanted to do math problems with him. And absolutely loved that he was excited about spending the night. If he had his way, this was the first of many nights both Bailey and Joel would be sleeping under his roof.

"Let's make the run to the pharmacy now before it gets too late. Then we can come back here and I'll start by showing you base six. Depending on how fast you pick it up, we can maybe get into addition and subtraction with it."

"Cool," Joel breathed before running off to find his shoes he'd taken off the second he'd entered the house earlier.

As soon as he was out of earshot, Nathan turned to Bailey, suddenly considering his home. It was small, but a perfect size for just him. Nathan's house was about twelve hundred square feet. It had a functional kitchen, a living area, a utility room that had a door to the side of the house, a master bedroom and two smaller guest rooms, two full bathrooms . . . and that was about it. There was a one-car garage and a yard that bordered an open piece of land. Nathan had planned on fencing it, but hadn't gotten around to it yet, enjoying the view of nature as far as his eye could see.

But now that Bailey was in his life, he realized that it wasn't big enough. He needed a home office, and Joel needed a place where he could play. Maybe a media room so they could watch movies or Joel could play video games and have friends over. He wanted at least a two-car garage, but a three-car would be better. Bailey should have space to tinker with a vehicle if she wanted to, and the extra space would give her room to store any tools that she might need. They also needed a bigger backyard. Joel might not be the most athletic kid, but it would be good for him to have space to run around so he stayed healthy and kept a balance in his life.

Most important, the master bedroom needed to be away from Joel's room. The last thing Nathan wanted was the little boy hearing his sister having sex . . . if nothing else, Nathan didn't want it to bring back any bad memories for the little boy.

As soon as the thoughts flitted through his head, Nathan shut them down. It was way too early to be thinking about the kind of future with Bailey that would include a new house. Sure, it seemed like she wanted to be with him, but he wasn't sure if it was just because he was there . . . with her all the time, or if she had more permanent feelings for him.

But just because he didn't know didn't mean he wasn't going to give their relationship everything he had and try to make sure Bailey fell as much in love with him as he already was with her.

"Thanks for letting us stay," Bailey said quietly, interrupting his silent musings.

"It's my pleasure," Nathan told her, the sincerity in his voice coming through loud and clear.

Bailey smiled then—a small, wicked smile that immediately made Nathan's cock hard. "I noticed you said that Joel could sleep in one of your shirts, but you didn't address my lack of clothes except for what I'm wearing."

Looking back toward where Joel disappeared, Nathan moved into Bailey's personal space, backing her up until she hit the counter. He bracketed his hands on the hard granite behind her, caging her in, and leaning toward her until their foreheads almost touched and his eyes held hers in an intense gaze. Her hands came up and rested on his chest, her fingers digging in as he spoke.

"You have a choice, Bailey. You can wear one of my shirts or sleep in your birthday suit."

"Hmm," she teased, "I typically sleep nude, but since I'm not at home and will be sleeping in a room next to my brother, I suppose I'd better wear your shirt."

"In case this wasn't clear," Nathan told her, standing up and putting some space between them, but leaving his hands where they were, "*you* will be in my bed. Not the second guest room. Not the sofa. My. Bed."

She looked taken aback for a moment before asking, "Where will you be?"

"Wherever you want me to be," Nathan answered immediately. "You know I want you. I want to feel every inch of your body next to mine. I want to be inside you more than I want to breathe, but it's your choice. It doesn't have to happen tonight. We'll go at whatever speed you need to feel comfortable, but I do want you in my bed. On my sheets. If you're not comfortable with that yet, I'll take the couch. But if you don't mind me sleeping next to you, but you're not ready for more, that's okay too. I'll take whatever you can give me."

Bailey's breath hitched, and Nathan hurried on. "There's no pressure. None. I'm not like the assholes you've been with in the past. If we make love tonight, great. If not, great. As long as I know you want it to happen at some point, I can be patient. I'll sleep on the couch every night until you're ready."

"Are you doing this because of Donovan? Because you think he's going to make his move?"

Nathan tensed, but forced himself not to move. Earlier that day he'd talked to Bailey about the discussion he'd had with his brothers about Donovan. She hadn't been happy to hear it, but hadn't really been surprised either. They both knew he was coming sooner or later.

"Absolutely not. I won't lie—sleeping under the same roof as you and Joel makes me feel better. But that's not why I want you." He moved a hand then, brushing the back of his fingers down her cheek lightly, then tangling them into the jet-black hair at the side of her head. He held her still as he looked into her eyes.

"I love you, Bailey Hampton. Without having made love with you. With Donovan waiting in the wings to fuck with you. I love how caring you are. I see the sacrifices you've made for your brother, and I know you're going to be an amazing mother. I don't even know if you want children, but the thought of you being round with my child makes me want that even more than I want my next breath. And I'll kill anyone who tries to take that from me."

When her eyes got wide with shock, Nathan hurried on. "My love for you has no bounds, and I hope someday you might return even a fraction of the love I have for you, but there is absolutely no pressure. And if after the Inca Boyz threat is behind you, you find you want to move on, I'll step aside."

"Nathan—" Bailey began, but he interrupted her by putting his finger against her lips.

"I mean it. No pressure. My love for you isn't dependent on you making love with me. Or sleeping with me. Or anything. It just is. Like we need air to breathe, water to drink, and food to eat."

Just as she opened her mouth to respond, Joel burst into the kitchen.

"I'm ready to go, Nathan!"

He quickly took a step away from Bailey, reluctantly taking his hands off her, and turned to the refrigerator to grab a bottle of water—more for something to do than because he actually needed a drink.

"That's great, buddy," Nathan told him. "Bailey just needs to put her shoes on, and we'll go."

He straightened and met Bailey's eyes for a moment. He had no idea what the emotions were that were swirling in her gaze, and her words didn't give him any clue either.

"The sooner we get going, the sooner we can get back here and you can start learning base six . . . whatever that is," Bailey told her brother.

Joel giggled. "Right. Let's go then, slowpoke."

Bailey turned to Joel and tousled his hair. "Who's calling who a slowpoke, slowpoke?"

Nathan watched as brother and sister headed out of the kitchen giggling and playfully shoving at each other. He took a swig of the water and closed his eyes. Every word he'd said to Bailey was true, but he hoped with all his being that she'd choose him. He hadn't lied. He loved her. More than anything. It was different from the kind of love he felt for his brothers and nephews. Deeper. More intense. And he knew without a doubt that if anything or anyone threatened either Bailey or Joel, he'd definitely kill to keep them safe.

Nathan didn't know what that said about who he was as a man. But he didn't care. It was as if he'd found the purpose to his life. Keeping Bailey and Joel Hampton safe and happy.

But first, he needed to get them toothpaste, a toothbrush, and shampoo. He'd figure out the rest after that.

Chapter Nineteen

Bailey had read the same page ten times, but she couldn't keep her mind on the romance in front of her. They'd gone to the store and gotten the necessary toiletries. Nathan went overboard and also bought her some makeup, bought Joel some strong-smelling shower soap he insisted "all the boys were wearing," and lotion, eye drops, cold medicine, and other various things one would normally have in a medicine cabinet.

When Bailey had asked him what in the world he was doing, Nathan had shrugged and said that it was better to be safe than sorry, and if any of them got sick, he wanted to have on hand what they needed to get better.

Bailey had stood stock-still in the middle of the aisle staring at Nathan as he put item after item into the basket. He was definitely buying too much, but she knew why he was doing it. His words echoed in her brain even now, hours after he'd said them.

My love for you isn't dependent on you making love with me. Or sleeping with me. Or anything. It just is. Like we need air to breathe, water to drink, and food to eat.

She'd never felt love like that. Not ever. She knew her pa loved her, but as she'd gotten older and harder to handle, mostly what she'd felt was resentment from him. None of the men she'd slept with had loved her like that, certainly not Donovan. All they'd seen was easy pussy.

But Nathan. *God.* She wasn't sure she loved him, but she wasn't sure she didn't either. What did she know about love? She loved her brother, but that wasn't the same thing. She'd practically raised him.

She'd sat on the couch and listened as Nathan had explained base-six math to her little brother, and it had totally gone over her head. But Joel seemed to grasp it easily, and he was currently doing both subtraction and addition problems with it—for fun.

Listening to how patient Nathan was with her brother and how he laughed with him made tears spring to her eyes. He didn't get frustrated with him when he didn't get something, he didn't belittle him or make him feel bad about it. He merely explained it a different way until Joel *did* understand it.

Nathan might be a math geek, but he was one of the best men she'd ever known. She had a feeling she wouldn't ever meet another man who seemed to care as much about her brother as he did about her.

"You about ready to call it a night, buddy?" she heard Nathan ask Joel.

"Aw, do we have to?" Joel whined.

"It's getting late. Don't worry, we can do it again later. Maybe we'll even give base four a try. It's trickier, though, because the base is lower."

"I can do it!" Joel said with enthusiasm.

"I'm sure you can. But you need your brain to be fresh before we start. Go on. Brush your teeth and get ready for bed."

"Will you . . ." Joel hesitated, then said quickly, "Will you come say good night?"

Bailey's head turned at that, and she caught Nathan kissing the top of Joel's head gently before he said, "Sure thing, buddy. I'll be in in about five minutes. That enough time?"

Her brother nodded happily, then sprang up from the chair and walked quickly down the hallway, disappearing from sight.

Nathan turned and Bailey stared at him for a long moment before whispering, "Your bed. Nude. With you next to me."

And the smile that spread across his face was worth any embarrassment she might've felt for being so bold in telling him what she wanted.

Nathan didn't come over to where she was sitting, though. He got up from the small dining-room table, carrying the glasses he and Joel had been using, and went into the kitchen. Bailey heard water running and the opening and closing of the dishwasher. She kept her eyes on the kitchen doorway.

Within moments Nathan came back out and stood with one hip resting against the table. His arms were crossed, and he held her eye contact for several beats before saying softly, "Don't move. Stay right there, just like that. I'll be back as soon as I get him settled."

"I can do it," Bailey said, just as quietly.

"I've got him." Nathan's eyes got soft, but they lit with an excitement and anticipation Bailey felt between her legs. "You have no idea how happy I am that you're here in my house. On my couch. And soon you'll be in my bed. I don't want to rush anything about tonight. We both might be exhausted tomorrow, but it'll be worth every second of lost sleep."

Bailey shifted in her seat and felt the wetness between her legs. Good Lord, the man was lethal. How in the hell no woman had snatched him up by now would forever be a mystery. No matter his concerns about his performance in bed, Bailey had no doubt he was going to blow her mind.

"Okay. I'll wait here," she told him quietly.

He nodded, and without another word strode down the hall toward the room Joel would be sleeping in.

Putting her book aside, Bailey waited for Nathan to return. As she waited, she realized that this was the first time in a long time that she'd felt excited anticipation when it came to being with a man, rather than resignation, antipathy, or even disgust.

It took longer than she thought it would, but finally Nathan was back. He settled on the couch next to her and immediately pulled her into his side, tucking her against him as he usually did. But it felt different this time, more intimate.

"What took you so long?" Bailey teased. "I almost fell asleep out here."

He grinned at her, letting her know he knew she was teasing before saying, "Joel had some concerns."

The small smile that had been hovering on her lips disappeared in an instant. "Concerns? About what? I should go to him." She made like she was going to get up, but Nathan tightened his arm around her.

"He's a lot more observant than I would've thought, but I'm not surprised after being around Donovan and his friends. He saw that I couldn't keep my eyes off you and wanted to make sure I wasn't going to do anything you didn't want me to."

"Holy crap. Really?" Bailey breathed.

"Really. He knows he can ask me anything, and I'll be honest with him."

"What did you say?"

"The truth."

Bailey bit her lip nervously. "And what's that?"

Nathan lay back suddenly and pulled Bailey with him until he was flat on his back and she was lying on top of him. They touched from thighs to hips to belly and chest. He pulled her up until his cock was under her pussy and held her against him with both hands at her hips.

"That I loved you. Have loved you since practically the moment I saw you. That I would never make you do anything you didn't want to do. I'd never hit you. Never hurt you."

Bailey stared down at Nathan. She knew her eyes were huge in her face, but she couldn't help it. Even though he'd already told her he loved her, she was still shocked every time she heard it.

"How'd he take that?" she whispered.

Nathan picked his head up and kissed her temple, then her cheek, then lightly brushed his lips over hers. "He wanted to know if I was going to take you into my bedroom. I told him yes. But if he needed you in the middle of the night, he was welcome to come find you. I only asked him to knock first."

"Donovan told him that he wasn't allowed in his room at any time no matter what he heard or if he needed anything," Bailey said softly.

"I know. Joel told me. That's why I wanted to make sure he knew that not only were you going to be in my room of your own accord, but if at any time he wanted to check on you, or if he needed anything, he was welcome."

Bailey felt the tears well up from her throat and swallowed hard before clearing her throat and licking her lips. "Should I be embarrassed that we're about to fuck when my brother is down the hall?"

Nathan immediately shook his head. "No, because we're not fucking. I can't say there will never be a time when we fuck, but tonight won't be that night. Bailey, I'm not an idiot. I know that Donovan probably went out of his way to be loud and obnoxious so that everyone around him knew exactly what he was doing . . . even if those around him were nine-year-old boys. That's not me. It's never going to be me. What happens between us is between us. Period."

"In my entire life, I don't think anyone has ever made love to me," Bailey whispered, then dropped her forehead into the space between his shoulder and neck.

She felt Nathan's arms slide up, not stopping at her lower back where he knew she was uncomfortable with him touching, and clutch at her shoulder blades, holding her to him. "Then I'm glad I get to be your first."

Bailey smiled at that and couldn't hold back the bitter chuckle. "That's hilarious, considering my background."

"Don't look back, Bailey. Look at today and tomorrow. Remember?"

"I remember." She picked up her head and raised up just far enough that she could reach his lips. She kissed him gently, then said against him, each word whispering against his lips as she spoke, "Take me to your bed, Nathan. Make love to me. I need you."

Without another word, he helped her to her feet, then grabbed her hand and clasped it tightly as he led the way down the hallway to his bedroom. They both walked on silent feet, and Bailey noticed that Nathan was careful to shut his door without a sound. The consideration he showed her brother never failed to make her thankful she'd stopped to help him with his car in front of the grocery store a couple of months ago.

He pulled her to the side of the bed and put his hands on her hips, once again pulling her into his body. Her belly cradled his erection as he looked down at her with a heat in his eyes that almost scorched her.

"You want to use the bathroom?"

Bailey nodded.

"Okay. I brushed my teeth after I tucked Joel in. Take your time. I'll be here waiting for you." He squeezed her lightly, then took a step back.

Bailey nodded and headed for the small bathroom tucked into the corner of his room.

"Bailey?"

She turned at Nathan's call.

"Thank you for giving me a chance."

Having no words to explain that it didn't feel like she was giving him a chance, but instead as if *he* were the one she should be thanking, she merely nodded, entered the bathroom, and shut the door behind her.

Five minutes later, Bailey stood in front of the mirror, naked. Her back was to the glass, and her head was twisted around, looking at the horrific words inked on her skin.

PROPERTY OF INCA BOYZ
D'S WHORE

Every time she saw it, it looked and felt worse. She shut her eyes and bowed her head in defeat. How could she even be thinking about letting Nathan make love to her? The memory of when she'd been given the tattoo sprung into her mind, and she gagged.

Donovan, Damian, Dominic, and whatever the name was of the guy who'd done the tattoo hadn't cared about her feelings. Hadn't cared that she'd begged them to let her up. They'd done what Donovan had wanted with no regard for her feelings about the tattoo. The humiliation of that moment was enough to bring her to her knees.

But then she remembered the look of uncertainty on Nathan's face. Realized that he was as nervous about this as she was. Realized that he had body issues as much as she did. He wasn't perfect, yet he was doing everything he could to make this moment perfect for her. For them. Hiding his own insecurities.

She wasn't ready for him to see the tattoo, but she could give herself to him. And in giving herself to him, she'd give herself a gift. She wanted to know what sex could feel like when the person she was with actually cared about her. About her feelings and pleasure. In return, she could help make Nathan feel more secure about himself. About his lovemaking skills.

Licking her lips, Bailey took a deep breath. She'd procrastinated enough. She would go out into Nathan's bedroom and make sure he knew that she only wanted to do it on her back. Under no circumstances would she get into any position where her tattoo would be exposed. And she knew Nathan would do just that.

She threw the shirt Nathan left on the counter over her body, its hem falling to midthigh, marched to the door, and threw it open before her newfound courage left her.

Nathan was sitting on the side of the bed, looking uncomfortable. His head whipped up, and he stood when she opened the door. He'd taken off his shoes and socks, had undone the button on his jeans, and his shirt was off. He stood there, shifting from one foot to the other as he stared at her.

Bailey's eyes roamed down his body, pleased with what she saw. Just as she had the day when she'd walked in on him changing, she noticed his uncertainty. Feeling as if she had the upper hand in the situation for once, she slowly walked toward him, making sure to sway her hips more than necessary.

Seeing his eyes go from her face to her chest and her beaded nipples poking through his T-shirt, then down to her hips, Bailey smiled.

She walked right up to him and stood on tiptoe. She put her arms around his neck and pressed her body against his. The warmth of his skin seeped through the material of the shirt and into her soul.

"Hey," she said softly.

"Hey," he returned immediately, his hands going to her hips once more.

She was more than aware that ever since she'd told him about her tattoo, he'd taken great pains not to touch her lower back when they cuddled together. It only made him more precious to her.

"I think I'm supposed to be the one nervous here," she told him with a small smile.

Nathan shook his head. "I want to make this good for you so badly. I don't want to do anything that will make you think about what *he* did to you, and I'm scared to death I'm going to screw it up."

"You won't mess it up," Bailey reassured him. "I can't promise not to have any bad moments, but I do know you aren't him. I could never mistake you for Donovan. Ever." She reached back, took hold of one of his hands, and flattened it against her side, then slowly moved it up her body until he was cupping her breast through the shirt.

Nathan immediately took over and gently squeezed her flesh, then used his thumb and brushed over her rock-hard nipple until it stood up even more prominently through the shirt. Without a word, he bent and took the bud he'd been teasing into his mouth, sucking on her through the cotton.

Bailey's head went back, and she moaned, clutching the back of his head as he bit, sucked, and teased her within an inch of her life. He pulled back, but his eyes stayed fixed on her chest. She looked down and saw that the white material was completely see-through now that it was soaked with his saliva. Even *she* had to admit it was as erotic a sight as she'd ever seen. Her dark-pink nipple stood out in stark contrast to the white of the shirt surrounding it.

Without a word, Nathan moved to her other side, treating her other breast to the same treatment. His hand went back to the now-neglected nipple, keeping it taut as he worked on its twin.

Finally, he pulled back once more and examined his handiwork.

"Beautiful," he murmured, running his thumbs over both nipples, now straining to break through the cotton shirt to get to him.

Bailey arched her back, pressing herself into his hands.

This time, it was Nathan who groaned. "You are so beautiful. Every inch."

She wrinkled her nose and gestured to her arms. "My tattoos are stupid."

"They aren't. They're a part of you." He intertwined the fingers of his right hand with hers and held her arm out to the side. Then he proceeded to blow her mind.

Leaning forward, Nathan brushed his lips against each tattoo on her arm as he spoke. "The first time I saw you leaning over Marilyn, looking at her engine, I imagined you here . . . in my bed. I couldn't take my eyes off these tattoos." He licked a rose on her bicep, then nuzzled it with his nose. "A rose for beauty." He traced the ink winding around her upper arm. "Barbed wire to keep everyone at arm's length, but getting under that barrier is the greatest gift."

His mouth touched the pistol, knife, and skull on her forearm. "So tough, yet tender at the same time." Nathan looked up at her then as his fingers traced Joel's initials on her wrist. Then he switched to her other hand, holding it just as tenderly as he did the right.

He continued to lavish affection on every inch of her arm. Not skimming over any of her ink, not even the stupid cartoon logo of the gang or the initials *IB*. Through it all he murmured beautiful words of love and adoration.

When he was done, Bailey felt like a pile of mush. No one had ever made her feel as cherished and treasured as Nathan just had.

Bailey brought her hands up to Nathan's chest, running them over the slightly scratchy hair on his chest until she got to his nipples. He returned his hands to her breasts, never taking his eyes from hers. She mimicked his movements. When he pinched her buds, she did the same to his. When he lightly caressed her, she mirrored his caress on his own body. Soon, his own nipples were tight and hard on his chest. Without waiting for his permission, she leaned forward and licked one. Feeling powerful as a shudder went through him, Bailey got serious and sucked his small bud hard, flicking it with her tongue as she did.

Nathan ground his cock against her belly and moaned out her name.

Bailey pulled back and smiled up at him. "Should we move this to the bed?"

"That's probably a good idea. I'm not sure I could've stayed standing if you did that much more."

"You liked it?"

"Bailey, I like holding your hand. Feeling your skin against mine makes my day complete. You sucking on my chest? It's fucking amazing."

Awed once more at his lack of artifice, she merely smiled and said, "If you think that feels good, just wait until I have your cock in my mouth. You'll think you've died and gone to heaven."

"I already feel that way. Lie back," he ordered, his voice only cracking once.

Without taking her eyes from his, she scooted up onto the bed and lay back, making sure to keep the shirt pulled down. It was ridiculous, they were about to have sex, but she felt extremely vulnerable for some reason and didn't want Nathan to see her tattoo. Not this time. Maybe not ever, but definitely not tonight.

He smiled tenderly at her and lay down next to her. He propped himself up on an elbow and used his hand to brush her hair away from her face. "You're beautiful, Bailey. Your hair is the first thing I noticed about you. How it blew in your face, and you brushed it away impatiently. It's shiny and so damn soft."

He moved his hand and started tracing the features on her face. "Your nose is literally as cute as a button. Your cheekbones make you look delicate and dainty, but it was a total turn-on to have you fix my car with a flick of your fingers. And your lips. Lord, your lips. Every time you get nervous and bite your lip, I want to run my tongue over it to soothe the sting you were sure to leave behind."

Bailey inhaled sharply as his finger ran over each lip, then his thumb brushed back and forth over the bottom one. She licked it, catching his thumb in the process. She brought her hand up and grasped his wrist, holding him still. Then she lifted her head a fraction and took his thumb into her mouth. His eyes dilated as her tongue wrapped around it, and she sucked.

"Jesus, Bailey. I'm supposed to be making you feel good. Much more of that and this'll be over before it begins."

She popped his digit out of her mouth and told him something she'd never told another man before in her life. "If you come first, you'll just last that much longer when you do get inside me."

"Fuck," Nathan breathed, then shifted quickly until he was kneeling over her. He took both wrists in his hands and held them flat against the mattress next to her head. "You are so damn sexy, you take my breath away."

"You swear more when you're turned on," Bailey observed with a smile.

"Can't fucking help it," Nathan said absently, his eyes once more on her hard, wet nipples. He let go of one of her hands and trailed his fingers down her side until they reached her thigh, then he slowly began to push her shirt up as his hand made progress toward her chest.

Her thoughts only on her tattoo, Bailey flinched and said, "Can we turn the light out?"

Nathan froze above her, and her eyes flew to his. She saw the hurt there before he banked it and nodded.

As he leaned over to switch off the lamp on the table next to the bed, Bailey said, "Wait."

He paused midlean and looked at her.

"I . . . you don't want the light out?"

"It's not the first time a woman has wanted to have sex with me in the dark," he said with no inflection in his voice.

Bailey inhaled in horror. She hadn't meant she didn't want to look at *him*. And she really didn't like how all of a sudden they were having sex instead of making love.

"Nathan, I want to see you. I want to see every inch of your body. I told you about my tattoo . . . it's just . . . it's big . . . and some of it wraps around my waist and can be seen from the front. I'm embarrassed about it, and you know I don't want you to see it. I know that it'll be impossible to keep it hidden from you forever, but for our first time . . . I wanted it to be just us . . . not Donovan or the Inca Boyz."

Nathan stopped reaching for the light and settled back over her on his elbows and knees. "Oh shit. I'm sorry. I made this about me when I swore I wouldn't. You want the light out? No problem. I'll do whatever you need, pixie. We have all the time in the world. If we make love in the dark tonight, it'll be just as perfect as if the lights were blazing." He kissed her forehead. Then her nose. Then her chin. Then finally her lips. "Whatever you need, Bailey. Whatever. Whenever. Wherever."

Bailey opened her mouth under his and kissed him. Hard. And he reciprocated. The kiss was hot, wet, and deep, and they were both panting when Nathan finally pulled back.

"I want to make love to you in every position we can think of, and more that we have to look up to figure out how to make them work," Bailey told him.

Nathan's eyes flared with lust.

She went on quickly. "But tonight, if we leave the light on . . . I need you to let me stay on my back. Not because I don't want you the other ways, but it'll hide my tattoo until I can be brave enough to show it to you. Is that okay?"

In answer, Nathan kissed her again. Once again, it was long, and they were both panting when he pulled back to say, "It's more than all right. Can I take off your shirt? Or do you need it to stay on?"

God. Seriously. How this man was still single, Bailey had no clue. He was amazing.

Taking a deep breath, she brought her hands between them, forcing Nathan to lean up to give her room. She grabbed the hem and quickly, before she changed her mind, lifted it up and over her head. She threw it to the ground, not caring where it landed. Immediately her arms went to her belly and crossed, using her hands to cover the letters she knew could be seen from the front.

With a tender smile, Nathan immediately lifted to his knees and pushed his jeans and underwear down and over his butt, falling to a hip and impatiently flicking them down his calves and off. Bailey only caught a quick glance of his cock before he was lying next to her once more. One leg thrown over hers, one hand cupping her breast, the other pressing under her arms to rest on her bare belly.

"There," he said breathlessly. "Now we're even." His eyes warmed, if that was possible, and he said, "The only thing I see is your beauty. I have no problem taking you on your back tonight, pixie. I can't wait to bury my face between your legs, suck on your tits, and believe me, the last thing I'll be thinking about the first time I get inside you is what is inked on your back."

Bailey nodded and licked her lips. Nathan kissed her quickly, then once more hovered over her and began to feast on her breasts.

Chapter Twenty

Bailey gasped and grabbed Nathan's head as her body readied itself for another orgasm.

Nathan smiled as he felt her fingernails dig into the sides of his head. He'd almost blown everything by not considering her feelings about the lights. All he could think about was his feelings, which was stupid. He wasn't the one who'd been raped. He wasn't the one who'd been forced to get a tattoo on his back. He needed to make this good for Bailey. His needs and wants should always come in second when it came to her.

He concentrated on doing exactly what his brothers had suggested, direct contact with Bailey's clit. He'd thought licking her folds would feel good to her, and it had, but he hadn't considered exactly how magical a woman's clit was.

Every time his tongue flicked it, she moaned. When he sucked on it, she squirmed under him and pushed her hips farther into his mouth. When he added a finger into his play, pushing slowly in and out of her, he could feel her muscles clench down every time he flicked his tongue against her clit.

He alternated with fast flicks and slow, long licks, giving her time to relax a bit, then bringing her back up with hard touches again. He'd never felt as powerful as he did right in that minute. His cock was as hard as steel, and he could feel himself leaking precome on his sheets, but he didn't care. Giving Bailey pleasure was as heady a feeling as he'd ever had before.

It was more important that she enjoy herself than it was for him to get off. He needed her to enjoy this. Deciding he'd teased her long enough, Nathan turned his hand and searched for her G-spot. His brothers had told him what it should feel like and approximately how to find it. They'd cautioned that he might not get it right the first time and that he shouldn't feel bad. But they'd said when he did find it, she'd let him know by her reaction, and Bailey would have the biggest, strongest orgasm he could ever imagine.

As he gently pushed his finger farther into her body and pressed into her upper wall with his finger, she suddenly stiffened under him.

Nathan lifted his head and pushed into her again, feeling the rough skin on the inside of her body. She jerked under him again. He looked up her body to her face. Bailey had propped herself up on her elbows and was staring down at him.

Her face was covered in a sheen of sweat, an ebony lock of hair was stuck to her forehead, and she'd never looked so beautiful to him. *He'd* done that. He'd gotten her so worked up by sucking on her tits that she'd pushed him down to her crotch and begged him to eat her out.

He'd complied, gladly. She hadn't had to give him too many instructions. His talk with his brothers had helped immensely. But she obviously hadn't expected this.

"That feel good?"

"Oh my God," Bailey wailed. "Fuck, that's amazing."

Nathan caressed her again, smiling when she jerked under him again. Wrapping his other hand under her ass and pressing her thigh to the side, leaving her as open as he could get her, Nathan dropped his head once more. Keeping his eyes on her face, he licked her clit hard and fast at the same time he pressed over and over on her G-spot.

Bailey's head immediately tilted, and she collapsed onto her back again. Her hands clamped down on his head, and she pressed him into her. The faster he licked and pressed inside her, the more her hips thrashed under him. Forgoing licking, Nathan attached his mouth over her hard clit, which was now sticking up out of its protective hood, and sucked. Hard.

That was all it took. She flew over the edge. She turned her head and moaned her ecstasy into the pillow next to her, muffling the sounds of joy that erupted out of her mouth.

Nathan stilled his finger, fascinated by the feel of her body gripping him as she orgasmed. He lightly licked at her clit, smiling as she jerked under him with every lick. It wasn't until she whispered, "Too sensitive," that he lifted his head.

He could feel her wetness on his face. He could smell her cream on his skin. And it was amazing. He'd literally bathed in her excitement, and it had only increased his own. Seeing Bailey lying still under him, breathing hard, a small smile on her gorgeous face, Nathan sat up.

Getting to his knees between her legs, he reached for the condom he'd put on the side table while she'd been in the bathroom.

For the first time in his life, he wasn't worrying about what he looked like. Was he too skinny? His legs too long? His cock not thick enough? Too long? All he was thinking about was getting inside the woman he loved.

He quickly sheathed his cock, wincing at the pleasure it caused, and shuffled forward on the mattress another few inches, pushing her thighs farther apart. Looking down, Nathan saw her soaking-wet folds open and ready for him. Her clit had receded a bit, but still could be seen sticking up from the hood. But it was the wet spot under her folds that made him lick his lips with lust, tasting her all over again.

Bailey Hampton was in his bed. Under him. And he'd just made her have two orgasms. It was as if he was having an out-of-body experience. He wanted to be inside her as badly as he'd wanted anything in his entire life. But she had to want it too.

"Bailey?" he called, his hands massaging her inner thighs. His cock throbbed, but he kept it from touching where it most wanted to go by sheer strength of will.

"Hmm," she murmured drowsily.

"Open your eyes."

Nathan watched as her eyes fluttered open. She looked confused for a moment, before realizing where she was and what had happened. Immediately her eyes dropped between her legs, and she gasped.

"Nathan. You're . . . huge."

He chuckled. "I'm not, but thank you anyway."

"I don't mean thick, but you're long. Really long."

Nathan shrugged. "May I?" he asked politely, wanting inside her so badly, but wanting her permission first.

Her knees came up, and she put her feet flat on the mattress next to him. She tilted her pelvis up and said softly, "Please. If you don't fuck me, I think I'll die."

"Fuuuuck," Nathan said, grasping his cock with one hand and propping himself over her with the other by her hip. "You need me to stop, I will. No matter what, pixie. I'd sooner die than cause you pain. Physically or emotionally."

"Let me," Bailey said, still not taking her eyes away from his cock and ignoring his words. She pushed his hand away and grabbed the base of his dick.

Catching himself with his now free hand, Nathan's head fell back and he groaned. Instead of guiding him to her immediately, Bailey's hand trailed up to the tip of his erection, then back down to the base. She did it twice more before dropping her hand to cup his balls.

"For the love of God, Bailey," Nathan begged, "I want to be inside you when I come the first time. Please."

Without any more teasing, she took hold of him and fit the mushroomed head of his cock to her sopping-wet hole. He pushed inside at the same time she raised her hips, and they both groaned.

"Jesus, pixie. I've never felt anything like you before in my life. You're so hot and wet. And you're sucking me in as if you can't live without me inside you."

"I can't. More, Nathan. Fill me up. All the way."

Slowly, Nathan pushed inside her, then pulled partway out. He did it again, going farther, before he pulled back. "Is this okay?"

"Stop fucking around and do it already," Bailey pleaded. "I'm fine."

"No bad moments?"

"No."

"I don't want to hurt you," Nathan bit out between clenched teeth. He hadn't lied. He hadn't felt anything as amazing as being inside Bailey's body. "I don't ever want to hurt you."

Bailey's hands came up, and she grabbed either side of his neck and forced him to look down at her. "You. Are. Not. Hurting. Me. Fuck me, Nathan. I want to feel your cock against my womb. Do it."

Before she was even done talking, he'd sunk all the way inside her. Burying his entire length inside her, then reaching down with one hand and grabbing one of her ass cheeks, pulling her farther open and letting him settle another millimeter inside her. Nathan let out a long breath and held still. Memorizing the moment.

He could feel his balls up against her asshole, the wetness from her earlier orgasm soaking him. The blood pulsed in his cock with the beat of his heart, and every time she tightened her inner muscles against him, he had to grit his teeth and think about adding three-digit numbers in base three to keep from exploding like the almost virgin he was.

"I can feel every inch of you inside me," Bailey breathed, staring at his face.

"Is that okay? Do I need to pull out?"

"It's more than okay. It's amazing. Fantastic. Phenomenal. If you pull out, I'm gonna have to hurt you."

Nathan chuckled, then gasped as the movement made her clench against him again. Remembering what his brothers had told him, and how she'd felt orgasming against his finger, Nathan had the sudden urge to feel her lose it on his dick.

He raised himself up, keeping himself planted deep inside her, and used his thumb to caress her clit. He tested the waters first, making sure what he was doing felt good and wasn't hurting her.

When Bailey's eyes widened in shock and she grabbed his biceps, he smiled and increased the speed of his thumb, but not the pressure.

Soon, she was squirming against him, trying to press up against him, wanting a firmer touch.

"You want to come again, Bailey?"

"God. If you'd asked a minute ago, I would've said it was impossible. But now I'm full of you, and it feels so damn good. Yes, I want to come with you inside me."

Wanting to be the one to give her another orgasm, Nathan was suddenly overcome with the need to thrust. His cock almost hurt with the amount of effort it was taking for him to hold back his own orgasm.

"I need to . . . dammit . . . can you . . ." His voice trailed off, and he felt self-conscious for the first time since he'd entered her. Was he supposed to ask her to rub herself? Maybe she didn't like doing that. He wasn't sure if she thought it was his job to make her orgasm or not.

But as usual, she didn't leave him hanging for long. Her eyes came to his, and she brought her right hand down between their bodies, pushing his out of the way. "I got this. Put a pillow under my ass," she ordered as she gently rubbed herself.

Nathan immediately reached for his pillow, and she helped as he shoved it under her. She was right, it raised her pelvis just enough to let his cock more easily penetrate her. Gritting his teeth, he bit out, "Now what?"

"Now you make love to me, Nathan. Do whatever feels good to you, because you inside me certainly works for me."

"I'm not hurting you?" Nathan asked one more time, wanting to be sure. "I've got some lube if we need it."

"I'm soaking wet," she reassured him. "We definitely don't need more lube." Bailey began to stroke herself harder and faster.

Nathan couldn't take his eyes off her fingers. She was using both her index and middle finger and was much more aggressive and rough than he ever would've been. He made a mental note for the future.

He vaguely noticed the black letters on either side of her waist, but at the moment couldn't care less, just as he'd told her he wouldn't. Whatever was inked on her back didn't matter. Not in the least. All that mattered was this. Was them. Being together. Coming together.

"Move, Nathan," she ordered in a croak.

He did. Pulling out almost all the way, then pushing back in until he couldn't get inside her any farther. He did it again and again, feeling her inner muscles flutter against his cock as he moved in and out.

She moved her free hand up to her chest and pulled at her nipple, hard. Again, making a mental note, Nathan lost his control for the first time. Seeing her under him, giving herself pleasure as he took her, was more than he could take. He shoved inside her roughly, grunting as his balls bounced off her ass. He did it again. Not pulling out all the way now, but keeping a constant friction against the sensitive head of his cock.

Every time he bottomed out inside her, she thrust her hips into him, forcing him to hit harder inside her than he'd planned. He wondered for a moment if he was hitting her G-spot with every thrust, but before he could experiment, she lost it.

"Nathan. God, yes!" she said as she squeezed the ever-loving shit out of his cock.

He managed four more thrusts, pushing through her muscles, which were strangling his dick, before he shoved inside her as far as he could go and let himself go.

The orgasm was longer, stronger, and more devastating than any he'd ever had in his life. His come seemed to erupt from his balls forever, filling the condom until he thought it'd either break or overflow. But throughout it all he kept his eyes open and on Bailey's face.

Knowing he'd actually given her pleasure made his orgasm that much better.

He pulled the pillow out from under her ass, then eased down next to her, putting most of his weight on his side, and turning her so he stayed inside her as they both came down from their orgasms.

"Holy crap," Bailey whispered when she finally caught her breath. "Are you even real?"

Nathan chuckled. "Have you ever seen the movie *Revenge of the Nerds*?"

At that, her head came up, and she looked at him as if he were insane.

"Uh, yeah . . . who hasn't? And what does that have to do with anything?"

"Betty asks Lewis if all nerds are as good in bed as he is. And he says, 'Yes, because all jocks ever think about is sports, and all nerds ever think about is sex.'"

Bailey burst into giggles before she said, "If you tell me you have a Darth Vader costume and you want to have sex while you're wearing it, I'm gonna have to pass."

Nathan smiled down at the woman in his arms. His heart hurt with how much he loved her. "I don't have a Darth helmet, but I'm happy to get one if you wanna play."

She giggled again and nuzzled her face into his chest, throwing her leg around his hip. "Thank you."

"For what?" Nathan asked, genuinely curious.

"For caring. For making that so wonderful. For not treating me as a hole to stick your dick into."

Nathan stiffened, but forced himself to relax. "I love you, Bailey. You and Joel mean the world to me. And anyone who does or says anything to hurt you will have to deal with me."

She picked her head up and kissed the underside of his jaw. "And I'll be there to deal with anyone who calls you a nerd or says shit about you, since I know you won't do it yourself."

"It doesn't bother me," he reassured her.

"I know, but it bothers me," Bailey mumbled.

Smiling, loving that she cared enough about him to give a shit if someone called him white trash, or a geek, or any other name. Nathan sighed. She hadn't said she loved him, but it was a start.

As he'd sighed, his now-soft cock slowly slid out of Bailey's body, and she giggled. Nathan mock-glared at her. "Not funny."

She rolled onto her back and reached for the sheet crumpled under her. "Go take care of that condom. I'll be here when you get back."

Nathan sat up, kissed her on the nose, and said, "You better be."

When he returned from the bathroom, he carried a warm, wet washcloth. He sat on the side of the bed next to Bailey and held it out, a little unsure. "I brought this for you . . . it's warm. I didn't know if you wanted to clean up."

She stared up at him, not saying anything.

"You don't have to use it," he mumbled and went to stand back up.

"Yes, please. I'm sorry, you surprised me. No one has ever done that for me before." She held out her hand, and Nathan put the cloth in her hand. It disappeared under the covers, and he held eye contact with her as she cleaned herself. She blushed and brought her hand back up and out from under the sheet.

He took the quickly cooling washcloth from her and dropped it on the floor without a thought. He pulled back the sheet and settled in next to her. He groaned in contentment when Bailey immediately snuggled up into him. Her head resting on his shoulder, her arm around his belly, and her leg hooked with his.

"Sleep well, Bailey," Nathan murmured.

"You too," she said back, already sounding half-asleep.

Memorizing the moment, Nathan lay awake for a long time, listening to Bailey's soft exhales as she lay boneless and trusting in his arms.

Finally, he closed his eyes and drifted off to sleep, happier than he'd been in his entire life.

Chapter Twenty-One

With every day that went by, Nathan got more and more tense. It had been more than two weeks since he'd spoken with his brothers about Donovan, and they'd made a preliminary plan. The fact that they couldn't find the gang leader was putting them all on edge.

The man was out there. Somewhere. And breathing down Bailey's neck. He knew it. She knew it. They'd had a long discussion the other night about what Donovan was capable of and what he was likely to do when he showed up.

As much as Nathan wanted to reassure Bailey that her ex wouldn't get his hands on her, he couldn't. They both knew it was simply a matter of time. They'd argued about what Joel should do when Donovan finally made his move. Bailey didn't want to talk to him about Donovan at all, while Nathan argued that he should have some idea of what might happen.

"He's not strong enough," Bailey huffed. "He's still having nightmares, and the psychologist says that he's still working through the shit Donovan exposed him to."

"I realize that, but do you really want the asshole to show up and not have Joel prepared? I think if we let him know what we're planning and give him a role, it'll give him a sense of empowerment. It'll make him feel less helpless. The last thing we want is for Donovan to surprise him."

Bailey had hemmed and hawed and finally given in. They'd sat the boy down and told him that they thought Donovan would be showing up soon and what they thought he wanted—namely, to use Joel to hurt Bailey.

The little boy had seemed okay with everything they'd said, but the next day around lunchtime, Nathan received a phone call from him.

"Hello?"

"Nathan?"

"Hey, Joel. Are you okay?" Nathan asked urgently.

"Yeah, I'm good."

"Should you be using your phone right now?"

"It's lunch. I'm allowed," Joel reassured him.

"Okay. What's up, buddy?"

He paused for a moment, then said quickly, "I don't wanna go with Donovan."

Nathan closed his eyes and silently sighed. He prayed he would say the right thing to make Joel feel better. "I don't want you to either. No way in hell. But, buddy, we should be smart. I can probably overpower him in the short term, but he won't fight fair."

"I'm scared," Joel whispered.

"I'm not all that thrilled myself," Nathan told him honestly. "But here's the thing. Between the three of us, I'm sure we can come up with a plan. I've already been talking to my brothers, and we have some ideas. One of them could work, but it depends on you to make it work."

"Me? Really?"

Nathan heard the interest in the little boy's voice and was glad to know he'd banished some of his fear for now. "Really. But it's tricky, and a little dangerous. Not to mention if Donovan figures out what we're doing, it could backfire."

"We can do it. He's not that smart. You're way smarter than he is," Joel said without an ounce of doubt in his voice.

The confidence Joel had in him made Nathan feel ten feet tall. He couldn't let him down. "Good boy. Okay, I'll talk to your sister in a bit when we have lunch." He paused, then asked, "You gonna be all right for the rest of the day?"

"Yeah, Nathan. I'm good."

"Okay then. I'll be there to pick you up in a few hours. Try not to worry. We got this."

"Yeah. We got this. 'Bye."

"'Bye."

Nathan had hung up the phone and clenched his teeth. He hated that Joel was scared of Donovan. Hated that he felt the tension in the air. But he really hated that he had to involve the boy in the plan to take down Donovan at all. But as much as he hated it, he knew using Joel was most likely to work.

Nathan knew something had to give with Bailey. She was at the end of her rope. He'd called Clayson and asked if Bailey could have the afternoon off, and he'd agreed, obviously knowing Bailey needed a break.

But when Nathan strolled into the auto body shop, calling out greetings to the guys, and told Bailey that he was taking her home for the rest of the afternoon, she wasn't happy, to say the least.

"I've got shit to do. I can't just leave," she told Nathan.

"You can. I already asked Clayson, and he agreed," he told her calmly.

"No fucking way. Rent is coming up next week, and I need to go to the store. Joel needs a new pair of jeans because he's growing like a weed, and frankly, I don't want to go."

Nathan walked right up to her, clasped his hand behind her neck, leaned his forehead on hers, and said quietly, "You need a break, pixie. You've been going a hundred miles an hour for over a week. Spend the afternoon with me. Just the two of us. We'll eat lunch, then we need to talk. After that we can spend the rest of the time we have until we need to pick up Joel in bed . . . and you don't have to worry about being quiet . . . yeah?"

As if his touch and words were magic, she melted into him, her arms going around his waist. Her eyes closed and she murmured, "I'm so tired."

"I know you are. Let me help. Lean on me."

"Okay."

"Okay." Nathan immediately turned them, wrapped an arm around her shoulders, and led her out of the large bay doors and into the Colorado sunshine. With a wave to Clayson, who was watching from his office door, he led Bailey to his car.

Nathan knew Bailey was irritable. She was irritable because she was stressed. And she was stressed because she was on edge. She was on edge because she knew Donovan wanted to get his hands on her. And because she was worried about her brother.

He wanted to give them both this time together. To talk about Joel and Donovan, but also just to relax for a couple of hours.

Nathan drove to her house since it was closer and got her settled on the couch with a glass of lemonade while he made a quick lunch of turkey-and-cheese sandwiches.

After they ate, Nathan pulled Bailey into his arms in their customary slouch position, and he got to it.

"Tonight we need to talk to Joel about what to do when Donovan shows up."

Bailey stiffened and sat up. "No, I don't want to—"

"He called me today," Nathan interrupted. "Scared out of his mind that Donovan was going to force him to go with him back up to Denver. If we could keep him out of this, I would do it in a heartbeat. I'd send him to live with Logan or Blake, but we both know that won't stop Donovan. He's out there. Watching us. I can feel it, and I think you can too. He's biding his time. He wants to torture you. Make you regret leaving him. He knows we're together, and I think that's why he's been holding off. He's trying to figure me out and make a plan. But we're running out of time, and the last thing I want is for Joel to freak when Donovan makes his move."

Bailey sank back into his arms and pressed her face into his neck. "I hate this," she said fervently. "I hate *him*."

"I know."

They were both silent for a moment before Bailey tentatively asked, "Do you have a plan?"

"I do," Nathan said immediately. "Logan and Blake helped me work out the kinks. I won't lie. It's dangerous, but in light of what Donovan wants—namely, Joel, and to torture you, I think it can work. But most of it is going to rest on Joel's shoulders. And before you protest, he can handle it. I know it."

Bailey was silent so long, Nathan wasn't sure she was going to respond. Finally, she said in a soft, pained voice, "This is all my fault."

"No," Nathan barked immediately, making Bailey jump. "Don't do that. You didn't ask for this. You didn't ask for Donovan to rape you. To mark you without your permission. To treat you like shit and try to corrupt your brother."

"But if I—"

"Bailey, no."

She sat up and tried to pull out of Nathan's arms, but he wouldn't let her.

"Let me talk! I—"

"I said no," Nathan interrupted once more. "You're gonna spout some bullshit about how you were his girlfriend and should've known better. Should've kept Joel away from him. Blah, blah, blah. But it *is* bullshit. He took advantage of you just like he takes advantage of everyone around him. He's an asshole. Not a good man. You were young and dealing with hormones, then later, the loss of your pa and trying to raise a little boy. This. Is. Not. Your. Fault."

Bailey tore out of his arms and stood. Without another word, she tore off her shirt and turned her back to Nathan. "Yeah? Then how's this. I was his whore, Nathan. An Inca Boyz slut. I let them use me. I let them fuck me any way they wanted, whenever they wanted. And I liked it . . . at least at first. But that doesn't matter. I was and always will be Donovan's fucking whore."

Nathan stared at the obscene words on Bailey's lower back.

PROPERTY OF INCA BOYZ
D'S WHORE

He wished Donovan was in front of him right now. He'd kill him. Slowly. The man was evil. Pure evil.

He had no idea what the right words were. No idea what to say to get through to her. To let her know that her past didn't matter to him, except that it made her the person she was today. The woman he loved with all his heart and soul. Nathan dropped to his knees and shuffled over to Bailey. She was breathing hard and had her arms wrapped around her waist defensively.

"This is what you've been hiding from me." It wasn't a question, and Nathan went on. "You are nobody's property, pixie. And you are certainly no whore. I have never met anyone who has impressed me with their strength more than you."

"I'm contaminated," Bailey said sadly. "I shouldn't have let you touch me."

"The last week or so has been the happiest I've ever been in my entire life," he told her honestly. "And it's not just because we've made love. What truly has filled my heart with contentment is you and Joel. Spending time with you. Laughing. Helping Joel with his homework and seeing his eyes light up when he understands a math problem for the first time. Seeing you sitting on the couch doing nothing but reading. Sleeping next to you. Feeling your heat against me, hearing you breathing as you trust me enough to fall asleep next to me. I've never had that. Not once in my life, Bailey." He leaned forward and kissed the skin on her lower back, not caring about the words inked there.

"I won't lie. I want to fucking kill that bastard. The thought of what you went through at his hands makes me want to hunt him down and kill him slowly and painfully. But that won't take away your memories. Won't take back what happened to you. But what he did makes *him* the asshole. Not you."

He paused, letting his words sink in, resting his forehead against the warm skin of Bailey's back.

She shivered. Maybe in revulsion. Maybe in response to his warm breath against her sensitive skin. He wasn't sure, but he wasn't going to let her leave until they'd hashed this out. Until she understood to the marrow of her bones that he didn't care about what her asshole ex tattooed on her skin.

"I'm afraid you're going to see it down the line and regret hooking up with a gang whore." Her words were barely audible, and filled with pain.

Staying on his knees, Nathan turned Bailey until she was facing him. He put his hands on her waist, his thumbs against her belly, and looked up. "There's *nothing* about you I regret. Not one single thing. Bailey, we are a product of our pasts. We can't go back and change that. My mom killed my dad. I'm the son of a murderer. Does that make you want to run?"

She shook her head. "Of course not."

"My mom used to beat me. Do you think because of that I'm going to start hitting Joel?"

"Nathan, no, but it's not the same."

"Our past is just that. The past. Our future is what *we* make of it. We can be bitter and pissed off . . . or we can move forward. I want to move forward with you, pixie. The only thing this tattoo on your back makes me feel is more anger toward the asshole who put it there. You are no whore, Bailey. Not even close."

"I didn't want him to do it, but he didn't give me a choice. He held me down and laughed when I cried. It's ugly. I hate it."

Nathan tensed, not wanting to hear the details, but at the same time needing to know exactly what happened so he could make Donovan pay for every tear, every mark on Bailey's body, but he held on to his temper.

"Bailey," Nathan said with all the feeling he could put into his words, "I *love* you. The good, the bad, and the ugly—not that you have much bad or ugly. I know you're not perfect, but this"—he moved his hands until they were pressed against her lower back—"isn't either. It's skin-deep. That's it."

"I want to get it covered," she said immediately. "Felicity said she'd take me to a guy she knows and trusts. I don't know what I want, but it should be something that represents my new life. Away from Denver. Away from the Inca Boyz." She took a deep breath, then said, "With you."

"I've thought about getting a tattoo myself. Maybe the date we met, so I never forget it."

At his words, the tears she'd been holding back sprang into her eyes, and she sniffled. "I don't deserve you."

"Yes, you do," Nathan countered immediately. "We deserve each other. We've had a hell of a life up to now, but it's time for us to have good. Don't you think?"

Bailey smiled through her tears and nodded. "Definitely."

Nathan smiled back, then leaned forward and rested his cheek on the bare skin of her belly, hugging her to him. They stayed like that for quite a while. Taking comfort in each other.

When it was obvious Bailey's tears had dried up and she was over the worst of her painful emotions, Nathan leaned his head back and looked up at her. "I'm sorry you went through what you did, but from this point on, no one is going to hurt you. You're going to have the life you should've had all along. I'm going to make sure of it."

Chapter Twenty-Two

Two days later, Nathan woke up with Bailey's mouth around his cock. Even though Donovan's arrival in their lives was hovering like a giant black cloud, his relationship with Bailey had never been better. It was as if showing him her tattoo, and exposing what she thought was her shame, had freed her to be who she was with him.

And she was an extremely sexual woman who loved to touch, and be touched, and she taught Nathan how and where. She hadn't lied when she'd admitted that she liked sex, and he felt like the luckiest man alive. Not only was Bailey beautiful, but she was sharing a bed with *him*. She liked to wake him by sucking him off, trying to see how close she could get him to exploding before he fully woke up.

This morning was no exception. His dick was fully engorged and halfway down her throat when his conscious mind realized what was happening. Instead of protesting, as he'd done the last two mornings, he went with it. Nathan grabbed her head and held on as she bobbed up and down on him. Within moments he was close, his balls pulled up tight to his body, the come churning inside ready to shoot out the tip of his cock.

"I'm close, pixie," he croaked in desperation.

In response, she closed her mouth around him and sucked—hard. That was all it took.

"God!" Nathan ground out between clenched teeth and did his best not to shove his hips into her face, choking her. It was several long moments before he could think clearly again, and when he could, he sat up, grabbed Bailey around the waist, pulled her up his body, and she eagerly straddled his face.

He'd only eaten her this way once, but it had obviously been something she'd liked as she'd ground down on his tongue and hadn't hesitated to use her fingers to rub her clit as he feasted. This morning was no different. She was obviously primed by sucking him off because she was dripping wet.

It didn't take long before she was undulating over him and high-pitched keens came from her mouth. She shook and shivered over him as she went over the edge, and Nathan licked and sucked every drop of her come he could reach with his tongue.

She fell to the side, her head at his hip, arm draped over his thighs, breathing hard.

"Good morning, pixie," Nathan said softly, knowing the huge smile on his face was being communicated in his words.

She chuckled, and he felt the warmth of her breath on his leg. "Good morning."

"I think I could start out every morning that way," he observed dryly.

Bailey lifted her head and looked up at him with her eyebrows raised.

He burst out laughing and hauled her up and around so her head was next to his. Then he kissed her. Not caring that he could taste himself or that she could undoubtedly taste herself on him as well. The kiss was easy and tender, and made his heart hurt with how perfect it was. She pulled away after a long moment and rested her head on his shoulder, running her fingers through the sparse hair on his chest.

"I can't do lunch with you today," Nathan told her. "But Grace said she'd love to get out of the house and meet up with you at Clayson's.

I think she's going stir-crazy with Nate and Ace and needs a change of scenery."

Bailey lifted her head and gave Nathan the stink eye. "You know I can't protest when you put it like that."

"I know," he agreed easily, his eyes sparkling with humor.

"Fine. But only because it's been too long since I've seen those adorable creatures."

Nathan kissed her on the forehead. "Go ahead and shower. I'll get Joel up."

She didn't say anything for a long moment, then finally said softly, still looking him in the eye, "Have I told you lately how appreciative I am of you?"

"Yeah, Bailey. You have."

"Well, I'm saying it again. Thank you."

"You're welcome," Nathan said immediately, then continued with, "But you know I wouldn't do anything I didn't want to."

"I do know it."

"Good. Now, go on, get up. Shower. Get ready. I'll go get Joel and start breakfast."

Bailey leaned up and kissed him hard. "Okay."

"Okay."

Nathan watched as Bailey climbed out of bed and headed for the small bathroom. They'd started spending more and more nights together at his house, partly because he had an en suite bathroom, and he thought partly because Bailey somehow felt safer there. The fact that she was okay walking completely naked to the bathroom, knowing her tattoo was on full display, made him all the more proud of her.

It was awful. Hideous. But that tattoo wasn't her. No, it was what Donovan tried to make her. But she was so much better than her ex would ever be that Nathan barely even saw the hateful words on her skin anymore. All he saw was her ass, and her slim waist, and the twinkle in her eye when she looked at him.

She hadn't said she loved him, but it was there. Nathan saw it in the way she looked at him, the way she made love to him, and the way she thanked him. Every day she told him how grateful she was he was in her life. He hoped, maybe foolishly, that every time she said *Thank you,* what she really meant was *I love you.*

Knowing he'd spent enough time lying in bed, Nathan climbed out and got started on the day.

Bailey glared at Ozzie. His one eye not covered by the eye patch twinkled with mirth.

"Don't know why you bother paying rent when you're practically living at Nathan's house."

"Shut up, Oz. I am not," Bailey protested. She'd just called Nathan and told him that she needed to stop by her house on the way home because she and Joel needed to get some more clothes. Ozzie had obviously overheard her conversation and was now giving her shit.

He held up a hand. "Hey, don't get me wrong. I think it's fucking awesome. I like him . . . even though he doesn't know the difference between OEM and aftermarket parts."

Bailey rolled her eyes. "There's more to life than fixing cars, Ozzie."

His face got serious. "You wouldn't have said that a few months ago. He's not a superhunk, but he's good for you, Bailey. That's all I'm saying."

"There's nothing wrong with the way he looks," Bailey huffed immediately.

"I didn't say there was. But he's not exactly Mr. Universe," Ozzie observed.

"So?"

"So nothing. Look, it's obvious the man cares for you, that's all that matters."

"He says he loves me," Bailey blurted, then closed her eyes in embarrassment. She so hadn't meant to tell Ozzie that.

"If he says he loves you, then he loves you," was Ozzie's response.

She wrinkled her nose. "It's soon. I'm afraid he's caught up in my drama and he's going to come to his senses as soon as it's over."

"I'm not dissing him, but men like him . . . they don't often get a woman like you to look twice at them. And this might be surprising, but men generally fall faster in a relationship than women do. Statistically they're more apt to say *I love you* first."

Bailey gritted her teeth. She was getting really sick of people dissing her boyfriend because he was a nerd. "Ozzie, I swear to God, you're like a brother to me, but if you say one more derogatory thing about Nathan, I'm gonna slug you. Yeah, he's a nerd. But who cares? He's got this inner alpha that comes out at the weirdest times. And I've noticed his confidence level over the last couple weeks has really grown. I don't know why, but it's sexy as hell. He doesn't give a shit what other people say about him, but I do. So don't diss him again. All right?"

Ozzie was smiling huge, and Bailey shoved her hands on her hips and demanded, "What are you grinning about?"

"Nothing." But he kept smiling.

Bailey rolled her eyes. "I'm outta here. Tell Clayson the Accord is good to go. It didn't need a new air filter."

"I will. Have fun with your boyfriend tonight," Ozzie called out.

She lifted a hand and waved at him with her middle finger without looking back. "I plan on it," she retorted, grinning when she heard Ozzie bark out a laugh.

Starting up the engine on her Chevelle, she thought about the night ahead. Nathan and Joel were planning on playing his *This Is War* game tonight. Even though Nathan sucked at it, he said he wanted to get better. And since he was teaching Joel math, it was only fair that the boy got to try to teach him to be a better video-game player. It was sweet, and Bailey knew Joel felt very important that he got to be an expert in something that Nathan sucked at.

Bailey had told Nathan she'd meet him back at his house after she stopped by hers to pick up some clothes, but he'd insisted on meeting her there. He'd said, "I missed you today. I haven't seen you in eight hours. Even going an extra thirty minutes is too long. I'll bring Joel, and we'll meet you there."

What could she do but agree? She'd missed Nathan too.

Being around him was amazing. She'd learned a lot about him simply by watching him interact with others. He stayed in the background a lot, especially around his brothers, but he was a great observer. He saw what a lot of other people missed. His analytical mind was constantly working.

What she'd told Ozzie was true. Over the time they'd been dating, she'd seen him break out of his shell. He was more outgoing with strangers, more protective of her and Joel, and he didn't put himself down nearly as much as he used to. She liked to think she'd had something to do with his growth.

And once he overcame his shyness in the bedroom, he had far exceeded her expectations. She'd always been fairly sexual, but over time, Donovan had squashed her libido until it was nothing but a shriveled mass in her belly. But Nathan's enthusiasm and obvious love for her had resurrected it so it was now stronger than ever. She hadn't thought about the awful things Donovan had made her do in a long time. She and Nathan had made love every night over the last week and a half, and she'd loved introducing him to new positions and activities.

In the past, she'd tolerated taking a cock down her throat, but hadn't really enjoyed it. But Nathan didn't hide his appreciation or enjoyment of her doing that for him . . . and he always came quickly when she put her mouth on him. She loved that she could make him lose control so easily.

She'd never been happier in a relationship. She sometimes felt bad that Nathan constantly told her how much she meant to him and she hadn't reciprocated, but she wasn't sure what she felt for him. She enjoyed being around him, respected him, liked him, but wasn't sure what love for a man was supposed to feel like. She didn't want to do anything that would hurt him, and telling him she loved him, then later telling him she'd been wrong, *would* hurt him.

All the way to her house, which wasn't really that far, Bailey thought about nothing but Nathan. She got giddy at the end of the day when she knew he'd be coming to get her, or that she'd be seeing him soon. It was ridiculous, but it was a good feeling.

Bailey pulled into her small driveway and smiled when she saw Nathan's piece-of-crap Ford already there. She bounced out of her car and jogged up to her door, eager to see the man who was quickly becoming the center of her world—in a healthy way this time and not something destructive, which she'd always had in the past.

Throwing open the door, she called out happily, "Hey, guys!"

The smile faded from her face as the scene in front of her registered. Nathan was sitting in one of her rickety kitchen chairs, his hands tied behind him, his ankles secured to the legs.

Joel was standing a couple of paces away from him looking completely freaked out.

And Donovan, fucking Donovan, was standing next to Joel. His hand around the back of his neck. Smirking.

"We've been waiting for you, Bailey. Now the party can start."

Chapter Twenty-Three

Bailey slowly closed the door, taking a big breath to strengthen her resolve before taking a good look at her ex.

Donovan looked like shit. Oh, he was still muscular, and still had that cocky grin he always thought got him anything he wanted, but his skin was pale, and he looked disheveled. She had no idea when he'd showered last, but it wasn't anytime recently. His jeans were dirty with black streaks and dirt. It looked like he'd lost weight as well. He shuffled from foot to foot as if he couldn't stand still.

Bailey's eyes swung to Joel. "You okay?" she asked quietly in a voice that was steady with resolve. They knew this day was coming, and even though it had surprised her, she'd do exactly as she and Nathan had talked about. She only hoped Joel was ready as well.

"Yeah," he said softly, and winced when Donovan squeezed his neck.

"You didn't think you'd really get away from me, did you?" Donovan asked casually.

Bailey shrugged. "I thought you'd be ready to move on when you got out of prison."

"Not hardly. You're the hottest piece of ass the Inca Boyz have. Even if I was ready to move on, that doesn't mean you'd get to go anywhere. There are other Boyz who wanted their turn."

Bailey forced down the bile that rose in her throat at his words. Unfortunately, he continued talking.

"From the second you waltzed into one of our parties when you were fourteen, you were marked. I knew I'd have you. I let some of the others play with you for a while. Teach you how to suck cock and get fucked. You're nothing but white trash, and you'll be nothing but trash for as long as you live. The only place you got is with the Boyz."

"Um . . . excuse me . . . are you talking about Bailey?" Nathan asked in a tone Bailey had never heard him use before. It was meek, and shaky.

Donovan turned to Nathan and, without a word, punched him in the face. Bailey cried out as his head whipped to the side with the force of the blow, and blood immediately began to trickle out of his nose.

"Owwwwww, that hurt," Nathan whined.

"Don't ask stupid-ass questions, and I won't have to hit you," Donovan retorted calmly.

Joel's eyes were wide, but he kept silent.

"I didn't know she was yours, man. She didn't tell me she was in a gang."

"What the fuck you think that tattoo on her back meant, asshole?"

"What tattoo?"

Donovan's arm shot out again, once more hitting Nathan in the side of the face, and once more his head flung to the side.

"Goddamn, stop it!" Nathan cried.

"Bailey, are you seriously going to stand there and tell me you're fucking this pansy? First, it's disgusting. Look at him. He's skinny as fuck and looks like a total dork. Let me guess, you're spending your time watching *Star Wars* or some shit? Where are his geek glasses?"

"Leave him alone," Bailey begged. She knew it was part of the plan, but she hated seeing the blood on Nathan's face. *Hated* it. She and Nathan had talked about letting Donovan think Nathan wasn't a threat, and the possibility of him knocking him around, but it was so much more . . . real . . . seeing the blood in person.

Donovan let go of Joel and stalked over to where Bailey was standing near the front door. He grabbed her bicep in his meaty grip and hauled her over to where Nathan was sitting. She refused to look at Nathan. She couldn't. It would kill her and she'd fuck up the plan.

Donovan spun her around, forced her head toward the floor with a brutal hand behind her neck, and whipped her shirt up her back.

"This tattoo, motherfucker," he snarled at Nathan. "She's *my* whore. I fuck her when I want, where I want, and how I want. And when I'm done, I give her to whoever I want. And she takes it without a fucking word. Because she's nothing but a dumb whore. A good-for-nothing slut. All women are good for is fucking and sucking. That's it. They're weak and nothing but a pain in my ass." He ended his statement by shoving Bailey as hard as he could.

She threw out her hands to try to catch herself, but wasn't fast enough. She hit the ground face-first and cried out as pain exploded in her cheek. She stayed on the ground and turned to look up at the man she'd once thought she was in love with.

Her jaw tensed. Donovan would not win today. There was too much at stake. Her relationship with Nathan, Joel's future, her own well-being. No, their plan would work. It had to.

"Look, man, I never saw that tattoo," Nathan said in the most pathetic voice Bailey had ever heard. "We only did it when she was on her back. She didn't want it any other way. I think that's the only way she can get off."

Donovan laughed at that. Put his head back and guffawed as if Nathan had said the funniest thing he'd ever heard. "Get off? You dumbass. There's no point in a woman getting off. Why you even care about that shit? No, man, you gotta fuck a chick the way *you* want, not how she wants it."

Bailey hated that Joel was hearing any of the vile words coming out of Donovan's mouth, but she couldn't do anything about that now. They'd deal with it after.

As if her thoughts about her brother were spoken aloud, her ex turned to the little boy and hauled him into his side with a tight grip around his arm. "Joel, did you miss me?"

He nodded quickly.

"You did? How much?"

"A lot," Joel murmured.

"Hmm, I'm not sure I believe you." Donovan scowled, his mood going from jovial to suspicious in the beat of a heart.

Bailey had seen this kind of unpredictable mood swing in the past. She glanced at his arms and saw the bruises inside his elbows and on the backs of his hands. Drugs. Somehow she knew without a doubt that Donovan had crossed the line he said he'd never cross. He'd always said drugs fucked people up. Made them make bad decisions. But it looked like he'd changed his mind.

"I-I found a movie like the ones you showed me online. I've been w-watching," Joel stammered.

Bailey's heart broke. Damn Donovan for doing this to her brother. Damn him to hell.

"Good boy," Donovan told Joel, tousling his hair as if he were a dog.

"Look, if she's your girlfriend, I didn't know," Nathan said quickly. "If you untie me, I'll leave. You can have her. I don't want to get into the middle of a gang situation."

Bailey's eyes went to Nathan, and she flinched. He was staring at her as if he didn't know her. She knew he was pretending. *Knew* it. But it still hurt.

"You think I'm dumb?" Donovan asked. "I'm not going to let you go. For one, you'd just call the po-po. For two, I know who you are. If you didn't call the police, you'd call your fucking brothers. The strong ones. The ones who have probably fought every fight for you since you were three years old. You're the weak link. And C, I'm not letting you go because it's hilarious as fuck to see your geek ass tied to the chair, and I like beating up nerds. They make such fun whimpering sounds." With that, he picked up his foot, turned sideways, still holding on to Joel, and shoved it as hard as he could into Nathan's knee.

Bailey looked away as Nathan screamed in pain. Donovan simply laughed. Then he did it again to his other knee. Again, Nathan cried out. Then he started begging.

"Please, don't do that again. Let me go. I won't call anyone. You can have her. She said I sucked in bed anyway. I'm begging you, untie me. Please."

Donovan laughed even harder. "Oh man, this is priceless. What? You gonna offer me up your collection of science-fiction toys? Give me your ticket to Comic-Con?"

"Anything, anything you want," Nathan cried out pathetically.

Bailey opened her mouth to stop this. The plan wasn't working. Donovan was really going to hurt Nathan. They had to do something different while they waited for the cops and Nathan's brothers to show up. But her brother spoke before she could get a word out.

"Donovan?" Joel asked tentatively.

"What?" he barked, obviously irritated at being interrupted.

"I gotta pee."

"Oh, for Christ's sake," Donovan swore. Then, grabbing Joel's arm in a steely grip that had the boy standing on tiptoe to try to take the pressure off his muscles, and pointing at Bailey, he said, "Don't move, bitch. You so much as move an inch, I'll hurt him." He shook Joel to make his point.

Bailey nodded immediately, frantically. "I won't. I swear. Don't hurt him, Donovan."

The gang member smirked then. "I'm not going to hurt your precious brother, Bailey. I've never wanted to hurt him. All I've ever wanted was for him to be an Inca Boy. Why do you think I kept you around for so long? Don't worry, he's in good hands with me. You ought to be worried about what I'm going to do with you, not Joel."

With that, he hauled the boy down the hall to the bathroom. He kicked open the door and quickly glanced in, obviously making sure there were no windows the boy could crawl out of. Seeing nothing but the nondescript bathroom, he swung Joel around and said, "Hurry the fuck up." Joel closed the door quickly, and the last thing Bailey saw was his scared, pale face looking out from the crack, before it shut.

Donovan stomped back into the small living room and went straight to Bailey. He hauled her off the ground and into him, his arm going around her chest, her back to his front. Then he licked a path from her shoulder up her neck, and across her face. He grabbed her chin with his other hand, turned her head to the side, and forced his tongue into her mouth. She struggled against him, hating the feeling of him inside her in any way. Not only that, but his breath was horrid. She gagged, and he immediately pulled back.

He didn't immediately say anything, but simply looked at her with an indescribable look on his face. Bailey remembered that look, and it didn't bode well for her. Not at all.

"You wanna know how Bailey here likes to be fucked? Watch and learn, pansy motherfucker," Donovan told Nathan, who was sitting silent, his head down in dejection.

When he didn't move, Donovan roared, "Look at me, asshole."

Nathan's head slowly came up, and his gaze locked on Donovan's. Bailey didn't see any emotion other than pain and fear in his face. He didn't look upset. He didn't look pissed. She was pretty sure he was acting . . . but suddenly wasn't one hundred percent sure.

Donovan's hand moved up her body, and he grabbed onto one of her breasts. Her heart sank. God, was this really going to happen? Was Donovan going to rape her in front of Nathan—and possibly Joel too? She'd been so brave when she talked about what would happen when

Donovan caught up to her, but the reality was so much worse than she remembered or thought it could be.

"Donovan—" She started to plead with him not to do this, but he didn't let her get anything out other than his name before he spun her around and hit her.

He'd hit her before, but it hurt more this time. Maybe because she'd gotten used to Nathan's gentleness. Maybe because she hadn't been expecting it. Or maybe because it had simply been so long since she'd been hit. Pain exploded around her eye, and she whirled around, tripping over the arm of the couch and ending up half-sprawled over it.

Exactly where Donovan wanted her. He put a hand on the back of her neck and squeezed at the same time that he pushed her down. Forcing her to bend farther over the arm of the couch. She could barely breathe as he was pushing her face into the cushion. She kicked out with her feet, but Donovan merely stepped closer into her, taking away her leverage and pushing her hips against the side of the couch in the process.

"You watching, nerd?" Donovan asked.

Bailey didn't see Nathan's reaction, but she assumed he nodded, because Donovan continued his instruction on how best to rape a woman.

"Here's the thing. Bitches want cock, even if they don't admit it. It actually feels better for her, and you, if she's dry. More friction, you understand." He paused and ripped her shirt up and over her back, moving his hand on her neck just long enough so he could push the material over her head before replacing it and pushing her back down.

She whimpered. God, this was so not part of the plan. It had been a possibility in the back of her mind, but she'd never said anything to Nathan. She couldn't bear this.

"The reason I had this slut tattooed with my name was so I could see it when I fucked her from behind."

"I'm done," Bailey heard Joel say in a small voice. No. God, no. He couldn't be there. Couldn't see her like this. Could not watch Donovan violate her.

"Good, come here, Joel. I want to show you up close and personal what it's like to fuck a chick."

Bailey struggled in earnest then. Thrashing in Donovan's grip as if her life depended on it. Screw the plan.

"Fuck," the gangbanger swore, trying to hold on to the wildly flailing Bailey. "Stay still, bitch, or it'll only get worse for you."

"Fuck you," Bailey cried, still kicking and thrashing in Donovan's grip.

Several things happened at once.

Donovan let Bailey go and screeched in fury.

She felt his weight leave her back.

Joel screamed.

Nathan grunted.

Bailey quickly brought herself upright and tugged her shirt back down so she was covered, and she turned around.

Just as they'd planned—okay, not exactly as they'd planned, but close enough—Nathan was dragging a struggling Donovan toward the bathroom. But the gangbanger wasn't cooperating. Whether it was the drugs in his system, or something instinctual that told him if he didn't get away, he was in big trouble, Bailey didn't know. But it was obvious Nathan was going to lose the battle with her ex if she didn't do something to help him.

Looking around, Bailey ran for the kitchen and grabbed the closest knife she could find. *This* definitely wasn't in the plan, but screw it. She wasn't going to leave Nathan to deal with Donovan by himself. She'd grabbed a steak knife. Not the biggest one she had, but it would have to do. She ran toward where Donovan and Nathan were wrestling and slashed at her ex's legs. She didn't want to stab him. Definitely didn't want to kill him—she had enough problems at the moment, and a murder charge wouldn't make her situation any better.

He yelped and kicked out, catching her in the side of the head. Bailey grunted, but ignored the pain and went back at Donovan. Slashing at him when his limbs were clear of Nathan's. Together they herded the man down the hall, and with an inhuman amount of strength, Nathan threw him into the bathroom and slammed the door shut. He immediately leaned against it with his entire body weight.

"Help me," he said urgently.

Bailey dropped the bloody knife and threw herself against the door, adding her body weight to Nathan's.

"Joel, you did as we talked about, right?" Nathan asked more calmly than Bailey felt.

"Y-yeah," the little boy stammered.

"And it worked?" Nathan asked urgently.

Joel nodded. "Definitely."

Bailey turned her head and saw a brilliant smile creep over Nathan's bleeding face. "Awesome. Run and find your phone, buddy. It should still be in your backpack. Make sure the others are coming, then stay outside. We'll be there in a minute or two."

Without a word, Joel spun and raced toward the front door.

"You motherfuckers! When I get out of here, you're dead. You hear me? Dead!" Donovan raged from inside the windowless bathroom. He coughed, then the door shuddered as he threw his body against it.

"I'm serious!" He coughed again. "I'm gonna knife that pansy-ass geek, then shove that blade up your cunt, bitch!" More coughing. "Then when you're pleading with me to stop, I'm gonna force your precious brother to use it to slit your throat."

There were a few more loud pounds against the door that Bailey felt reverberate through her body, but between both her and Nathan's body weight, the door didn't give. They heard more coughing, then swearing, then wheezing.

"Slow your breathing down, pixie," Nathan said softly, the tenderness in his tone almost breaking the control Bailey had been holding on to by the barest margin. She looked over at him. He had blood streaming down his face from a cut on his cheek. His nose was oozing blood as well, and he had bruises all over his face. But he was looking at her and speaking with her as if they were sitting next to each other at Scarpetti's, having dinner.

"It's working. Joel did it. But we can't move until we're sure," Nathan reassured her.

"Are your brothers coming?" Bailey asked.

"Absolutely," Nathan affirmed immediately. "I saw Joel hit the silent alarm when Donovan first pushed himself into the house. As we thought, he was more concerned about subduing me than paying attention to Joel. They should be here any minute."

He coughed then, and Bailey realized that her eyes were burning. She looked down and saw a slight fog coming out from under the bathroom door. She turned panicked eyes up to Nathan.

"It's okay. Stay calm." Nathan coughed, then went on. "Just one more minute, then we'll join Joel outside."

"I love you," Bailey blurted suddenly.

She watched as his eyes got big, but she went on before he could say anything. "I do. I know I haven't said it, and that wasn't fair of me, but I wanted to be sure."

"And you're sure now?" Nathan asked softly between coughs.

With her eyes watering from the toxic fumes coming out from under the bathroom door, Bailey nodded. "When I saw you taking those hits from Donovan to give the cops and your brothers time to get here, I knew. There's no one I'd rather have at my back when shit goes down than you. You can outsmart anyone any day of the week, and that is sexier than anything else I can think of."

"Let's go," Nathan ordered, standing up and grabbing her hand as he towed her quickly down the hall, into the living room, which looked as if a tornado had moved through it, and out the front door. He shut it firmly behind him, closing Donovan, and the deadly chlorine gas Joel had created in the bathroom, inside.

He immediately knelt and caught Joel, who had flung himself at him, and Bailey dropped down next to them as well.

They stayed huddled together for another minute or two before they finally heard sirens.

"Here they come," Nathan murmured. Then he pulled back and took Joel's shoulders in his hands. "You did it, buddy."

Joel didn't look anywhere near ready to smile or to stop being freaked out, but he did manage to nod. Nathan gathered him into his arms and stood. Joel's legs went around his waist, and the little boy buried his face into Nathan's neck.

"Are you okay? Should you be holding him?" Bailey asked worriedly, as her aches and pains started to make themselves known. Nathan had been hurt much worse than she had. It had to be agony holding her brother. He wasn't exactly a lightweight.

"Honestly? I hurt like hell. My knees feel like they had spikes hammered through them, and my face is so painful it hurts to talk. But one of two things that makes me feel better is feeling Joel against me, and knowing he's okay."

"What's the other?" Bailey asked, resting her hand on his forearm.

"You in my arms. Come here, pixie," Nathan ordered, holding an arm out.

Bailey immediately snuggled in next to her brother and the man she loved.

Chapter Twenty-Four

Bailey sat nervously next to Nathan at the Castle Rock police station. They weren't under arrest, but they had to give their official statement to the cops. Blake and Logan were also in the room. Standing against the wall, their arms crossed in front of them, scowls on their faces. If she didn't know them, Bailey would've been scared to death, but since their ferocious looks were because their brother had been used as a punching bag, she supposed they were entitled to their scowls.

Joel was in another room with Felicity, Grace, her babies, and Alexis. Bailey had been reassured several times that he wouldn't be questioned without her there, but she was still worried that somehow Child Protective Services would take him away from her.

They'd been seen by the paramedics at her house and been patched up. Even though they were both hurt, Nathan and Bailey decided not to go to the hospital.

Donovan hadn't been so lucky.

Now they had to tell their side of the story. Bailey hoped like hell either she or Nathan didn't end up getting arrested by the time it was all said and done.

"We know you've been watching Donovan for a while now," the detective said gently. "Why don't you start at the beginning and tell us what happened tonight."

Nathan put his hand over hers on the table and immediately spoke, not giving Bailey a chance. She sat back in relief and listened to him recount the last couple of hours of their lives.

"We knew Donovan had Bailey in his sights. He was pissed she broke up with him when he was in prison. When he got out, you're right, my brothers were keeping their eyes and ears on Donovan. He tried to get the Inca Boyz gang back up to what it used to be before his brothers were killed. Our connection on the gang task force up in Denver, Ross Peterson, told us weeks ago that he'd disappeared off their radar. He wasn't sure where he was or what he had planned. You can verify all this with him, of course."

Nathan took a deep breath, glanced over at Bailey, squeezed her hand, and continued. "We knew he'd be coming for Bailey, so me and my brothers made a couple of plans, just in case."

"Why didn't you come to the cops?" the detective interrupted to ask.

"Because all we had was a hunch. You wouldn't have been able to do anything with just that."

"We did warn a few SWAT members about a week ago that we thought Donovan would be in the area and out for revenge on Ms. Hampton," Logan broke in.

The detective eyed him for a moment before nodding. "Okay. Go on."

"Anyway, so we had plans for what we could do if he kidnapped Joel from his school and then contacted Bailey, or if he showed up at her workplace and threatened her coworkers. And we also concocted a plan in case he showed up at either of our houses," Nathan explained.

"And what was that plan?" the cop asked, leaning forward, his eyes narrowed.

Bailey spoke up before Nathan could continue. "You have to understand what he did to my brother. He showed him porn. And forced him to smoke a joint!" she blurted. "He was trying to mold him into one of his gang members. That's mostly why I left Denver. I didn't want that for Joel. And it messed him up. He's been seeing a psychologist here in Castle Rock, and he's been doing great."

The detective's eyes gentled as he looked at Bailey. "I'm sorry you had to go through that. Adults can make poor life choices, but they shouldn't affect innocent kids."

Bailey winced as if the older man had slapped her. She knew without a doubt he was talking about her being involved with the Inca Boyz and Donovan in the first place. She wanted to defend herself, but couldn't. He was right.

"That was out of line," Nathan growled. "You don't get to judge Bailey, and if you're going to continue to have this condescending attitude, this interview is over."

The officer held up his hand. "I'm sorry. Please continue."

He didn't look very sorry, but Nathan hurried on with the story, obviously wanting to get it over with. "We knew Donovan would take one look at me and dismiss me as a threat. Joel and I walked into the house, and he slipped in behind us. While I fought with him, Joel pushed the silent alarm."

Blake broke in at this point in the story. "Logan and I both got the alarm on our phones, and we immediately called SWAT."

The detective's head swung back to Nathan as he picked up the story. "We knew it would take around thirty minutes for anyone to arrive. So we had to stall. Donovan overpowered me, and tied me to a chair. I'd been carrying a pocketknife in my back pocket, just in case. So, I played the pathetic, scared victim, all the while pretending I was still tied securely when in reality I had cut the ropes and was just holding them in place. I let Donovan feel superior and pound on me, hoping to keep his attention away from Bailey and Joel."

The tears that had been gathering in Bailey's eyes spilled over. God, it had hurt to see him pleading with Donovan.

She put her head on the table and cried silently. Without stopping his story, Nathan put his arm around her shoulders, and scooted closer to her, holding her as she wept.

"Joel was the key to taking out Donovan as a threat. I think it was Logan who suggested ammonia and bleach."

The detective looked surprised. "What?"

"He knew all about chlorine gas from his time in the Army," Nathan said without emotion. "So Joel and I practiced mixing the chemicals. When we had it down, we put bottles of bleach and ammonia under the bathroom sinks in my house and Bailey's," Nathan explained.

"So what happened?" the detective asked.

"Joel asked to use the restroom. When he was in there, he plugged up the sink, poured in the bleach and ammonia. Then did the same in the toilet, and left, closing the door behind him."

"Jesus," the cop swore softly.

Nathan nodded. "He walked back into the living room where Donovan was trying to rape Bailey. He wanted Joel to watch. Luckily, I'd long since cut myself loose of the ropes, and I jumped him. I was trying to push Donovan down the hall to get him into the bathroom, but he walloped me pretty good, and I was weakening. Bailey came to the rescue and cut him, not to kill, but to distract. It worked. We got him into the bathroom and made sure he stayed there until he was incapacitated."

"Then we showed up," Blake said succinctly.

"And SWAT," Logan added helpfully.

"And the ambulance," Blake said.

The detective looked from one man to the other, then his eyes went to Bailey, who had finally lifted her head. She was clutching Nathan as if he would be ripped out of her arms at any moment.

Finally, the officer said, "Donovan's in critical condition at Denver Regional Hospital. The doctors think he has chemical pneumonia, which is incurable. If the paramedics had been even five minutes later, he would've drowned from the fluid in his lungs."

Bailey flinched and finally spoke. "Everything we did was in self-defense. Donovan was about to rape me in front of my boyfriend and little brother. Then he was most likely going to take a blowtorch and try to remove the tattoo he had inked in my skin. I believe he's been doing drugs since he got out of prison."

The officer nodded and remarked, "Toxicology showed that he did have heroin in his bloodstream. It's not helping him now."

"Please," Bailey whispered, "I knew he'd be coming for me. He wasn't going to let me leave him. He flat out told me that more than once. I knew if he found me, he'd kill me. It was my idea to lock him in the bathroom. I didn't know the gas would kill him, but I knew it would slow him down and give me a chance to escape."

She ignored the insanely tight grip Nathan had on her hand below the table and kept speaking. "If he dies, and you should charge someone, charge me. It's my fault. I was the one who dated him. I was the one who left him, and I was the one he came for."

The vibe in the room was electric. Bailey didn't dare glance at Nathan, who she knew was glaring at her. Not to mention Logan and Blake. They definitely weren't happy. But she'd be damned if she let any of the Andersons take the fall for Donovan. It was time she stepped up and made the right decision for once in her life.

The detective heaved a huge sigh, then said, "It's more than obvious what happened in your house tonight was self-defense. The evidence at the scene corroborates what you said. I'm not saying you did the right thing, but it was effective. We found Donovan's car about a mile down Wolfensberger Road. He had a blowtorch, more rope, a shovel, a box of garbage bags, lye, and a map."

"What the fuck?" Logan breathed at the same time Blake said, "Jesus!"

Nathan didn't say a word, but when Bailey glanced at him, his jaw was ticking as if he was clenching his teeth.

The detective continued. "We believe his plan was to kill you, then bury you up in the mountains. Then take your brother back to Denver with him and do as you said—make him an Inca Boy."

Bailey met the man's eyes steadily. She was afraid to hope.

"From what you've said here tonight, and from what we've learned from the Denver PD Gang Task Force, you're lucky to be alive. I ask that you don't leave town and make yourself accessible when we need to speak with you. The DA will be in touch."

Bailey closed her eyes and sighed. She knew she wasn't exactly off the hook, but as long as she didn't have go to jail over someone like Donovan, she'd be okay. She turned to Nathan and threw her arms around him.

His arms immediately tightened around her waist, and he held her to him.

"Are they free to go then?" Logan asked. "It's been a long night, and we all could use some sleep."

"Of course. If we need to contact you tomorrow, I have your number."

"We'll be at my house in case you need to see us," Nathan volunteered.

The officer nodded, then stood. "I'm sorry about everything you've been through."

"Thanks," Nathan said, nodding as he stood, still holding Bailey in his arms.

Blake and Logan shook the officer's hand while Nathan led Bailey to get her brother. They were battered and bruised, but safe.

Later that night, as Bailey lay in Nathan's arms, she turned her neck to look at her brother, who was sound asleep on her other side. They'd all piled into Nathan's king-size bed, none of them wanting to be away from the other. It had been a close call; they all knew it.

"I'm free," Bailey whispered into Nathan's ear.

He didn't respond with words, but the kiss on her temple and the way he squeezed her waist was all the response she needed.

Epilogue

"You feel all right?" Nathan asked for the tenth time that afternoon. He knew he was being overprotective, but Bailey had just gone through a four-hour session in a tattoo chair earlier, and she had to be hurting.

The day after Donovan had passed away, Felicity had taken her down to Colorado Springs to talk with the tattoo artist she'd recommended.

The tattooist had taken one look at the awful words on Bailey's back and curled her lip. She'd looked Bailey in the eye and swore, "I'm gonna make this the most kick-ass tattoo you've ever seen. And it's on the house."

Bailey had protested, but the woman hadn't budged.

Today wasn't the first time she'd had the tattoo worked on, and it wouldn't be the last either. The words Donovan had tried to brand her with were gone, transformed into swirls and shading of three mountain peaks. There was the start of a brilliant sunset behind the mountains, and, at Bailey's request, there were small birds that matched the ones Grace and Logan had inked on their skin.

"I'm fine, Nathan. Seriously," Bailey said with a smile.

They were sitting on the bleachers in the Castle Rock gym watching Joel's robotic team compete. In the three months that followed their ordeal, Joel had continued to see the psychologist, who said he was coping remarkably well, most likely because he'd had a part in helping save his sister. With Nathan's prodding, he'd tried out for the robotic team. To everyone's surprise, he'd excelled at it, earning a spot on the middle-school team.

Bailey had experienced nightmares for weeks, but it had been more than a month since she'd woken up screaming Nathan's name in terror.

Nathan grimaced, remembering how helpless he'd felt when he couldn't make her nightmares stop, but when she snuggled into him so quickly and trustingly, it soothed that ache. It didn't hurt that not a day went by that they didn't say they loved each other.

I love you fell from her lips as easily as it did his. And last night, for the first time, Joel had told Nathan he loved him.

Bailey had made her views on marriage quite clear. She didn't think she had to get the government's permission to officially tie herself to someone she loved. Nathan didn't care. As long as she loved him, and he loved her, he didn't need the paper. He'd already changed all his documents listing her as his next of kin. He didn't have the heart to tell Bailey that, according to the state of Colorado, they were as good as married.

She'd find out the first time they needed to pay their income taxes that they had a common-law marriage and could file as married for their taxes. Since they lived together, people believed they'd eloped and gotten married since they both wore a ring, and had certainly consummated the relationship.

Nathan smiled to himself. Bailey was his. He had one more surprise for her today. One he hoped she'd like. Getting back to the topic at hand—namely, if her back was hurting after the work she'd had done on it today, he asked, "Are you sure?"

"I'm sure. But thank you for caring."

He smiled tenderly at her. "I more than care, pixie."

Nathan knew they didn't exactly match. Bailey with her dark hair and bright tattoos on her arms, and him a tall, slender geek, but he didn't care. Bailey loved him. He loved her. That was all that mattered.

A loud cheer went up in the bleachers around them, and they both whipped their heads back to the competition. Joel's team was high-fiving each other and smiling. Their robot sat motionless in the center of a circle surrounded by what was obviously the parts of their competitor's robot.

Bailey leaped to her feet and cheered along with the other parents around them. Nathan kept one hand on the back of one of her thighs to hold her steady and beamed down at Joel. When Bailey sat down again, she leaned over and said into his ear, "Guess all those video games were good for something, huh? He's got a mean competitive streak."

Nathan smiled back at her and kissed her quickly. "I'd say so," he told her, still smiling.

"What are you all smiley about?" Bailey asked suspiciously. "What are you hiding from me?"

Figuring this was as good a time as any, and not able to keep the surprise to himself any longer, Nathan reached behind him and pulled out his driver's license. He handed it to Bailey without a word.

Her brows furrowed in confusion as she looked down at the plastic card in her hand. "I don't understand. What's the big—"

Her words cut off suddenly as she saw what he'd done.

"Since you felt it was disrespectful to your pa, and to Joel, to change your last name to Anderson . . . I decided that as a nonwedding gift to you, I'd change mine. As much as I loved my dad, being one of three Anderson triplets hasn't always been a walk in the park. I've been compared to them my entire life, and through no fault of their own, always felt as if I didn't measure up. I thought that becoming a Hampton would be kinda cool."

Her eyes met his and were filled with shock. Her hand came up and covered her mouth as her lip quivered and her eyes filled with tears.

Nathan put his palms on the sides of her neck and speared his fingers into her hair. "I love you, Bailey. The best day of my life was when you took pity on me and my poor car and helped me out. No, the best day was when you let me spend the day with you and Joel on his birthday. No"—he shook his head—"the best day was when you lay in my arms and whispered that you were free. We can't look back; we can only look forward. And the only thing I want to look forward to is a long life with you at my side. Do you mind that I'm now Nathan Hampton?"

"Mind?" she asked incredulously before throwing her arms around his neck and hugging him tightly. "I'm blown away. Flabbergasted. Shocked. Excited. Thrilled." She leaned back, keeping her hands locked together behind him. "I love you. You couldn't have given me a better nonmarriage gift. Thank you."

"You're welcome, pixie."

"I have something for you too," she said coyly, a smirk on her face.

He couldn't help it, his erection pulsed with excitement as he asked, "Yeah?"

"Yeah. But it'll have to wait until tonight. After Joel is asleep."

"Does my present have anything to do with you being naked on our bed and letting me have my wicked way with you?"

"Maybe," she drawled, then got serious. "I didn't know I needed a man like you until you pestered your way into my life. You were content to be nothing more than my friend, when I needed a friend the most. Thank you for being patient. Thank you for loving Joel as much as you do. And thank you for making me the luckiest woman in the world."

They smiled at each other, ignoring the couples around them, ignoring the next heat of competition starting on the gym floor in front of them, content to simply be with each other.

The next day, a man stepped out of his sleek, black Mustang and calmly walked down the sidewalk in downtown Castle Rock. More than one person did a double take when they saw him. He was a little over six feet tall, with light-brown hair. He had a heavy five-o-clock shadow on his jaw, hiding his full lips. He was wearing a pair of black jeans and a black T-shirt. Even though he wore steel-toed boots on his feet, his steps were almost silent. He was a man on a mission, and no one wanted to get between him and whatever he was focused on.

He stopped outside Ace Security and seemed to hesitate. He shoved one hand into a front pocket of his jeans, and the other clenched into a fist at his side. Ten minutes later, he was still standing there.

Grace Mason walked up beside him and said softly, "If you stand there much longer, you'll grow roots."

Obviously startled by her presence, the man turned his head and nodded. "Mornin'."

"Good morning. Going in?"

"Yup."

"Great. Me too."

And with that, the man moved. He reached for the door and held it open. He gestured for Grace to enter ahead of him. He took another deep breath and followed her in.

"Logan!" Grace called. "Someone's here!"

Seconds later, Logan came out of the back room, which held their offices, and greeted the man.

"Hello, welcome to Ace Security. I'm Logan Anderson. How can I help you?"

"My name is Ryder Sinclair. But my friends call me Ace."

The silence was so thick in the air, the man knew he'd be able to hear a pin drop. He continued. "My mother's name was Patricia Sinclair, and I'm your half brother. Ace Anderson was my father."

"Fuck," Logan whispered. He sized up the man in front of him, then said, "I'd like to blow you off. Tell you to not let the door hit you on the ass on your way out, but I can't deny the resemblance. I assume you have proof?"

"I have proof," Ace said with a nod of his head.

"Grace? Lock the door. We're closing early today. I'll call Blake and Nathan. Looks like we're having a family reunion."

Later that night, Felicity ignored the ringing of her phone. She knew it would probably be Grace, again. She'd called earlier with the news that Ace Anderson had apparently had an affair, and the result of that dalliance had strolled into town wanting to talk to his half brothers. As much as Felicity wanted to know more about what was going on, she had more important things on her mind at the moment. She knew going to Chicago earlier in the year had been a mistake, but she'd done it anyway. She sat on her twin-size bed in her small apartment and stared off into space. She didn't seem to be aware that she hadn't turned any lights on and she was sitting in the dark. She was lost in her memories of a time she'd tried to desperately put behind her.

Felicity couldn't see the letter she'd read hours earlier, now lying facedown on the floor in front of the bed, but the words on the plain sheet of paper mocked the progress she'd made over the years. Mocked the safety she'd just begun to feel with her friends in Castle Rock. Everything she'd worked for had crumbled with the words. Every iota of peace she'd fought for, every memory she'd banished from her mind, came back in Technicolor.

Hey, sweetheart. Did you think you could get away from me? I told you I was an expert at Hide and Go Seek, but you just never learn. I'll be seeing you soon.

Acknowledgments

Sometimes writing can seem like a solitary job, but in reality, there are a ton of people behind the scenes. I want to give a shout-out to Elle James, Beth Neal, Chas Jenkins-Patrick, Marie Brown, and every blogger who has picked up the books in this series and let me know how much they've enjoyed them.

I would be remiss if I didn't mention my Montlake editors as well. Melody Guy has had nothing but wonderful suggestions for tightening up and tweaking my stories, and Maria Gomez has always been supportive and encouraging as we go through the process.

And finally, to *every* one of my readers, you're the best. I know this series came out of the blue, but you embraced it and ultimately loved it. I can't tell you how much that means to me.

Acknowledgments

[illegible]

About the Author

Photo © 2015 A&C Photography

Susan Stoker is a *New York Times*, *USA Today*, and *Wall Street Journal* bestselling author who loves hot alpha heroes. She debuted her first series in 2014, and quickly followed it up with her SEAL of Protection series and her Ace Security series, which includes *Claiming Grace* and *Claiming Alexis*. She is addicted to writing and creating stories readers can lose themselves in.

Susan considers herself an all-American girl with a heart as big as her home state of Texas. Thanks to her Army husband, she's lived in several different states. Now that he's retired, however, it's *his* turn to follow Susan around the country.

Discover more about Susan and her books through her website, www.StokerAces.com, or follow her on Twitter (@Susan_Stoker) and Facebook (www.facebook.com/authorsusanstoker).

Connect with Susan Online

Susan's Facebook Profile and Page

www.facebook.com/authorsstoker

www.facebook.com/authorsusanstoker

Follow Susan on Twitter

www.twitter.com/Susan_Stoker

Find Susan's Books on Goodreads

www.goodreads.com/SusanStoker

E-mail

Susan@StokerAces.com

Website

www.StokerAces.com